Tan

CRACK APPLE and POP

Rock & Rebellion

Saira Viola

Saira
Nov. 2012.

Kite and Key Publishing
Cleveland, Ohio

Published by Kite and Key Publishing, 2012.

Cover design by Unitas Quick

A CIP catalogue record for this title is available from the British Library.

ISBN 978-0-9850003-5-6

Kite and Key Publishing
Cleveland, Ohio, USA
www.kiteandkeypublishing.com

FOREWORD

Occasionally, if you're lucky, you come across a writer that really makes you sit up. Not because of a great story line, horror, or sex themes set to shock and outrage but because that writer has a way of stringing words together, that is unique, almost as if they have invented a new language.

Saira Viola is that *writer. Her style is truly different because she uses everyday words with a twisted meaning but somehow you understand her straight away. She is also very fond of street slang but there again, she makes it her own.*

This story is an allegory of a dark criminal underworld complete with guns, crack cocaine and a thumping soundscape of London town.

The pace is fast and there is a definite beat to the book that keeps you guessing, keeps you involved and connected as if you're right there in the folds of the action.

Saira's main talent is the way she uses words, invents new expressions out of old ones, recreates the vibe of the street with words that would not even enter the mind of most writers.

She takes you into **her** *world in* her ***own*** *way without the reader ever realizing that he has left his own behind.*

This glorious individuality and the impressive cast of characters who inhabit the subterranean cosmos she draws us into include a spiritual Yardie gangster, a set of Dominatrix twins hell bent on scamming their way to the top and a recovering Heroin addict who has an appetite for rubber love dolls.

Viola writes of immigrants, misfits, the damaged and the privileged then presents us with a social landscape that obliterates all of the clichés by keeping it real.

One of the key strengths of this book however, is its universal appeal: whoever you are, whatever your background, you always know exactly where *you are. Reading Viola's prose is like a roller coaster ride: a well-known attraction but always a different experience, she does it by slightly tweaking words: Be prepared for something new it won't always be pleasant but it will shake rattle and stun.*

At its epicenter, all art poses the same question how should we live what are our moral and humanitarian obligations, how does our history shape our present.

At the centre of this novel Viola repeats this theme revealing the class and racial tensions that have scarred a nation and in doing so exposes the living truths of the world today.

Viola does not flinch from controversy or hide from contradictions .This is a novel of exceptional promise and intense complexity, a snake pit loaded with social commentary beautiful imagery and brave ambition .

You've already bought the ticket now take the ride and enjoy CRACK APPLE AND POP!

Marc "Frenchy" Gloder May 2012

CRACK APPLE and POP

"Superman don't need no seat belt."

Muhammad Ali

Chapter 1

The gut wrenching screech of a siren: emergency lights and a swerve of brakes. An ambulance pulls up on the West side of the street opposite a Shell garage. The pavement flooded with the crimson rush of human blood. It was a cut-throat Monday evening around ten thirty five p.m. in Streatham South West London, and Tony had just taken the very first beating of his life.

Six skinheads crocked on glue and racist yip were pummelling the neighbourhood gunning for hate. They stank of *Thunderbird, B & H* and too many *white noise* meetings.

"Oi you what you lookin' at too dark to see too dumb to talk nigger coon flake!" A red haired thug with a fascist smirk, wearing groin busting denim and a Fred Perry tee, bashed the air with stewed spite.

"Fuck off!" Tony's gutsy throwback landed him a steel toe kick to the stomach followed by a crow bar blow to the head. He sank to the ground. He could feel the leather strop in their voices as they held him down and mashed him to jelly. Now he was nothing more than a pulping mass of puss and wounded flesh: a requiem of gore. He had become a *Francis Bacon* skull mixed with the tortured splay of broken bones.

On arrival at St. George's hospital, he had already been resuscitated three times. Lying on the gurney his mother, Elizabeth an A& E nurse stopped by to make a routine check on new admissions, as she peered closer her face blanched with terror.

"Oh Jesus, that's my son" She gasped.

"Oh my God, that's my boy – my Tony – look at him, my Lord, my God. Dear God who - who did this to my son?" she surged.

A junior doctor rushed to the trolley.

"Elizabeth, please come away from there," he spoke with a clinical density and detached toughness cultivated after several months of practice, but Tony's mother was shut down with shock trembling and shaking, her insides raw and jagged, like cut glass scraping on a wheel. Tears streaming from her eyes she sobbed hard without any let up, a plateau of pain glutting her soul. Her heart staving a beat and her mind shrinking, with fear.

"Please leave me, let me be with my son I need to be with him," she wailed, blue with anger.

"Please, just let me be close to him, I must stay with him," she fell to her knees as the doctor tried to scoop her away.

Bang Bang pretty pretty, all the colours weep for a mother's love that rocks you gently to sleep.

Tony had a nine-hour operation and for six months was force fed through a straw. His mother swore he would never be a victim again.

Chapter 2

When Tony reached the second floor of the Half Moon pub in Herne Hill the first sound that greeted him was the ding ding of the boxing clock chimed to go off every three minutes.

The main training area was rammed with fit young men, cut lean, muscle tight with firm brawn and plenty of gold ambition. It was a mosaic of rip and burn. Guys all over the gym were limbering up, doing stretching exercises, pulling, shadow boxing or juicing the jump ropes.

Fifty Cent was blaring out of the sound system, with speed bags and hand weights scattered over the wooden floors. Long line target mirrors and framed photographs of the world's greatest hung regally from the bouncing walls. Hand wraps and dozens of pairs of boxing gloves were strewn on the ground. The air was thick with the crackle of energy. All of the boxers were sweating success and T wanted more than a mouthful.

"You must be Tony," a tall good-looking black man of around thirty came towards him. He was *Promax* thin and chiselled to perfection. He spoke with a Jamaican *lilt* that hummed palm trees and tropical sands. A former heavyweight champion, he had the pretty- boy charm of a young Ali with the laid-back ease of Sugar Ray Leonard. He would be Tony's mentor trainer and surrogate father for the next year of his life.

"I'm Clayton," he put his hand out warmly, and T took it gladly.

"Confidence is what it's all about, turns a boy into a man son. If you want to make it in the ring you need focus, you need drive, and a sense of purpose. Most of all you need that hunger, the fire in your belly boy to make somethin' of yourself you has to catch that fire and do somethin' you can be proud of, that comes with *confidence.*"

Tony had never listened to such inspired jabber but he wanted to hear more and was glad he was there. He was keyed up and ready to flip but didn't want to make a fool of himself in front of so many sculpted Apollos.

"First off, let's do some easy stuff. We're gonna warm up do some straight stretches then later maybe, we'll try something more if I think you got that fire we talked about boy," instructed Clayton, with a soft pedal tone.

Tony was relieved he had a chance to get used to the whole idea of boxing before working the ring.

"Okay now watch mi Tony, knees bent, arms to the side, just follow my lead this is a very simple basic warm up, now keep your body loose, keep focused, and look this way," he signalled. Tony leaned into the routine with a natural fluency and gently Clayton took him through his paces like a Prom date's first dance; it was a gracious beginning.

"Okay that's good now one of the most important things I'm gonna teach you is how to wrap your hands before you go into a fight. Even before, you enter the ring or any of that stuff you have to know how to protect your hands. You must know what to do to keep your hands safe and prevent any snapped bones or violent breaks understand? Your hands are your weapons. Inside the ring they're capable of killing a man and you yourself, could be knocked out by a man's hand so you gotta keep them safe wherever you are d'ya get mi? Outside, inside wherever, man, you gotta shield them from any kind of danger or harm. Think of them like the crown jewels of your body – know what I'm sayin?"

"Yeah," Tony nodded with secret awe.

"Okay, so first wrap 'em like this" Clayton demonstrated.

"Strap the hook around your thumb and your second finger then move the cloth back to the outside of your hand like this," he continued.

Tony slowly wrapped the bandage around his hand until he had formed a distinctive criss- cross shape the rest of the bandage slipping nicely over his wrist.

"Good that's good, now you gotta check that it's tight enough so it won't slip off."

"Yeah fits good" Agreed T switched on and alert. He was fast on the draw, sapping up knowledge like a starved sea sponge.

"It should fit solid all the way around you know real snug." He flexed his hand over.

"Right, now if you were jammin' the ring you could strap on your gloves and protect yourself, but first let's see you on the jump rope and then we'll check out your position you get mi' I mean your boxing style." He threw Tony a skipping rope.

"Ever done this before man," he asked with a foxy grin.

"Nah" T replied with buttered- up shyness and looked away. He had the classic gaze of Snow White's *Bashful* with the whopping frame of Vin Diesel.

"Okay let's do it without the rope first, just step lightly from side to side and keep your wrists loose."

Tony deftly play- skipped without the rope, he was surprisingly nimble and had the natural agility and elegance of a young Darcy Bussell. Clayton knew within seconds that T was a champ' in the making.

"Good that's good now let's bust some moves."

"Yeah sweet."

"Okay, let's work out a regular boxing position. Your shoulders should be above your knees and your left hand should come smooth near your cheek okay now copy me," he signalled with his hands pointing to his eyes. "Just do the same as I do- good, now take a swing from there."

Tony took a shot.

"Not bad Tony, not bad at all." Clayton could see he had a powerful left hook. He moved to his right and placed a speed bag in front of him.

"Now Tony I want you to aim for the ball just like we practiced."

Tony pounded the bag with his right fist- he was too close and it slammed back at him with whizzing fury.

"Think of it as close to your chin son," Clayton explained.

"Right step up – not too close, Tony – now step away a little more, one two and jab, one two and hit that's it. Now, move your hands to the centre of the speed bag and on three get into the flow."

Tony hammered the bag first with his left hand then with his right. The lyrical symmetry of his footwork mirroring the beat of the one two jab.

"Now slide up, dip and drag- that's it drag with your feet good, slide dip and drag this is a three beat rhythm son."

Tony's body was moving like a jet stream throwing left jabs and right hooks while all the time his head was a perfect union of bob and weave.

"Okay that's great Tony you got your footwork tight now let me see you throw a few punches, come over here by the mirrors and watch me." Tony stood aside, as Clayton showed him which way to move his head, punch, and pace his footwork all at the same time in unbroken harmony.

"These head target mirrors show you exactly where to move your head, you got to cover yourself you know, in the ring you got to duck your head and attack so now you try. Step to the side and step in – keep your knees bent now go back so you won't get hit so much inside, see."

Tony was dipping in and out, dodging and diving.

"That's great you do your damage and then step back- to protect yourself."

Clayton beckoned him over.

"See this it's your best friend – the heavy punch bag. Your punches need to be fast but firm you know close, from the body. You're a heavy hitter but your punches shouldn't loop. The way to do it is to hit from the shoulder and keep the punches close and tight then step away out of range of your opponent – you slam it now."

Tony was sonic- burst happy he wasn't a *try- hard* now, he was a contender.

Every day it was the same routine. Up at five with a three mile jog to the gym, and six-hour training session. He would fuel his body with whole grains, yams and beans overdosing on chicken and tuna, and eggs and steak. A protein shake during exercise bouts added to the general gash and mend body regime he had adopted. He would eat six small meals a day and run solid, a deluxe build up for the Southern Counties Heavyweight tournament. In the shadows of Ali, Tyson, and Lewis, T was on his way to championship glory.

Chapter 3

T's professional debut was held at the legendary York Hall; Bethnal Green the "spiritual home" of London's boxing elite. All of the world-class fighters had graced its' hallowed ring and jacked its' golden ropes with meat and muscle. T was on the under card playing handmaid to the pros and the undefeated Cuban Alexi De Morra.

It was a ripe, spanking night the wind slapping the skin of the trees and hurling the leaves from top to bottom in a spin rush, shading the Autumn sky with thick brush strokes of colour, a post impressionist hue of twilight beauty.

Tony stared with wide- eyed wonder at the commanding edifice and extensive red frontage of the plinths and cornices made from Portland stone. It was a voracious testament of prize fighting history. From Charlie Magrit to Terry Spinks and beyond they all had a similar story starting out as amateurs from local boxing clubs to claim their place on the world stage.

T's supporters were out in full, a chopping symphony of friends, family, fellow fighters and street kids all hoping to goose his punch. York Hall was battered with press and product sponsors ready to net some fresh talent. The major event that night: a headline fight between Alexi De Mora and Russian explosion, Sergi Olov. The air was fever- pitch high spitting excitement and bubbling with testosterone. Would this be victory for T? Would he secure his professional ranking in the mighty York Hall? All eyes were on him and his rival, twenty five year old Joss Bullie, known for his deadly right hook and big hitting style. As T stepped up to the ring in his flash spot trunks he was all sparkle and shine. He boogied down the aisle to the hardcore rap of Slim Thugs: *Like a Boss.* Joss strutted forward; listening to Ozzie Osborne's *Paranoia* together, they weighed more than five hundred pounds. It was gonna be a pow- wow night full of split and slit. Their ref' was in a cream coloured mood, inscrutable but composed.

"In the blue corner weighing in at two hundred and twenty five pounds we have the London Truncheon Tonyyyyyyyyyyeeeee T, and in the red corner hitting the scales at just under two hundred and twenty three pounds the Belgian Messer Joss Bullllllllie!"

"Now gentleman touch gloves, I want a good clean fight and above all protect yourselves at all times."

Tony came out slam- bam hot with a left right left turning his body to flex, jab and swing curving from his cheek nice and tight. He was bruising his way to a comfortable first round. Straight long punches, working a waltz: slide- dip and drag all the time bob and weave bob and weave. The pace getting faster and faster. Duck! Tony blocking the socking thump of Bullie's right hand. Even paced and pushing for a hard left off T's rib cage the Belgian was not giving in. Tony was gliding around like a figure skater, his footwork smoother than a *Pink Floyd* baseline and twice as chilled. Clayton at ringside was steaming guts and fire, chomping out positivity and pepping him up, while his drill coach gave him a much needed shoulder rub and pat down.

Why's he doing that, doing what I'm doing he asked himself with crushing anxiety. Then, T missed several punches and Bullie took maximum advantage of his growing nerves Bullie, pressed barred and finally sandwiched him to the ropes. Their heads locked like two butting rams. T with an open cut to his cheek, showing extraordinary strength by doing his utmost to stop, block and defend. This was an epic challenge and T was caving in, run over by Bullie's defensive grit – but still it was game on. An inspired right hand- left hook combo' on Bullie struck the closing bell, now Tony's eye was popping. In the fifth, the Belgian took the lead, T's eye swelling up like a globoid balloon. Clayton was rightly stressed.

"His eye is growing a mouse," he said quietly.

"We have to get him out of there," he sighed, ready to give up, but T was spunked to the max rapping Bullie with a blitz of body shots and head knocks.

"I wanna stay," he rushed, his words dropping, as he chunked for air.

"I wanna go on – don't get me out I'm staying." T refused to break.

Bullie had the upper hand in round six, Tony's eye softening his rhythm and wearing him down. Then his gum shield dropped out. He scrambled to replace it, but within seconds, Bullie had launched an impressive volley of punches on T's chest, head and chin. T was now in massive trouble. A final double right hook thrust him to the canvas. Limping to his feet like a wounded animal, he was a drowning reflection of a *Herman Nietzsche* liturgy. More than blood was on the line this was a battle for a man's soul. Tony lay slumped on the ground, he was finding it hard to breathe and his eyes were blurred and addled with pain.

"I don't feel my body, I don't feel my legs," he choked. The medics laid him to one side so he wouldn't swallow his tongue, but, there was just nothing, no response. Blacked out, and bloodied to the bone his dreams of a better life now a shattered pastiche of severed glory. It was worse than a bad break it was a Broadway Tragedy.

Tony suffered a detached retina and a fractured cheekbone. A botched operation followed, leaving him permanently blind in one eye and killing all hope of a future comeback.

I got a fist full of misery and a chain of suffering he surmised with sterling poignancy.

Chapter 4

Enter: March Aloysius Clarence a Jamaican Elder, an original Yardie gangster, now CEO and operations Director of one of the most feared criminal enterprises in South London. Don March was a *boom boom shake the room* kind of guy with dreadlocked hair, pimp cane, 20 ounce and pinkie ring, displaying more bling than *Mr. T* of the *A Team*. He was cool as shit and had a talk- sexy charisma that made him slick with the ladies and emulated by men. A money-baller, he commanded respect and malice in equal measure.

He was resourceful and knowingly opportunistic. In Tony, he saw a bright, high-spirited individual with natural charm and a self-possessed easy approach to life. He wanted him for his crew.

Soon after T's stay in hospital, he invited him to breakfast at the Wolseley in Piccadilly London. Tony knew who Don March was, he also knew he couldn't take a crumb and crust job as a working stiff in regular employment. Tony wasn't built for service he had a more laissez – faire attitude with a hint of aux-abois speculation. *Being is what it is*. Tony's *Sartre* perspective on life had always worked well for him in the past and he was counting on it now.

Don March was seated in the lavish grandeur of the Wolseley like a Roman Emperor presiding over his kingdom. Before him, a full English breakfast comprising of scrambled eggs, bacon, sausage, baked beans tomato, black pudding mushrooms and tea. An august feast fit for Tiberius and his dynastic family. He waved him over grinning gold and glitter he was bling-dazzle hip.

"Rude Bwoy! Come sit wif me man come on over 'ere-man run tings 'ere man you like this man this is fine man, best place to eat breakfast bwoy."

"Respeck man." Responded T with veritable reverence.

"This is fine as hell man check out the ceilings, the lights, the floors man, best place to start the day. When a man has a strong start to the day and a big breakfast there's nothin' he can't do d'ya get mi ' bwoy."

"Yeah it's bad, fine as fuck." Agreed T still checking out the crisp white linen, bespoke table and silverware. His eyes fixed on the symmetrical sweeping staircase, chinoiserie and Venetian themed chandeliers. The Wolseley's noble heritage, Doric pillars, thirty-foot ceilings and opulent design, a permanent reminder of Italian artistry. The waiter was buddy-buddy helpful. Don March had a quality reputation as a bountiful tipper and fix – it guy he was popular and well- known there. They even kept a special bottle of West Indian Econa pepper sauce for him to use on his food. Don March liked the fact that he and T were the only black people, in a washed sea of white faces.

"Good morning, Sir, well now what will you have today?"

"Yea, I'll have the full English," smiled T.

"Yes Sir good choice and will you have tea?"

"Yeah and orange juice."

"Certainly Sir."

"You like this Tony, you wanna 'ave some of this bad bwoy mi cargo is fine huh?" exulted Don March.

"Yeah man nuff respeck. Like- this? Who wouldn't like it man?"

"Check in deep man soon come, this shit is real you know it."

"Yeah man."

"Come here bwoy come look 'ere see da picture of mi, this is mi other family man see that wiv mi horses and ting. Mi got private schools for mi childrens, and look man a white woman. She makes me credible you know what I'm sayin' man."

"Where's that house then?" Asked T more impressed with the layout and size of the home than the *trophy* white *bitch*.

"Me live in a stoosh place the house is a remade castle man in Surrey I built it miself. I got mi two lives one here in London and one in Surrey – it stays private what no one knows about."

"And what your wife tink you do?"

"Oh man she tinks mi a music producer mi keep it low – key in Surrey you know just chillin' wit the local people and ting. Music producer man is the best front there is for this kind of work. It allows you to operate at night and keep some glamour pussy near by y'a get mi?"

"Yeah" T nodded.

"So now, let mi tell you the story of Don March: anyting is possible here man. I came here with nothin. I was the original no-moneyman. You get mi, I was on the run man from back home Trench Town. Those days man I was a fool runnin all over town so mi got 'ere, mi had nothin so mi had nothin to lose understand.

Mi only 'ad one choice man: SURVIVAL. Mi had me crosses to bear and mi didn't want to be down pressed all mi life d'ya get mi?"

"Yeah man" Replied T listening intently.

"Well I got to Croydon and stayed with mi posse they gave me areas to run you know what I'm sayin' from da time I got there to now only been five years man." He raised his hands and showed five digits to re- emphasize the point. "Now look at mi I got mi own liccle Empire and people runnin for mi now." He leant back in the gilded chair and slapped his knee beckoning T closer:

"If you do it good you can 'ave it all man everyting cook and curry man cook and curry."

"So..."

"So you get it by starting small then when bizzo falls into place and you get the trust from the people we take you all the way man all the way to the Top Table understand?"

"Yeah man."

"Well what you tink then man you in?"

"It's a good life man."

"Yes indeed."

"Don March?"

"Yes man."

"Why does the waiter keep calling you Lord March?"

"Hee Hee," he rolled with laughter.

"Yes mi bought the title man mi is a *Lord* right and proper."

Don March even had a soubriquet of Viscount March that was more than a little ironic as there was a real Lord March in the actual House of Lords.

"Yes man mi tinks me is Viscount March I paid for it, paid to play the money game and take my seat at the Top Table man. I *paid* to *belong.*"

Viscount, Lord, what did it matter the fact was Don March was top dog and Czar of South London

"So all them other..."

"Businesses."

"Yeah businesses what are they in?" Asked T with frank gullibility.

"Hee he it's everyting wanti wanti can getti getti no want understand ?"

"Yeah."

"It's bitches, betting, chop shop car deals, money from the street, ID scam everyting understand all part of March's bizzo but we don't cheat the street understand we don't take from our women or children never sell to anyone under age understand they have to be fully **grown** to take **it** home get mi?"

"Yeah, so was it hard back home?"

"Lord God man yes I was only a yout of ten when mi earnt my stripe as a shotta but it was the only way for mi to get outta the ghetto. Listen to mi you had tree choices: You played football, you sang songs or you become sponsored by a Drug Don and you know we give back to our own man that's the way it happened to mi. Just a bullet a bag and a dream that's all I had and now mi got all of this oh yeah zimm zimm zimmer sweet"

"I'm only dealing to the *bashment* crowd no children, no hard ups that's the way I wanna roll," T explained.

"Yeah that's safe man you got to have your line and stick to it man you got to ketch man make it real get mi?"

"Yeah man."

"All that's between you and all of this is a Ratchet and a Mac 9 that's the way we spell Front Line - Stonebridge where all our people is at man but if you screw the market it's easy to score. There's so many big rich people to pork man – then you can get everyting man and a liccle bit extra trust mi."

"Yeah soon come ay say this is the life I'm lookin' for man this is it," T concurred in thoughtful mood.

"Y'ar know you could have been a real mamadoo a top boxing champ man, shame about your eye – but it's SURVIVAL bwoy listen chicken merry da hawk is near understand?"

Tony put on an earnest face but was unsure of some of the more colourful Yardie terms and just fudged it not really understanding everything that Don March was saying.

"Soon come and remember T got to keep running costs low in the city yeah run it low keep your overheads minimum."

"Yeah I get that."

"You got to take it easy – small at first then one cocofil up a basket."

"Aay say."

"Now what mi gonna do is put you in wit de baddest rude bwoy there is dem is liccle B (Big Bernie) they call him but don't you be callin' him liccle B not yet not to his face otherwise he gonna mash you up. You know Bernie he got plenty of Bandalu bizness to get you earning. He's one sharp cookie y'ar know he's got plenty of bandulu bizness to get you grafting but he's not a blabba mout and 'ee's got it all, knows his figures, what scams to run knows what works and what won't then soon you'll be a Don Dadda that's the way to do it man. I'll hook you up with liccle B and soon you'll be badder than Don March hee hee!"

They continued eating and mixing dialects Patois and English in the velvet luxury of the Wolseley toasting T's entry to the good life and sorting out the meat and potatoes of their undertaking. Don March would take a ten percent cut of all bizzo for the first six months and thereafter the deal would be re-negotiated.

"So, now I got a place for you to stay – nice flat on the South Side. Your crew has to be tight man, dem has to be people close to you dat you can trust wit your life man, people who you keep clamped to your chest, know what i'm sayin, no harries no worries everyone joins the party, get mi? No time for diva attitudes we run a tight crew get mi?"

"Yes man."

Chapter 5

The chunking groove of the Croydon nucleus was a hive of bars, clubs, pubs and house parties it was a microscopic speculum of Caribbean street life so at the start T served the local community with marijuana and cocaine never dealing crack unlike other West Indian dealers.

Then, under Don March's private tutelage, he began supplying the clubs and bars and VIP holes of the London glitterati, moving up the criminal career ladder and making a name for himself as someone who could be trusted and would deliver.

T's business was open 24/7 and busier than Billingsgate Market. Everyone was buying coke: those that were blessed with diamonds on the soles of their shoes and those that were cursed to the netherworld. T soon pegged that cocaine was a universal, multi- user cross- cultural high and stopped selling weed altogether.

The coke profits paid for more than his rent, sundries and upwardly mobile lifestyle, they paid for social acceptance and a plausible identity. From now on Tony was no longer a boxing dead -beat he was an entrepreneur, a Record Producer, a Promotions Dealer, and low –level investor. He had a prime appetite for success and the Einstein precocity in Bernie, was particularly impressive.

T was different to other dealers he hardly ever used drugs for personal consumption and was diversifying at terrific speed. With Bernie's lissom bizzo flair and T's princely charm, they became a hit amongst the Bugatti classes taking themselves out of the ghetto and into the Rich Man's Club of uptown. T was looking for more than just a *pimpster's paradise*, using *dirty cash* to free himself of *white lines* and a bread and butter existence.

That night while they were counting their monies, they were cut short in their calculations by the shriek and shrill of Tony's former girlfriend mother of his child Amber. "Toneeeeeee it's me Brittne!" she raged.

"We can't let that psychotic bitch in she'll get fed up soon man."

"You think so bro' the woman is like one serious evil bitch."

"She'll get tired soon man."

"You sure, she's like a roasting hog about to frazzle man."

"I can't talk to her right now let's move this gear somewhere safe."

"She's holding up bizzo man.Your space should be free from such fuckery man serious, can't stand that bitch."

T's crew were all inside they needed to drive into West End Central and score the door of L'equipe before midnight but the stupid slag wouldn't let up.

"You guys go through the back – you know the side entrance," directed T

"And I'll deal with this, but the griping slut was still whining through the letterbox flapping it noisily.

"If you don't open this door right now I'm gonna blow it off!" She oinked.

Tony did his best to ignore her.

"She's scaring me," muttered Bernie under his breath.

Within seconds, she had dropped a homemade grenade through the letterbox. It was more of a firecracker than a missile but the kitchen and storeroom were sparking flames.

"What the fuck! Phone the fire brigade now man."

Bernie lobbed the phone at him.

"I'll go check on the merchandise."

"Yeah this is 53 Addington New Road my ex has tried to burn mi house down."

Tony's principal priority was the money and the stash of coke hidden underneath the floorboards in his bedroom. The Fire Crew caught the blaze just in time. Minutes later, it would have spread through the entire house.

"That insane bitch. Why the fuck do I do this job man?" T was feeling the pressure of keeping one kilo of coke worth £26,000 safe from the crazy slut.

"She slashed Dipsy's tyres and threw all my clothes away and now she does this says she wants to get back together again. I've had enough it's too much of a gamble to stay here." T was carving a rep as a big shark in a local pond; he was making tracks breaking ground. The last thing he needed was cuckoo bitch screwing up his chances.

There was only one option he had to move into the West End or Soho that's where most of his customer base was concentrated now anyway and where he could increase, and expand operations without any trailer trash interruptions. The stench of dry smoke and charred tinder were chugging his throat with corrosives.

"Can you fucking believe that man – we have to thank God and count our blessings that we still got our stuff and that everything is safe. We could 'ave got busted or the bitch could have made me lose it all man in the friggin ' fire she could 'ave created havoc man take mi bread my living man, and fucked me up big time."

"Yeah man she's like fucking radio rental we gotta get out."

"Yeah time to leave the fucked up country dive of crappy Croydon and boogey on down to the West End of London now that's what I'm talkin' about man."

"You'll 'ave to tell Don March."

"Yeah I'll call he's got a place for us right in the centre of coke central."

"Cool."

"Still can't believe what that crazy whore was gonna do she's Amber's mother you know she's totally crazy, man one crazy coconut know what I mean, no way back for her selfish bitch and I'm gonna get my baby girl off her too if she carries on – I mean it. It's *always* about her, she's always looking for *her* cut, *her* steal of the deal, *her* way out."

"Yeah she's fuckin' dangerous man."

"Serious brov."

"Hey Don March it's T man. Yeah everythin' is fine man everythin' is safe but we wanna move now you know it's aggravation station with the bitch man she's walking down ruination line man so we wanna move like today you know in the place you got in the West End. There's too much nastiness it's gettin' in the way of bizzo the sooner we move the better I'll feel."

They took the blow, their guns, two cases of amo' some clothes, and shut the door on suburbia for good.

Chapter 6

At least three, sometimes four, and even five times a day, casual builders, rising pop stars, and slick-suited Essex blokes making their way to and from Bank Tube Station would whistle, wave, or hoot their car horns to try and get Eva's attention.

Eva was a "hot" blonde with glamour girl curves and an irresistible innocence about her. She spurned them all. She had an exclusive attachment to a certain someone. He was special: brave, good, and true, a modern knight, someone who believed in her and made her feel a perfect ten. It was a cliché, she was quietly smug about. She hung onto that feeling for days.

Eva had always thought of herself as a maverick actress, and at work, she would while away the day playing with different scenarios in her head. She likened herself to the tragic femme fatales of the fifties and sixties. She was cool, edgy, sometimes angst ridden, and had no sense of "self," just like Garbo and Monroe, or so she thought

"I can be just like Marilyn," she rippled as she applied her Perfect Red YSL lipstick with a slightly affected air and carried on with her work. Eva Potoski, twenty- four and originally from Lodz in Poland, lived in Battersea now with her two sisters and an aging aunt. She had been a paralegal with Deschamps Bouverie for eight months. She was congenial and, for the most part, easy going with her work colleagues, all, that is, except her Senior Partner, Richard, for whom she had a seething dislike. He was always lying to her.

He never wanted to do any work, and he was always at lunch. She felt like spilling the beans to her other bosses and letting them know about his four- hour trips to the local lap dancing bar in Holborn Circus, and his stealthy comings and goings to the office at night. Why did he even bother showing up at all?

She had to do all the donkeywork; Francesca would type it up and he would sign it in the firm's name. He appeared to do very little except wax lyrical about his pension and tax liabilities and his plans for a retirement home in the south of France. Richard Davey, Senior Partner at Deschamps Bouverie, at thirty five years old, a bit too chubby now to be considered "phowar" but attractive, nonetheless, firm, and round of face.

He had a happy, ruddy hue and sharp blue eyes that seemed to say, "How much am I worth?" They really said, "Hello, goodbye." Not yet married, he had too many encounters of the wrong kind with female clients, female work associates, and sundry females whom he met by chance on the street.

Richard enjoyed the power of being a lawyer and not much else. He liked the way it sounded to his erstwhile friends who had never made the grade, those that had to settle for less and were never part of anything more than the daily grind. Richard, on the other hand, believed he was affecting change where it mattered; he was making shit happen.

Why, then, did he feel like the "Man on the Hill," out of reach, out of touch, and, worse, out of control? Richard was up to his neck in it, that's why. Nobody knew about the spiralling debts, his secret connections with the criminal elite, and the coke demons and whiskey goblins dancing in his head.

Chapter 7

"Come in, please sit down" Richard was being as pleasant as his money mouth would allow.

"I understand you are a business man and property magnate in Mumbai is that right?"

"Yes...I have lots of what you might call big wheel enterprises from rice export to Bollywood movies"

"Indeed, so what is it exactly can we do for you here at Deschamps Bouverie. We of course, handle all kinds of commercial, tax, investment and other areas of corporate practice that may of be use to you."

Poncho leaned forward getting as close to Richard as the desk that separated them would let him:

"I would like a *yes* man" he proclaimed with a sneaky look in his eye.

"Excuse me" Replied Richard in a startled tone.

"You heard Richard – let's not um how is it you English put it beat around the bush. I want a nodding poodle and I choose you. You will take care of all my deals, set-ups, ventures, buyouts; buy ins, and so on. I will pay you for all the work and, pay the professional fees of your Firm upfront with special consideration for you and that sum will go directly to you"

Richard was stumped by such a forthright proposal and the dictatorial almost bullish hostility expressed by Poncho. He had nailed Richard in one and he knew Richard was too yellow-bellied to ask any further questions of him. Richard needed that money like a needle needs a spoon.

"I will arrange some tranches of money to be delivered to you, I expect you to return the monies to me minus your administrative fees, and will be in touch with all the details shortly."

Richard stared at him in abject horror, knowing this man would string him up like a worming chicken, if he dared to disobey. With bootlicking subservience, he answered:

"Yes Sir Mr Khan."

"You and only you will deal with my matters, the suitcases of money will be delivered by my right- hand man Mungle as and when, and *you* Richard will be my personal guest in Dubai next weekend at my Gold Palace where I will give you a very special Bearer Bond to hold for me. Do we understand one another?" He got up to leave.

"Can I um ask Mr Khan what would my percentage fee be for the financial transactions?"

"Oh the usual."

Richard looked at him quizzically.

"You know ¼ of a penny on the pound twenty five per cent."

"Oh right" Acknowledged Richard.

"And um how much do we anticipate?"

"Oh maybe twenty or thirty million a year obviously you are competing with other top lawyers I have retained and instructed several firms all over the world including Bangkok the

USA, Vancouver and most of the Capital cities of Europe all of them trade dirty."

He sat back down again and peered at him with open revulsion.

"You don't have the guts to tell me you don't want any part in this. It's a global enterprise. Now, please be a good boy and bring me a Black Label Johnnie Walker." He ordered, with bitter relish.

"Um it's only 11.30 am."

"Yes, I know," Answered Poncho with a note of contempt.

"I always have a Malt Whisky before lunch now jump to it and go get me a bottle."

Richard clipped the intercom button and gave Poncho a reassuring look.

"Get me the keys to the drink's cabinet they're in Mr. Wiesel's room."

"Yes Sir Mr Davey." Eva replied with the cut- and dried competency of a cube slave.

A few minutes later she bunny- hopped back into Richard's office with a Monroe tease clutching the key to her chest.

"Here it is," she buttered quietly.

"Thank you Eva – this is Mr Khan, whenever he or anyone representing him visits the Firm regardless of whether he has an appointment and irrespective of what time of the day it is you must ensure you let me know."

Eva did her wink- wink nudge- nudge routine and left.

Richard poured a glass for Poncho and one for himself

Poncho took a beefy slurp, stood up and tipped Richard two thousand in cash.

"For your time today – the first of the suitcases will arrive tomorrow at noon."

Chapter 8

When T got the keys for the flat in Denmark Street, someone was already waiting for him.

"You Tony? Don March told me I could crash here for a liccle bit, the name's Keggs."

"Yeah yeah that's cool – you look rough man" Answered T looking at him shifty eyed.

"I'm waiting to crap."

T turned towards Bernie then they both fixed their eyes on Keggs.

"Mi don't get ya?"

"Yeah what it is man is, right at this moment I've got twenty two condoms of uncut cocaine in mi I need a potty and some of those like rubber gloves ooh boy yes indeed."

T signalled to Godwin to get the requested items who sent Sabbatini to the local Robert Dyas.

"Be about ten minute's boss."

T was used to the insane and sketchy going on but this was seriously nasty and although he knew he couldn't cross Don March he wasn't overjoyed at the prospect of a white Jamaican fresh from Tivoli dunking his gear into a toddler's training box.

Keggs flopped onto a chair causing Bernie to remonstrate in protest:

"No man get up from there bro you'll 'ave to go outside when you're ready you know until then I think it's best to like just stand."

"Yeah okay, all mi money is back home y'know the movie *countryman*?"

"Yeah."

"That's mi, man that's mi life right now got into a gun fight and now mi on da run not just from dem yardies but dem Columbians too."

"You what?" Grieved T in alarm.

"Well bro' de Columbian's supply chain was broken, mi broke it off just like that snap!" He gestured as if snapping apart the head of a chicken.

"What you did?"

"Mi knocked out the cardinal man – he was onto mi for supplying and cutting him out so mi whacked 'im out crucial boderation man!"

"You Is de original hot stepper!" Remarked T, with grudging respect.

"You getting this Bernie man Keggs is taken out the Cardinal."

"I hear man," Bernie was poised but quietly concerned.

"So mi cash keep getting taken from mi understand I have everyting in cash."

This was customary among Yardies, who had a vicious disrespect and well- known suspicion of all or any type of banking or financial institutions and were fiercely opposed to storing their money there.

"This is mi second time here – last time was about seven years ago mi was charged with robbery but mi brief got mi off dat charge. Anyway back to now, I left home and got a boat from there to Haiti, there mi bredren got mi to Miami where I lay low for a long time."

"I's gonna sit now."

He was leaning against a wall, and then carefully sat down.

"I was in hiding you know from the big bout the Columbian and I was doin' my thing. Y'ar know mi is smooth with dem ladies there was this one hot biscuit man you never did see such a sugabomb she was wit mi y'ar know we were in one of the baddest clubs in South Beach. Mi remember it so clear in my head. It was boonoonnoonous, de club was cork up and me and her was rump- shaking, doin it fine then big bout storms de club and everyting go chaka –chaka..Next ting I know my bredren is down serious, he shoot 'im in de back so mi just fire snap crackle and pop!"

"Dat's serious boderation man."

"Was easy to get out man got a fake passport and mi here now dem no check mi. Too busy lookin' for coolie types y'ar know dem terrorist ones so mi not get checked at all."

"How you feelin' now?" Asked T nervously.

"Mi okay, mi know when it be ready..."

"You alright for money?"

"Oh yes man mi 'ave a liccle bit on mi and mi get paid for muleing dis coke over mi get to take mi cut y'ar know. Mi get Western Union to wire mi money over and bein' a mule will help me buy- live and supply, mi not stay for free and mi only stay a short time man. Mi give you and Don March your respect man."

"Yeah safe man what's the plan?"

"Well when mi ready mi do my business then mi cook it up and turn it all into rocks."

"Yeah that sounds bad man have you done that before?"

"Yes bro mi do it lots of times its safe man."

"So you just have to wait now?" Queried Bernie.

"Yes man let nature take its course sit on the potty bowl then it can be cleaned and cooked up."

"Well when you're ready let Godwin know there's a safe place to do it outside and then it won't be so rank in here man"

"What will you need?"

A pan, a liccle baking powder and the luck of dem Irish !"

"It's easy to get wrong." Cautioned T

"Mi done it many times bro' so long as you get those bubbles down when it's cookin' you got to keep flattening it out, then when it's pure white and solid you lay them to rest and drain them out."

"Then what?" Asked Bernie, interested in the science of it all.

"Then you put it in the freezer for a good thirty minutes or so and abracadabra you got yourself your first cash call of the night."

"Nice but we don't do crack 'ere man this is strictly a one-time deal get mi?"

"No problem bro I don't wanna show you no disrespect man but I'ave to pay my dues and this is what mi got."

"Yeah man but I don't deal crack and I don't make crack so this is it if you wanna deal it you do it understand mi?"

"Yes man no need for any aggravation I'll be able to roll to mi own yard in a couple of day's man."

"Sweet one time only man nuff said" Reinforced T.

"When I'm ready I'll shout for Godwin."

"Godwin!" T hollered.

"Yes Boss."

"When Keggs is ready take him and the potty outside near the rubbish bins and keep guard then when he's done his business get him everyting he needs to make the crack hear mi."

"Yes Boss."

Within forty-eight hours of Kegg's arrival, he had quadrupled his initial fee of twenty thousand as a mule by splicing up the drug and pushing it on the street. He had made enough to start his own mafia family and pay his dues to T and Don March it was Tony Soprano sublime.

Chapter 9

Richard was tripping the morning away. Plugged into Queens of The Stone Age on his iPod he had his feet on the desk and was lolling back in his office swivel chair thinking of a coconut breeze, the hot bang of his favourite club chick and his growing profit margins.

"Mr Davey a suitcase has arrived from Mr Khan and there is a gentleman in reception with it shall I?"

"Yes send him in straight away."

Richard jerked his legs straight and disconnected his ear piece shuffling the papers on his desk then straightening his tie attempting to exude an air of importance and proficiency.

"Heeello," Gruffed a small bespectacled Indian man: A mixture of Joe Pesci and Mahatma Ghandi with the perma grin of an Insurance Salesman He spoke with a scratchy lisp that reminded Richard of hissing beetles.

"Hello, please sit down can I er get you anything to drink or?"

"Oh no trouble Sirrrr perhaps a little chai and something sweet like a Rich Tea biscuit I very much enjoy Rich Tea biscuits one of those would be most delightful."

"Yes of course" Richard replied with anodyne civility.

"Now Mr. Richard I have been a self taught Accountant in Mumbai for many years and I have been Mr. Khan's assistant for several moons and so I know a little bit about banking and so on but I just want to check some things out okay?"

"Yes of course."

"Now from what I understand in England if you bank more than ten thousand pounds in cash the Bank of England make a note of it. They make a note of where the monies come from and they report the provenance of it if you will, and that is noted to Scotland Yard and so on, that the cash is banked if it is ten thousand pounds or more am I correct in this assumption?"

"Well yes ordinarily that would be correct Mr..." Richard paused so that he could wait for a name he didn't want to offend with an incorrect pronunciation.

"Just call me Mungle."

"Yes well, ordinarily that would be the case but solicitors' client accounts are in fact exempt from the rule, as the authorities rely on the honour and integrity of the legal profession to do the necessary. Should the lawyer feel there is a danger of suspect funds then it really is up to the lawyer to make that judgment call."

"Yes very good- this means that there will be no notifications made on the credit lodged with your bank through your Firm's client account."

"None whatsoever."

"This is most excellent – very good thank you and my humble thanks for the chai it was very enjoyable – just how I like it, oh before I forget here is the Bearer Bond please store it safely and guard it with your life. Poncho or I will be contacting you again shortly, for now goodbye and safe tidings, and remember: If you live in the river you should always make friends with the crocodile goodbye." He coiled out of the room sissing to himself in Hindi.

Richard opened a file and had the trunk of money sent to the bank and lodged on the Firm's account after taking his cut. Within seven days, he had laundered it better than Jeeves of Belgravia, running it through the Firm's Client Account and returning it to Poncho starch pressed and stain free. He made an entry on the Firm's books that the matter had been aborted. Now it was time for a coco- cola break *just for the taste of it* nothing like the *real thing*. He checked that no one was about and then went to his sealed, side cabinet and took out his private stash. Inside, approximately three grams. He discreetly unwrapped it then remembered his door was unlocked so quickly bolted it shut letting Eva know he was not to be interrupted under any circumstances.

Once settled he put the coke on a flat part of his desk, removed his American Express Black card from his wallet and frantically started cutting it getting ready for a hit. He searched again for his silver Tiffany straw but couldn't find it so made do with one from Pret- A- Manger snipping the ends off so he could do some lines. He looked like Gordon Ramsay chopping parsley. Once it was all separate and he had enough laid out to get wired he bent down and huffed in for the win.

Richard was breezing the moment with that *nothing's gonna touch me* feeling, his soul whispering the lyrical passion of the sweetest sonata as he got coke bomb high – he juiced up his iPod and started hammering the lyrics to U2's *First Time*

"For the first time I feel love...my father is a rich man he wears a rich man's cloak..."

His Bono polemic scaling alarming heights when he started aping the lyrics to *Stuck in a Moment You Can't Get Out* Of It. Unlike Bono's chiffon drawl, Richard sounded like a diseased tabby gulling for food. Things got progressively worse with his theatrical improv' of Barry White's: *You're the First, The Last, My Everything* just as he reached the middle eight, in full flow he, unbuckled his suit trousers, and flung them onto the back of his chair while doing the stirring- the- pot dance routine dressed only in his yellow Calvin Klein Hipsters. As he moved around the office waving his arms in front of him, his hips and body were rolling in the other direction. He was wasted on the music.

He seized his dictating machine using it as an impromptu microphone and bellowed the song lyrics out : "The first my last my everything and the answer to all my.......my kind of wonderful I know and with you I found so many things can't you see it's you you're like a first morning dew. You're my reality."

He looked like a humpty – dumpty version of Tom Cruise in *Risky Business* and just at that point in came Richie's cousin Josh, a Jesse Eisenberg wannabe complete with a movie – star Jew fro and smug little grin. He was also, unlike Mr. Eisenberg a wizard shoplifter. Richie had been asked by his uncle Marvin to look after him, but he was out of control, the door on the lock proving no obstacle for his Cracker Jack fingers.

"Why thank you Richie, I'm touched oops I did it again busted you when you were hitting up the white lady, awh and you 're so sweet chanteusing Barry's love tracks a moi."

"Shut it – shut that fucking door now," boiled Richie.

"Sure" He replied with deliberate tedium.

"Hurry up fuckwit."

He scrambled for his trousers and wiped his desk clean of all the drug paraphernalia.

"What the fuck do you want anyway?" He snapped.

"I just thought I'd let you know I intend doing a bit of shopping today and I want you to be around, you know just in case anything should occur." He spoke in a hammed up Stephen Fry accent.

"Don't be fucking silly – you're not thinking of doing that?"

"My weapon of choice for today will be this." He twirled a large candy striped umbrella in the air and made a D'Artagnan swipe at Richie.

"How much do you want?"

"No it's not about want Richie it's about desire the ride, the thrill understand?"

"The only thrill you'll be getting is a kick in the kishka!" He bristled.

"Look Richie I don't want the money to buy, that defeats the whole purpose of my afternoon just be there for me ta ta for now."

"Wait – please you little shithead come back!"

It was too late he left the office and made straight for the Piazza in Covent Garden.

About thirty minutes later Richie was summonsed to the Paul Smith shop on Floral Street.

"My lawyer." Smirked Josh.

"What seems to be the problem?" Queried Richie.

An over groomed sales assistant with stuck –up –cunt syndrome, neo- punk hair and Goth- sauced nails was holding a pair of signature chintz wool trousers in her right hand and a mobile phone in the other she was ready for action.

"This person I believe was intending to steal these," She gloated as if she had unmasked a dangerous killer.

"Could we go somewhere more discreet?" Richard asked softly.

"Er yes okay my office."

All three of them entered a small back room at the far end of the store.

"I understand your position Madam but my client says that he was merely trying to view the item in daylight with respect it's hardly aglow with luminosity in here is it?"

"The shop has a themed decor and the lighting is part of that," Replied the sales woman stiffly.

"You said on the telephone that my client opened his umbrella and you discovered the trousers in the rib of the umbrella but it was possible, was it not that he was merely carrying both items and checking the trousers in the light. He never left the store with the trousers, and so, contrary to your somewhat misguided assertion he had no *intent* to actually steal those trousers."

"I suppose that could be true," she agreed sorely.

"I suggest then in the interests of saving time, money and a nasty fracas in the shop we simply put this incident down to a regrettable misunderstanding."

"Fine."

Richie turned to his cousin.

"Would you like those trousers?"

"Nah they're too shiny" He retorted wrinkling his nose up at them.

"Right then we'll be off."

Outside the store, Richie was fuming.

"You fucking cretin, Meshuggina, you will be punished for this I'll let your father know. Go home now!" Demanded Ritchie

"Or what?" Josh ribbed.

"You'll see."

Josh wasn't going to wimp out on the threat but knew he had stepped out of line.

"Okay I'm gone I'll be home in like ten minutes."

"I'll be checking with uncle Marvin to make sure" Richie knuckled, he was all played out and tired of all this fuckery.

What right have I got to set the moral code I'm NOT A REAL MAN a real man makes an honest living

Chapter 10

What a bastard awakening! No safety of the radio today because the fuse had gone.

The familiar sounds of urban beats: Hip-hop tunes denouncing war and rough justice were not there to distract her racing mind. She had to face change. Today was a God-awful day and it was going to get heavier.

The air was like molten lead with the stale sharpness of a small town funeral. There was cold, unadulterated fear in her eyes, the blunt realism of no money—no cash, no checkbook, no credit, simply no way to get any food today. She would starve quietly, gently with dignity and a lying smile on her face. Her throat would be dry all day and slightly hoarse, her breath sweet. Her middle class defiance pushing her on.

She began making frantic telephone calls from her mobile phone, her hands trembling slightly, in a last ditch effort to rustle up some cash, but then frustration kicked in like a mocking school friend who had already discovered the truth about Father Christmas.

She looked away from random passers-by, office people, and hotel staff fresh from their two weeks in the sun, munching sandwiches and scoffing daytime trivia. She sat alone with her thoughts, alone with her pain. Her isolation was shielding her from the shame of it all. She was in her fifth decade and resolute in her conviction to carry on.

Her head hurt; she felt light, giddy, and weak. Gentrified poverty was a bind. Desperate to taste the numbing sweetness of a Fry's chocolate cream or the temporary kindness wrapped up in a Marks & Spencer's Cherry Jam Slice. That would sooth her anxiety; allow her two short minutes from her broken existence. Damn, she was unable to find the lousy £2.50 she needed to change her sullen mood.

What would she do all day, now that she was bereft of purpose? How would she cope? She continued watching those around her, those with jobs, and those who had a reason to get by and get along, those who had a daily rhythm. She was missing the beat of life. How she envied the dulling frequency of normality. Mrs. Calibresi had a tough existence but braved it through as best as she could. She only knew how to work.

Now, with the collapse of the family business and being overloaded with debt, she was lost without it. She could do nothing else; all she ever did was work. Without work, her soul was empty and her mind bleeding for hope. She thought back to easier times. She had missed so many opportunities: a promising film career and a string of affluent admirers all thrown to the wayside. If only she had married a real man, someone she could depend on, someone she wouldn't regret. Someone, who was worthy of her love.

Instead, she was lumbered with a no -no man. He was spineless, afraid of getting his hands dirty, and content to play the female role. He was just a filthy excuse for a "man." It was up to her now to make things work and save the rest of the business for her family. She hoped that she would be able to stay in the game long enough to make everything all right. As she turned her gaze away from the crowds in front of her, she saw her grown up son approach her.

He made her believe in fairytale endings and new tomorrows. She worried about him all the time. Even though he was in his third decade, she felt for him as you would a six-year-old child. Seeing his beaming face made her think back to happier times when she was young and fresh faced with a fragile vulnerability; now her silent beauty was etched with grey, the grey you find in the lost eyes of sacrifice. He moved closer, his warm smile lighting the shadows behind her. He had won £100 at Corals, a local Bookie's, and so, another little miracle guided her through the day.

Chapter 11

A serial womanizer and brilliant architect of self-induced misfortune and neglect, Scoot' had spent the last twelve months of his life living like an overindulged South London Street pimp. He was searching for that elusive "something," that hidden factor to life. He loathed his existence and felt as if the world owed him big time or at least the world owed him a house in St. John's Wood, a modest flat in Puerto Banus and a Ducati 900.

His body hurt. It was overloaded with toxins: alcohol, drugs, and over-processed food. He looked every bit a wasted man. Scoot was always making excuses about his predilection for easy lays, cheap takeaways, and hazy Mondays. He always saw everything in Matisse shades of blue and nothing was ever clear, nothing ever simple. He claimed to have a "highly addictive" nature and it was in his genes that he would always succumb to temptation.

He continued to search for that unobtainable "high" yet was already approaching thirty-three years of age. It took him a while to work out where he was.

He felt so tired. He could hardly breathe. He sighed; it drained him of all his energy. He needed to make it back home, where he felt wanted, back where he belonged. He would try again tomorrow; he just had to get through today. He cast his mind back to the night before and laughed out loud.

He had taken one of his "straight gimpy" friends Tom, a young twenty-something recruitment consultant, to spend time with Tony and the guys at Tantra. They ended up taking Tom back to Tony's. Janet Ebowe, a fifty-five-year-old Nigerian prostitute, was there, with a bright yellow weave on her head. Janet was all sass and no style, though her crazy *Butlins* Cabaret, moves were definitely worth seeing. She would herald her arrival to all and everyone, by singing that old Shirley Bassey classic "Hey Big Spender." She sang it very loudly in a harsh West African accent with an exaggerated hip swivel and flutter of her false eyelashes.

In his naivety, Tom truly believed that Janet was a former glamour model and now a "consultant" for an American Adult Entertainment Company. Scoot had left Tom with Janet while he and Tony had gone to The Sanderson Hotel on a coke run.

Four hours later, he returned to find Tom in the warm embrace of Janet, clutching the garish yellow hairpiece and wrestling with Tony's white kitten. It was a *Dali* moment. Janet tried to straighten herself up; she was skimpily clad in a leopard print bra with matching knickers. Her short, coarse hair was tied back and one of her bright red fingernails had snapped off and ricocheted off the bed onto the table next to a half drunk, bottle of Sancerre.

Scoot was rooted to the spot. He looked at Janet, then back again at Tom, and then fixed his gaze on the ugly, chipped fingernail. Janet was smiling coyly; Scoot, still staring in utter disbelief at the image before him, tried uncomfortably to exit the room. The closest Tom had ever been to a real life black woman was watching the Notting Hill Carnival on television and ogling

Halle Berry in *Swordfish*.

Tom felt awkward, a minority player in a bigger drama; he made his excuses and retreated to the comfort of his family home in Godaliming Surrey. As he left, Scoot signalled he would call him later.

Chapter 12

There was nothing like the feel and taste of "real" money in your hands. A tight wad of filthy lucre in your pocket felt beautifully corrupt. When you'd done without it for so long, it was infinitely better than a line of coke and twice as sweet as virgin pussy.

Today, Scoot had some cash to play with. Today, he would live a little, kick back, and enjoy the easy debauchery of the night. Accompanying him into the pleasure dome were two hardened street thugs. They had an attractive and pleasing gentlemanly way about them but were London gangsters nonetheless. Scoot affectionately referred to them as "Dipsy" and "La La," who were two characters from a popular children's television show.

Dipsy was around six-foot-two, with tufts of platinum blonde hair arranged in a wavy setting along his crown and forehead. He had weak blue eyes that became strangely distant and vacuous when he attacked you or when he became angry. He was well built with a sturdy girth and natural muscle tone. When preparing to smash someone's head in, he would grin sheepishly and exclaim, "I'm going to give you a potato head." With that, his big fat fist would come crashing down on the hapless victim and all else would fade to grey.

La La was exceptionally well dressed, with a definite sartorial air about him that made people stop and stare. He enjoyed the attention and didn't have to work too hard at getting what he wanted. With his cinematic good looks, boyish smile, and "Sauf" London charm, he exuded a roguish grace that made people warm to him. He was an expert knifeman and a good conversationalist.

Dipsy and La La enjoyed the sumptuous luxury of the exclusive Home House on Portman Street. They entered it with awe but soon settled down to the cosy celebrity of it all. Their money was good here and they would get their worth tonight. Hundreds of pounds later, in high spirits and laughing like two school oiks they ran amok in the men's bathroom:

"Ere, watch out," cried Dipsy as La La pushed and shoved him around.

"Nah, leave it out. C'mon, La, don't do that, leave that alone." It was too late. Smash, crash! The boys were on the lash, cooking up a right storm as they teased fellow patrons of the club and jumped about, horsing around. Then, with one feisty blow and a duck to his head, Dipsy managed to shatter an original French Artisan mirror, the frame thudding to the ground and shards of glass lying strewn all over the expensive, mosaic floor tiles.

They stared blankly at each other for around three seconds in a *South Park* moment.

"Only proper t' pay for it," remarked Dipsy.

"What's right is right," agreed La La.

"And what's wrong is no man's right," chimed Dipsy. They were a "class" act. The sound of falling glass had attracted the attention of the immaculately dressed Club Manager. He had an exclusive title in an exclusive location, and dealt strictly with "exclusive" people. Everything about him was exclusive, everything, that is, except the embarrassing rash at the base of his balls. He reminded Dipsy of an Irish Pall Bearer he knew from Kensal Rise. He threw a look of disdain their way and beckoned Scoot over. Visibly wincing, he demanded that he remove his "guests" before they went "too far." Scoot apologized for his friends' behaviour and tried to reassure the Club Manager that there would be no further trouble. Dipsy and La La agreed to leave after a spot of impromptu karaoke.

Anyway, they'd just coughed up seventy-five "squiddleys" for a round. Two seats away, the former members of an eighties girl band were enjoying some light conversation and a few drinks with friends. In "tribute" to them, Dipsy started singing his own rendition of one of the group's most famous tunes: *Robert De Niro's Waiting*.

He was off key, out of synch, and kept burping and hiccupping in between mouthfuls of San Miguel beer. Several onlookers and patrons of the club, though grossly irritated by this yobbish spectacle, didn't dare raise an eyebrow. The warbling continued for another two verses until one over drunk and irate *Throne Ranger* pleaded, "for God's sake and for the sake of everything that is alive from here to Lake Como, please shut the fuck up!"

Being sworn at like that by a proper "plum" girl was "well cool" to Dipsy. She sounded like Princess Diana, he thought, and then he pondered over the whereabouts of Lake Como. He asked her politely if she fancied a drink and obediently stopped his caterwauling. She acquiesced with a smile and an order for a Rose's Vodka Lime and Soda, the favourite tipple for girls on the go. Georgie was typical of that crowd, a Harvey Nicks chick with throwaway morals and a Trust Fund appetite.

Dressed in faded blue denim, with obligatory Saint Bart's tan on her long, lean legs sporting a seductively ripped angora knit that hung delicately off her burnished shoulders, she was unlike any of the women Dipsy knew. Her soft, Navaho suede boots and her creamy pink lip-gloss said everything is comfort; everything is where it should be. With her, another "Throne Ranger," Kamilla (Kami for short) slinky and kissable, in cowboy boots and tight skinny jeans. Her hair expertly arranged in a high ponytail, her tan fading a little, and her Harry Winston watch making a tinny bleeping sound to remind her to take her new herbal veggie caps. She had a bored, distracted look to her upper crust face. Slowly, she took a drag on her Marlboro light to boost her confidence. She wondered why she was even there tonight. Her boyfriend was shooting a perfume ad in New York and she wondered if he'd think about her at all, wondered if he'd be shagging someone else instead of her, someone better than her, someone with a real name perhaps?

As they stumbled out of the "A listed" security of *Home House*, Dipsy and La La decided it was time to head back to the baked bean reality of East London and get themselves a Donor Kebab and some chips. First, though, they'd swing by Tony's and say hello. Scoot, meanwhile, felt he must pay his aging mother a visit. He was consumed with guilt; he knew she was crippled financially and he knew he should have given her some of the money he had scored that night, but Scoot lived in the moment. The moment was all he had.

Chapter 13

The mournful lament of Dido coming out of the sound system was at odds with the rock and roll setting that greeted Scoot the next evening when he rolled up to Tony's place. To get access to T's flat you needed to be in- the- know and you needed to have the magic password for the day. Ordinarily, it would be random lines from any one of Bob Marley's back catalogue of hits and there was nothing as surreal as watching a mishmash of grown men and women spewing out the lyrics to one of these tracks outside the sober-fronted Mews building. Scoot started singing, "Get me guava jelly for my rubber belly" to the beat of "One Love" into the door microphone.

Thereafter, he was greeted by a huge, swarthy black man of Caribbean origin, who was in truth an unwitting caricature of his own character. Grinning broadly at Scoot, he buzzed him into the flat. He was known simply as Godwin; nobody was actually sure of his last name, but that didn't seem to matter much. Godwin often suffered bouts of epilepsy and was frequently seen hurtling away from A&E at St. Thomas' hospital in Waterloo. It was quite common for him to be spotted in local streets with a cropped trouser leg or shorn off shirt after one of these "episodes."

He told visitors to the flat and neighbours that he suffered from "electrical" fits. As Tony's "maintenance man," Godwin spent much of his day or at least three quarters of it anyway making and drinking soup. He had a liking for spicy meaty "caribou" soup, known as frou frou juice. It was particularly flavoursome and reminded him of sunnier days back home. If Godwin didn't know you, however, or you failed to try the password for the day, access to the flat would be emphatically denied.

Lounging in soft leather chairs Scoot spied three famous actors and their "significant" others. He was always secretly impressed by the fact that people like *them* knew people like *him*. Everything equal in a drug den. Up close, all of the famous faces turned to red eye and sunken spirits. They belonged to the drug now. Scoot said his cheery hellos and then embarked on a long soliloquy about the good and the bad. The art fucks around him seemed to like this type of inane chatter. They could "relate," "understand," and "get connected" to this loquacious prattle. They welcomed "open" conversation and bought every single word. "It's like if you do something bad to someone, it's going to come back on you."

Scoot felt justified and almost liberated by the power of his uncomplicated sentiments. Emilia, a young theatre actress, and understudy for a London Musical, nodded furiously in agreement whilst rolling a "spliff" and popping some veggie caps into her mouth.

She felt she understood the laws of the universe and the significance of "karmic" retribution. She had always been somewhat of a hippie anyway having been brought up in a liberal household while growing up in Brixton village. She loved the idea of ready packaged purity and swallowed some more veggie caps. No artificial flavours, no additives, and no MSG. She was grateful to Tony for selling them and she would definitely buy more. She especially liked her pink silk threaded friendship bracelet that you could choose with the Herbal Starter Pack.

Her sister Chloe had opted for eco-friendly green. You were not meant to remove the thread from your wrist once worn; it was meant to age naturally over a period and she thought that was super, super cool. Anyhow it was "bags" cheaper than Kabbalah as you didn't have to part with 10 percent of your income to any central organization and it still made her feel good, strong, and wholesome.

Emilia didn't want to feel like she had to pay too much to belong in her quest for spiritual satisfaction and the herbal capsule met all of her needs. As she got ready to leave, Darius entered the room.

Outside, the streetlights had been switched off and the pigeons were feasting on yesterday's chicken, chips, and stale leftovers of rain-soaked lettuce and bits of onion. Scoot was easily annoyed by Darius but tolerated him anyway. Tony said he was "good" for business. He always spoke such bull crap it might be entertaining to hear him mouth off for a while, he thought abstractedly.

Darius seemed to have it all: a hardworking wife, lots of uber chic friends, and even two young children. Something was amiss, though; something had to be wrong. If all was chocolate and roses, what was Darius doing in a West London drug den at five o'clock on a Tuesday morning? Darius fooled himself into thinking he was there to observe, to enlighten, and to educate. He was going to use all of these urban misfits for his next "big" project, a movie he had in "development." They would all serve their purpose in the end.

Darius was the only black man in the room who appeared completely white. His speech was white, his mannerisms were white, and his clothes were a white parody of what a black pimp might wear circa 1978 in London's Bedford Hill. Yes, it was probably an Oswald Boateng suit: trademark loud colours, clumsy tight fit, and experimental fabric. It was meant to be an example of revolutionary styling but lacked the exquisite tailoring of Italian design. Yes, you could really feel the "ghetto" in the fibres of an OB suit. Scoot much preferred the quiet understatement of a classic Canali any day. Scoot was watching Darius who then became very aware of how bizarre he looked in the presence of his Brit chic friends. Half of them lived in Clerkenwell alongside media luminaries and respected thespians. The rest seemed to permeate the other smart locations like Notting Hill Gate and further north Primrose Hill. Well, if it was good enough for Princess Sadie, it was good enough for him, Lysette, Amy, Gerry, and the like.

Darius was jacked up on *"charlie"* and seriously buzzed out. He was feeling the urge to talk. He wanted to let loose, to express himself. He started bellowing at the top of his voice (only it wasn't that loud due to his exaggerated English demeanour). He began giggling helplessly at a hand trick he had perfected with a toy finger puppet, a freebie given to him with his petrol from his local filling station.

Scoot was not even slightly amused. He was, however, appalled at the slavish mediocrity of the man. Frankly, such lack of imagination was distasteful. Even so, he laughed really hard, which encouraged the rest of them in the room to laugh: bit players, part time somebodies, "trustafarians" affluent Jo's and Josephina's, ex—offenders, pretty dancers, hardened city rats, musicians, artists, and a whole line-up of mischief makers laughing like an affected chorus of damaged sea gulls smashed on ecstasy. It was an unsettling sight to behold and reminded Scoot of a scene in the movie *Natural Born Killers*.

He tried to get the images of Juliette Lewis out of his head. Suddenly, their unnerving cackle cut short by the sound of a loud buzzer. Godwin signalled to Tony that one of his friends had arrived. A young woman of around twenty-three came through; she was a recording artist and a bit of a computer geek. She had known Tony most of her life. She had fiery red, wavy hair and spoke with an authentic Jamaican accent. She wore a very short black skirt and white fishnet stockings with orange high-heeled shoes. She was tall, with an ample cleavage and had applied bits of fishnet to her torn, frayed tee shirt emblazoned with a picture of post-war revolutionary Zimbabwe. She never appeared in public without her impressive collection of headbands.

Today was no exception; she wore a bright turquoise towelling number appliquéd with colourful fake rhinestones. Tony had asked her to drop by to help him with some research on capsule making machines for his burgeoning health business.

Her name, Zhy, was also out of place on her milky white complexion and her clear set, green eyes. Zhy would often engage herself in conversations littered with common Jamaican Patois: the language of Black London. She would thank "Jah" for life, and the love she felt in her heart. She adored Snoop Dogg, an infamous American rap star known for his subversive song lyrics and his anti-establishment style.

She claimed that one day "real soon" she would get to

meet Snoop Dogg as "Jah" decreed. Some people, on meeting Zhy for the first time, even a few of those in the room now, thought she was a "wigga," an American term used to describe white people with culturally black or "nigga" like tendencies. In London, Zhy was considered by some to be a "Jafaikan," ghetto slang for "fake Jamaican."

Raised on a diet of black music, black food, with black friends and a largely black church community, as well as having black adoptive parents, Zhy felt completely disenfranchised from her white counterparts. She could not relate to *white* pop music like Busted or MacFly and had no respect for progressive rock or the Jonas Brothers. She came by to pick up a computer, so she could begin sourcing out potential capsule makers for the business. Tony filled her in with the specifics, removed twelve £50 notes from the inside of a Sly Stone record sleeve, and then she left.

Meanwhile, on the other side of London, not too far away, an armed gunman had found his way into the entrance of a Jeweller's in Hatton Garden. It was small in comparison to the others dotted along the road but nonetheless housed an impressive line up of diamonds, watches, and gold. Bessie passed all of them by and headed straight for the safe. His head was throbbing; he felt nauseous and his breath was bitter from two days of not washing. He smelt like the inside of a public phone booth on the Old Kent Road: stale perspiration, old piss, and garlic. He was unaccustomed to such slovenliness but had been unable to get home for two days because of his stakeout of the store. He was going to throw up soon and that would make a lovely mess of things. The piercing sound of the shop alarm caught him off guard and reminded him of a screeching woman in the night.

He would sort that out no problem. He moved deftly to his feet and disengaged it as if he were performing lifesaving surgery. His mother had always said that he had "beautiful hands." He apparently took after his uncle Harry, a concert pianist. Once the deafening howl had stopped, he quickly gathered the haul into his arms and stuffed it into a plastic bag. He lit a cigarette and walked calmly into the cold night air.

Chapter 14

It was a big night tonight: Tony's birthday, which meant that everyone who was anyone and all the nobodies in between would be around. He would celebrate privately with members of his immediate family over the weekend. Nothing was planned as such, and business would have to be sorted out first before the fun could begin. Everyone knew, though, what the night would hold—lots of D& A (drugs and alcohol) and plenty of T& A (tits and arse). Scoot, Dipsy, La La, Jimmy Irish, Vinnie Diego, and Big Bernie were all seated with Tony in Gossips, a grungy rock and roll bar off Dean Street. It served as a makeshift office space for Tony where he could talk freely about his plans without any unwanted interference from the police or others. It was cold and damp inside with crates of beers stacked up in large columns to the left and right of the dimly lit room.

It looked like an underground cavern with small twisted passageways running from the centre. Streams of thin watery sunlight tried to break through the tiny slattern windows at the back of the club but lay trapped in diluted rays by the heavy wrought iron bars. The walls smeared with fresh tobacco stains and small, rounded wads of thick, sticky chewing gum flecked with gunk and sawdust. On the grey stone floor, cigarette butts and coasters lay strewn about, a grim reminder of the heaving sweat pit it had become at last night's Libertines gig. The manager, Johnny Ashton, looked jittery and confused. Years of cocaine and heroin addiction had bloated his over-red face and left him scored with purple veins and premature lines. Not yet, thirty-two, he looked like a man of forty-five or older. Wearing a loose fitting, ACDC tee shirt and some crumpled black jeans, the ends frayed and layered in dust and filth, he moved sharply around the room scuffing his red Converse Trainers, another old school, retro throwback to his "wannabe" rock star existence.

Oasis were playing on the jukebox, Liam's overstretched elasticized vocal blunting the thick furry air. Johnny didn't want to see Tony right then. He owed him money, but he couldn't exactly ignore him either. He fumbled around nervously with his lighter and took out a pack of Marlboro Reds. He was oblivious to everyone else seated at the small table. Everyone, that is, except "Big" Bernie, who glared at him menacingly. He tried to avert his gaze and walk out casually with a cursory nod, but then T motioned him over. Johnny was stumbling with his words.

"Hi T, whassup, man?"

"Listen I, er, got to go, go see Heather, but I'll be back in like thirty minutes," Tony pulled him closer and said,

"Yeah, that's cool, Johnny. Take your time; take your time, 'cause I ain't going no where. I'll be here." He leant back in his seat and the rest of the gang settled down to an afternoon's drinking. Jimmy Irish changed the music and stuck a *Big Youth* song on. The lilting beat of the reggae dub was soothing away the uneasy tension between Tony and Johnny. As the group sat there laughing and joking they began discussing their next move.

"Big" Bernie as Don March had explained was actually

three-foot-four inches tall with a Mohican haircut coloured blue and green, at only twenty- seven-years-old he was a Mensa maths genius who took care of all Tony's outgoings, expenses, deposits, savings, and money draw-downs. By ensuring Tony had a number of legitimate investments including shares in a modelling agency, London record company, and two profitable hair salons it gave T and the crew a reliable front. It was "Big" Bernie's job to satisfy the Tax and VAT people. Unfortunately, "Big" Bernie was also highly superstitious with a morbid fascination for the Occult and Voodoo. He had a seriously violent temper at times, was a killer shot at darts, and was having an obsessive relationship with a nineteen-year-old Australian underwear model and former boy band star. Bernie could also be highly neurotic and was, in short, a bundle of loaded dynamite. He insisted that they shouldn't leave, without getting their money from Johnny.

The others agreed. Scoot said nothing, but Jimmy Irish, a former welterweight boxer and one of Tony's muscle men, piped up: "That tosser's taking the piss. He 'asn't paid for over seven weeks now." Jimmy Irish was a tall, striking man with a mop of dark hair and a taut, strong physique. He looked like Monty Clift on a bad day.

"We can't let 'im take liberties like that, Ton. It's fuckin' serious."

"Don't worry about it. Stay cool, he'll pay," drawled Vinnie, a Spanish-born record producer with a sculpted, bronze torso and the face of a young Louis Prima; he was a beautiful cultural stereotype of a Latin dream. After a stint as an international DJ, and several small film roles, he was now managing T's record business. Scoot changed the conversation to the elusive search for the capsule maker. He was, in truth, uncomfortable with such heavy talk and not usually around for the blood and boom.

The plan was, of course, to have their own capsule Plant, and Distribution network. They were latching onto the dearth of new age philosophies and natural ways to get high. They already had a willing and gullible market through Tony's drug clientele, plus streams of punters who wanted some of that "feel good" vibe.

All they needed to do now was soup up their operation to satisfy demand. Zhy's research efforts had only turned up small mobile capsule makers for home and personal use. They had then looked into the possibility of buying a large industrial-sized machine but found that most of the suppliers were based in India or China.

"What I really want," began Tony,

"is the Caps-Dynomore."

"Yeah, it's really high tech, state of the art, bro," enthused Dipsy.

"Yeah, amazing capabilities," joined in La La.

"Yeah, top of the range, man," confirmed Jimmy Irish.

"It makes nine thousand capsules a minute," stated Bernie.

"Fuck, man, nine thousand. Every part of fuckin' London could be high and France and Italy and fuckin' Berlin, Prague, everywhere could get caps, caps overload, man!" beamed Tony.

"Yeah, you could go on QVC and sell it to the people. *Legal highs, legal* highs, *touch the sky with legal highs*" slurred Vinny. His voice smooth like brandy butter.

"How much is it?" enquired T.

Bernie got out his portable mini Vaio and started opening files and looking intently at a very long balance sheet.

"The damage on that particular model is a cool £245,000."

Vinnie whistled and Dipsy started swearing:

"Fuck, fuck, 'ow much? £245,000 are you sure?"

Bernie ignored them and carried on jotting down figures using a small handheld calculator. The others kept on talking while Bernie continued to work.

"What we could do is move the bizzo to a ware'ouse, you know, a lock up in Kent or somefing," volunteered Dipsy.

"Yeah, maybe," replied T.

Bernie was still crunching numbers and made some more rapid computations. Then, with a loud sigh, he put his pen down:

"It's not gonna be possible at that price," he said ruefully.

Once they'd factored in the shipping, packaging, and import costs, they were looking at serious money, not to mention the fact that customs and excise might find it a tad unusual to see a super-sized industrial capsule making machine being wheeled into the country.

"The import tax on such a colossal machine will kill the deal," explained Scoot.

"He's right," agreed Bernie.

Darius walked in. He had done his "work" for the day and had managed to screw up two routine bail applications and failed to save a suspected illegal immigrant from Deportation. He was a useless "brief" and unaccustomed to winning anyway.

"Hey, bro, Scooter, all right, chaps." He nodded to the rest of the gang then, pulled up a chair sat down and helped himself to a beer.

"Big night tonight, bro?" He smiled, looking up at Tony.

"Yeah, man, gonna be wicked tonight, y'ar know."

"Darius, you know how we can get this capsule maker for

cheap?" asked T.

"I've actually got some friends who might be interested if you cut them in on the deal. They're rich Indians into import, export. They have some resort centres and hotels in Goa and Mumbai Let me ask them."

"That sounds good."

"Yeah, but we need to move quickly, otherwise business will turn cold," added Bernie. Scoot thought this was just another example of trite gabble from Darius who was always making huge promises and never following through with any of them. He was quietly irritated and knew that the only reason Darius was even there was to score free cocaine and booze all night. He stood up and got some beers for the others.

Their talk gradually drifted away from the logistics of the capsule maker to the hot summer night ahead. Outside, the sun was setting like a huge orange flame caressing the horizon, and all around them the heave of rush hour, distant shouts, police sirens, car alarms, doors banging, buskers singing Bob Dylan tunes, weary half smiles, and a hundred yesterdays drowned in a sea of noise like hordes of geese clinking to the shore line. Johnny came back biting his lip.

"Tony, over 'ere, man. I'm gonna 'ave to run the boss's credit card on the till and get you the cash that way."

"Whatever man. I just need the money. It's been about seven or eight weeks now."

"Yeah, I get it, man. Fuck, I hope I'm not busted over this. It's not authorized."

"Neither is taking four ounces of 'C' and not payin' for it," added Bernie sharply.

"Yeah, an' I hooked you up with Cameron for your disco

biscuits," warned T.

"I'm grateful, Tony; it's just that I don't wanna lose this gig. I'm trusted here."

"Look, just swipe the card, open the till, give me my cash, an' we'll be on our way."

"Yeah, yeah, okay." Johnny did as he was told and handed over £4000. He put the amount down as "sundries" on the till slip and sloped back to a corner of the bar.

The rest of their business would just have to wait. It was T's birthday and they were gonna let rip.

Chapter 15

Ever wonder why drug dealers, politicians, models, the super rich, the super bad, the fame whores, the great, the greedy, and the Godless all end up at the same party? They all want to get high; twist the melon. That's why Tony always had the "best backstage pass" to the most exclusive, most happening, most coked up parties in town. He also had at least half the door and bar staff at these glitzy venues on his payroll. All rock and gravy, if they weren't there, the gig would be a blow out.

First stop: China Whites. Tony and the guys were ushered through the back entrance. Outside, the line snaked around the corner for at least half a mile. It was a mixed crowd: there were the "do-anythings" for fame brigade, usually twenty-something or younger. They had trademarked, clipped Essex accents with wealthy Jewish or South African parents and tended to have big hair and even bigger attitudes. They all seemed like sisters of Danni Behr with the usual French Manicure and pot roast hue. Then there were the "has beens" out for a laugh and a shag. Clothes too tight, make up too bright, Caprice-style hair extensions, wearing horrible pointy shoes with Cruella de Ville heels.

No "Sandersons" or "Louboutins" here, just "Faith" and

"LK Bennett." What was it with that tired, old, *Sex and The City* look that women over a certain age love to ape? It was like an enforced uniform courtesy of *Marie Claire's* fashion team. Fact: Puffball skirts and pointy vamp shoes look awkward and clownish on anyone without SJP's, lean trim torso, or the curvaceous femininity of Kim Cattrall.

Jostling alongside these groups of over eager club "chicks" were the "fellas" of the night, either aging lotharios from the music biz well past their sell-by date, now donning nervous eye twitches and "coke bloat" stomachs, or the usual city boys: Traders, Investment Bankers, Account Executives, they had Florida tans, shiny hair, and snappy let's-get-high suits on. Close by, a peculiar breed of straight hairdresser, complete with gold wristwatches and boy band hair teased and gelled into easy lay creations. Also in line: super toned, fit, gay, boy toys under twenty-five wearing low-waisted jeans and tight-fitted tees with crass slogans. Some of the crowd brandished neon-coloured VIP wristbands and others had enough cash to try and bribe the bouncers to get in.

This was all theatre, of course, just hype, for the real "stars" of the night were already ensconced in the hip VIP enclosure downing bottles of Roderer Cristal and sipping on chocolate martinis. Tony found himself seated next to a member of the Saudi Royal family and a well-known soap actress. Jimmy Irish was wedged between a provincial "wag" and a London rap artist. Bernie and his boy toy lover, Christian, were holed up in a private booth. Scoot and Darius were busy chatting up a couple of "Page 3" models and Dipsy, La La, and Vinnie were getting friendly with the cast and crew of a reality TV show.

Outside still in the queue were Mandy and Eva, they had

been waiting in the cold for over twenty minutes. They were tired and impatient. Finally, they got to the entrance, only to be told by the Resident Door Gestapo that the club was "full, their names weren't on the list and they couldn't come in." The Door Gestapo took their jobs very seriously indeed. They tended to be surly faced minder men sporting the same po-faced scowl, black knee length Crombie coats, and the collective brainpower of a toddler of three. It was a crushing blow to Eva and Mandy, who had been looking forward to this night all week. As they turned and walked away, Eva heard her name being called. She looked up to find Nathan, a friend of Richard's, smiling at her from inside the club.

He pushed aside the door goon and escorted her and her friend through. Eva felt really cool. It was notoriously difficult to get into China Whites, which boasted one of the biggest celebrity drop-bys in London. But even here, the celebrities were on a sliding scale and you certainly wouldn't find the likes of a Tom Cruise or Beyoncé Knowles slumming it at "Whites." No, they'd probably be partying in Lake Como or somewhere equally lush. Still, sports personalities and television actors were commonplace and Eva thought what fun it would be if she could bag a footballer for the night.

On the other side of London, Boujis on the Fulham Road was getting ready to welcome a dazzling array of assorted Royalty, Trustafarians, Throne Rangers, Models, Pop Tarts, and Dot com billionaires. Boujis was awash for the main part, however, with quiet old money. It had a pedigree and refinement that was hard to match in the rest of London. Nestled in between the innocuous Money Exchange shop and the cheap telephone place on the Fulham Road, you'd never dream it was such a favourite haunt for the Chelsea smart set.

Still, it was only a stone's throw from Kensington Palace and just minutes away from the fashionable SW1 and SW3 areas. After a sess' at Boujis, you could always nip down to the Kings Road and get a lovely fry up at five or six in the morning. It was safe, convenient, and deliciously up market. Richard sat back on an Arne Jacobson-inspired egg chair smoking a Cohiba cigar. It was still a bit of a novelty to smoke cigars in England but he had acquired a taste for them while working in New York and partying in Havana.

He found them extremely satisfying and the drag gave him an enjoyable buzz. One of his wealthier clients, a British Muscovite and heir to a plastics company, had brought him to Boujis. He was impressed with the "we're too rich to give a fuck" vibe and the uber cool décor inside. He ordered a Jack and coke and took a long swig from the glass. Refreshing and sharp, it stung his palette into play. He had a look around the club. A famous "celeb" pop tart was holding court at the bar. She had climbed her way through the charts screwing various A and R men and even some women. Still going strong, without any musical ability to speak of, she was propped up beside her influential gay music maestro who gave her credibility and validation. Richard thought her swollen hamster cheeks were a definite "Botox" giveaway. Talent by association made him nauseous.

He noticed several rich Asians, probably from India or Pakistan. Ever since the English Football Manager had confessed to bedding an exotic beauty of Bangladeshi origin, it had been quite en vogue to have a South East Asian girlfriend. Generally, though, Richard didn't stray too far from his own type. He wasn't racist but didn't like working too hard to get laid. You knew where you were with a proper English "slapper," a night's worth of drinks and fifty quid for their cab ride home the next morning: sorted. Even posh "totty" like those in tonight could be persuaded to give it up; you just needed a little bit of charm and a big fat wallet. Those foreign types, different ball game altogether. It was all in the chase with them. They wanted you to prove your worth. A tall, Padama Lakshmi look-a-like caught his eye, but she was already taken.

As he scoured the room for other hopefuls, a brunette brushed past him. *Fuckalicous*, thought Richard. She had a raw, untamed, dirty sensuality that oozed from her "Porn Star" curves: Big boobs, tiny waist, and a tight toned tummy with a firm, round arse all silhouetted through her black silk satin dress. He sidled up to her and introduced himself, trying hard not to stare. It was always the same robotic speech:

"My name's Richard. I'm a lawyer."

"Oh very impressive" she smirked with a rolling eye motion that said the exact opposite."

"I'm Odette and I'm a surgeon."

Richard was lost for words and very annoyed. How was he going to shag her now?

"I'm sorry, you seem a little, how can I put this, surprised, are you okay?"

"Yeah, I'm fine. I thought you were a Russian model or something."

"I'm Latvian or something," retorted Odette. She loathed men like this.

Richard rarely got close to women. He was a fuck-and-go type of man but he was genuinely overwhelmed by Odette's quick wit and "come screw me" look. He made a mental note never to judge a book by its cover a clichéd saying he swore not to use again. He wanted Odette now, right there in the club more than a fantasy screw with Jordan a glamour model he always had a secret "thing" for. He wanted to feel how wet she was, how tight, and slip his hand through that silk dress.

Odette, meanwhile, had other plans and Richard played no part in them. She had seen an Indian businessman whom she met earlier and with whom she wanted to reconnect. He was good looking and funny with a great body and strong, powerful hands. Anyway, how could she ever date a man like Richard? He was so painfully transparent. Then there were those unsightly skin tags visible for all to see. It was a curious pet hate of hers. As a qualified surgeon, she would always recommend removal. Skin tags and warts were unnecessary and she felt unable to forgive such a flaw. Scars, crooked teeth, big noses, pockmarks, and blemishes were all preferable to visible skin tags. She felt horribly shallow but chose to be truthful.

"I'm afraid I'm not looking for any type of relationship, so excuse me, if you will, er, nice to have met you." Richard, unabashed and buoyed on by the throbbing Jay Z rap tune, continued with his hackneyed sales patter and all the while he wanted to tongue that bitch. He looked pathetic to her and irritated the hell out of her. The skin tags on his upper left eyelid and to the right side of his neck were getting more and more prominent. Odette felt an incredible urge to lance them off without aesthetic. She bit her lip slowly and remained calm however.

"Really sweet of you, Richard, but I'm just not interested, you know. I'm just here to enjoy myself with friends. Please excuse me."

With that, she flounced off into the private area of the

club, wiggling to the sound of over-dubbed Dr. Dre. Richard hot-footed it behind her, collapsing in a nervous heap on a plush velvet armchair. Ulrich Solinsky, his client, was snogging some twenty-something double barrelled named society princess. He waited until they stopped.

"Ritchie Ritch."

He saw him staring at Odette, who turned away from him immediately.

"She's definitely out of your league, Ritch. I'll fix you up with someone else who's just as lush but not so fucking clever. The girl I have in mind was even chosen for a shoot in "Horse and Hound" and she was "papped" at Tatler's Little Black Book Party. She's super hot and super cool." Ulrich spoke with an edgy chic, trying to mock the "wide boy" Cockney English accent. This style of talking had now left the confines of leafy Sloane Square and filtered down to the Home Counties. Richard thought it was messed up. Why would someone who'd benefited from a seriously expensive private education pretend to be an East End urchin? Ulrich continued with his drunken talk, his arm around the pretty, angel-faced girl. His hand, now resting on her thigh:

"Richie, baby, come on, ask Tasha, sweetheart. Natasha, isn't Kamilla great? She's lovely, right?"

Natasha smiled and in between snoggs slurred, "Yeah, man, she's like really, really hot."

Richard feigned fake interest but demanded Odette's phone number, as it was Ulrich's party he was bound to have her contact information. Ulrich got out his Blackberry and read out her numbers.

"Don't fucking embarrass me, slick dick." He carried on kissing Tasha, sliding his hand up her skirt, then motioned Richard over.

"Got some killer Charlie, man. Let's go."

They left the club and the girl. Then they moved to the back of the Fulham Road where Ulrich's car was parked. They sat in the privacy of his XK8 Jag and both snorted several lines. As the orgasmic rush of the drug hit, they collapsed into an ice Elysium. This stuff was off the hook. The streetlights were casting an intrusive white glare into the front mirror of the car. Richard ducked down, shielding his face from the unwanted strobes. They snorted some more. Richard became energized, upbeat, and scathingly witty, as if he had just taken a shot of purity. His mood switched; he started to talk animatedly about nothing, making it all sound unbelievable and spectacular.

He was in a coke dream now, where he was better than anyone, better than everyone. He was "God" supreme; that's what Coke did for him, that's how it made him feel like he had divine grace. He watched Odette out of the corner of his eye and wondered how many men she'd pleasured.

Chapter 16

Bessie had been keeping a low profile ever since the snatch at Goldman's jewellers in Hatton Garden, but he knew it was Tony's birthday tonight and felt like getting loaded. He was relieved that, among the usual stash of diamonds, gold designer watches, and other trinkets, he had found the piece of paper he was looking for with the small rectangular-shaped key, the top of which was embedded with tiny emeralds and rubies.

He stared at it quizzically, then carefully wrapped it up in tissue and folded it away. The paper with the key felt old and worn. He reflected over its contents and made a mental note to himself to show it to his friend Deepak. If he couldn't decipher it, he would take it to his Sikh friend Manju at his local curry house. No need to let on he had it just yet; everything in its own time.

For now, he would have it "large" and celebrate Tony's birthday in style. First, though, he thought about banging some "sort" at his local strip club just off Tottenham Court Road. He was a regular at Spearmint Rhino. Although this wasn't a typical British lap dancing club, he enjoyed it anyway. Smiling to himself, he liked to think of it as the "McDonald's" of Table Dancing—fresh, healthy produce always competitively priced with guaranteed satisfaction. The club was close to Oxford Circus and boasted an exotic variety of international beauties. It had warm, sepia-toned lighting, a leopard print carpet, flash trash mirrored walls, and a filtered down private vibe.

Outside, the resident bouncers were beefed up, bald, and bolshie. They let Bessie through without paying as he was a regular. Once inside, he recognized the sexy beat of Prince's "You Got the Look." There was a floor show on.

He saw his favourite dancer sliding her legs up and down a long, silver-coloured pole. He would ask her for a private dance later. To the right of him at the far end of the club was Leroy the black D. J. He wore his hair braided a la Terence Trent D'arby. He waved and smiled at Bessie as he got closer to the bar. Behind him were a mixture of suits and wide boys wearing Ben Sherman and T. M. Lewin shirts, cheap brands for an easy night out getting pissed. Some women were sitting close to the action right in front of the stage. They had "tango" tans and big boobs. They were laughing loudly, making rude noises. Most of them dressed in Karen Millen or Morgan.

They all had blonde highlights and fake Louis Vuitton purses. They were tipsy now and gradually getting drunker as the evening wore on. A couple of guys sat directly opposite him, and in front of them were two dancers provocatively peeling their clothes off to a new, slow beat dance track, their silicone breasts and long, silky hair creating playful shadows on the softly lit walls.

Alex, the club manager, told him there was a launch party in Shepherds Market Mayfair to find Britain's *Best Nude Dancer*. Bessie liked the sound of that and decided to check it out after a private dance with Amazon. He called T from the men's bathroom to check on his whereabouts. He found him in high spirits. He was obviously tanked up, having started the day on Sol and Corona then, advancing to Cristal, Tequila Shots, Vodka, and Mojitos. There was even talk of some of the crowd doing Absinthe.

Ten o'clock the next morning, Bessie was stretched out on a king-size bed. He reached over for Amazon's warm-body and found her lying naked beside him. A newspaper had been slipped under their room door. *Britain's Best Nude* was in all of the press and on television. Bessie tried to think back.

He vaguely recalled a highly respected MP getting frisky with one of the contestants in the show but everything was a blur. The pictures in the tabloids, though, were of two European socialites tonguing one another and giving each other blow back. Now there was a scandal and allegations of a drug-fuelled orgy to contend with. News hounds, all they ever wanted to do was squeeze the sleaze. He woke Amazon. They showered together. The water was soft and warm, bouncing in long splashes across her swollen nipples. Turned on, he leant down to fuck her, his mouth closing in around her huge bosoms, pink from the heat of the water. Silicone humping gave Bessie such a rush.

Later that morning, they enjoyed a light breakfast of coffee, fried eggs, toast, and fresh juice. Then they left Berner Street and the cosy confines of their luxury hotel and went their separate ways.

Chapter 17

When he got home in the early hours of the morning, Scoot was careful to tiptoe up the old wooden stairs, but each one was creaking loudly, cutting the early dawn stillness with an ugly squeak. Suddenly, out from nowhere came the soft pitter patter of tiny feet.

"Oh, my boy's home. Thank God he's safe. Hello, hello, my

bushka.Are you all right? Do you want some food?" Caught in her maternal grasp, Scoot enjoyed all the fuss and bother as Mrs. Calibresi clucked around him, making him comfortable and safe.

"My sweet, precious bambino." Now he would get to eat some of mama's finest homemade fare. She busied herself in the kitchen fetching and carrying big bowls of hot spaghetti and heaps of freshly warmed bread topped with lashings of garlic butter. It was around 6:00 a.m. on a Friday morning, but nothing was too much trouble for her dear boy. She was just so glad to see him, thanking God that he was alive and in one piece. Playfully she tugged at his hair and pulled his cheek.

He was relieved that his friend's associates and "blood brothers" of the street were not there to witness this avalanche of affection. Scoot's parents lived in South East London, Dulwich, to be precise. It had a quaint village type of atmosphere but was not too far away from Central London and in easy access of Mrs. Calibresi's former work place.

She used to be a Company Director but had lost the business and all of her clients when she had taken a gamble on her shares and the market had plummeted. Paper losses were in the millions and she was now facing bankruptcy and high stakes litigation on several fronts. She still however, had assets to save that had tangible value and she was not afraid to fight. Today was court day for Scoot's mother; that's why she had been up so early, pacing around, trying to work stuff out. It was partly the reason why he had gone to see her; he wanted to show his support for her even though he wasn't going to make it to court.

Mrs. Calibresi had successfully postponed this hearing no less than ten times but now she would have to face it. She was also representing herself, having dispensed with her legal team who she felt were just feasting on her misery like overfed cockroaches. They were too expensive, clocking pounds and sense by the hour, more concerned about paperwork and procedure rather than actually winning.

Her stomach was churning slowly inside her, like the cogs of an old fashioned windmill, slow grinding movements that bruised her intestines and made her slightly short of breath. Frozen in time, her thoughts now lay scattered through her brain: an incoherent maze of disconnected facts, legal decisions, and distorted confusion. She walked with a defiant pride and fragile vulnerability. On the surface, her cool aloofness belied the sickening anxiety in her irritated bowel.

Waiting outside the entrance to the court were an assembled team of busy bodies. All were wearing the nondescript colours of navy blue or black, the sobriety of their attire souring the already austere atmosphere that clung to the building in muted tones of conservative gloom. This was a court of law and the bleakness of it a cutting reminder to all who visited there that they did so at their own peril. The opposition had gathered in a small, tight huddle at the far end of the room.

One man stood out from the throng. Dressed in a cheap pin stripe suit, he resembled a nobody man trying hard to be a somebody. He was openly smug and looked like a gerbil on heat. His hair was close shorn and he had pockets of fat around his midriff and his arms. He was a useless fuck and spent most of his nights alone, downloading Russian Porn and watching "slasher" movies. Scoot's mother wondered how he had ever become a lawyer and remained convinced he was nothing more than a legal clerk, possibly a legal "assistant"; he was a definite non entity.

Of course she was right, the cheap suit; the unsavoury arrogance, and the bullish hostility were all give aways about him. They showed a flawed and broken character; seething with class issues, petty jealousies, and a virulent, almost "biblical" dislike of minorities. She knew she would have a tough time appealing to his sense of "fair play" and "justice."

He was probably a paid up member of the BNP. He loathed the fact that she was representing herself and it annoyed him that she had the cohunes to do so. He was the kind of person who used racist slang in private and didn't have the balls to repeat it in public. He would try to win the argument with swathes of legal papers, a document war, which was almost entirely technical. She would have to develop a more textured response and explain why her papers were so thin on the ground.

"Can you tell me why we need to go through this section

of the matter when it appears you have now abandoned your application, Mr. Bonnet?" asked the judge, with a steely look on his face. He did not appreciate having his time wasted by irrelevant paper wars and knew that the large firm had sent a paper "Joey." He knew that the firm had access to a troop of lawyers and pen pushers and expansive resources, and they were merely flexing their legal muscles because they knew they could. They wanted to bully and intimidate Mrs. Calibresi and take advantage of her because she was there by herself and she spoke with a pronounced Italian accent. The judge was tired of these slimy tricks in the legal arena. He waited patiently for an answer:

"Please, your Honour, we, er, have indeed abandoned that part of the claim, Sir, but we felt that you should know about it anyway, Sir."

"Are you suggesting, Mr. Bonnet, that I don't read all of my papers?"

"Er, no, not at all Sir," stammered Bonnet.

The judge continued scowling as if he had taken a bite out of a very sour cherry. His thin, purple lips and hollow, creased cheeks showing a line of irritation stretching across his already furrowed brow:

"That's enough, Mr. Bonnet. You're wasting my time and the court's time. I am therefore ordering a Wasted Costs Order against your firm for £2000."

"Yes, Sir. My apologies, Sir."

Mr. Bonnet had gone from a parading peacock bursting with false pride and tacky arrogance to a silent and servile house mouse. His big talk and self-satisfied smile diffused into regret. The Judge further allowed Mrs. Calibresi's application to go through, which meant that she had saved her family home once again from a horde of slippery debt collectors and bailiffs.

All's fair in love and litigation, she thought as she made her way back home.

Chapter 18

On his way to score some gear from Tony's, Luke remembered seeing him and some of his "associates" at a private launch party in Shepherd's Market Mayfair. He thought of Georgia and Kamilla getting it on for the cameras and smiled to himself, thinking of how the media might react: "Posh totty tongues out," he could see the headlines now. He also remembered how Jimmy Irish and Big Bernie kept banging on about their new health drug and how it was going to revolutionize club land. *Natural Highs*: all legit and ready to use. He thought he would ask T about it. Luke had a real talent for making money and was adept at get- rich-quick schemes. With trunkful's of easy cash courtesy of his inheritance, he was more than eager to capitalize on this new age phenomena as he had already seen the potential of nouveau "feel good" products on the Pacific Coast. When he got to the flat, he began singing "Johnny was a good boy, yeahhh," a Marley classic.

Once inside, he found Janey and Sarah there, two highly respected television presenters with a serious coke habit. They were sitting at a large wooden table in the kitchen. With them was Christian X, a well-known Australian underwear model and former Chart Topper, now on the hunt for a solo deal and more money. They were laughing and joking about an actor friend of theirs called Rufus. Apparently, he had been "papped" the other night outside Home House "French kissing" a notorious pre-op Norwegian transsexual "Angie."

His fiancée had seen the story and was threatening to call off their wedding. In the adjoining room, opposite sat a grim-faced Bernie seething with jealousy and envy. Why was Christian so into this Brazilian fashion designer? In his hand were a set of pictures showing Christian and the mystery guy together. He scrutinized each shot carefully: Christian and "friend" sharing lunch, Christian and "friend" frolicking around London Zoo, Christian and "friend" snogging outside *Punk* night club. The guy in the photos with Christian was known as Estevez, a gay fashion student from St. Martin's College of Art who was now the darling of the fashion world and showing to all the big names, for his Final Collection.

He was tipped as a future star of the clothing industry and had already tasted success when a well-known actress had worn his designs to an awards ceremony. Bernie was physically disgusted: shot after shot of his adorable Christian playing around with this gay Casanova. Bernie had now reached boiling point. He knew that Christian was unreliable, narcissistic, and dreamy, but he thought he would at least play the game and pretend to love him. All Christian however, wanted from Bernie, was free booze, free gear, and a celebrity-fuelled lifestyle, as well as a fast track connection to a major record label. Bernie's cousin Alex was in the music business and could make stuff happen for him if Bernie gave the all clear.

Christian could think of nothing worse than spending the rest of his days with a self-confessed depressive maniac who had a disturbing violent streak and a list of neuroses that made even

Woody Allen in *Manhattan* look sane. Christian was biding his time, waiting for his next big break. Until then, he was content being used, as the resident porch monkey by T and the others. Bernie got up and moved slowly to the door. He decided that Christian had crossed the line. Enough was enough; he would call Dr. Johnson his "witch doctor" for a solution.

Tony stepped out of a room to the left of the flat. "Yo, Luke, how are you, man?" "Yeah, good, thanks, T," he replied brightly. "I saw you guys down at Shepherd's Market at the private launch party." "Yeah, that was blindin' man, sweet, really good, y'ar know. Was you there when they took pictures of Kamilla and Gerorgie? They were first at Café Boehme and then they were goin' at it together, but it was the papers that made 'em do it. They were kissin' and all sorts, the two of 'em."

"Yeah, I don't think Kamilla's father will appreciate the publicity. Listen, man, I saw Bernie and Christian down there. They said something about you needing Investment Funding for that veggie cap business: *Legal Highs*?"

"Yeah, that's right. Caroline's sister works for that bank, y'ar know the one." Tony looked around him for help with the answer of what bank it might be.

Sarah chimed in with the usual "Barclays NatWest HSBC?"

"Nah, none of those. It's like a private bank. Anyway, she's gonna look for funding from them."

Luke looked politely towards T : "How much are you looking for?"

"About 350k to start with, the biggest expense is the capsule making machine."

He called out to Bernie, who was on his mobile in the next room.

"Bernie, come here, man, get off the phone man. Luke is here and he needs figures and a bizzo plan for the veggie start up."

Luke was clearly startled by Tony's informed chatter. He knew that he was a smart guy; well, he must have been to have evaded police arrest for so long, but he had wrongly assumed that he was similar to most gangsters and street criminals in that he lacked real intellectual capability. He was completely unaware of the fact that T had only turned to drug dealing as a means of *survival* when his boxing career had nosedived and he had needed more than just government handouts to support his extended family. T's ultimate plan was to downsize the drug business and then retire altogether. He was counting on the natural high venture as a real alternative to cocaine and cannabis.

Bernie shuffled into the room. He was dressed in an open-necked shirt and some indigo blue jeans that matched the colour of his Mohican. Luke bent down and embraced him, taking the business plan at the same time. Tony left them alone while he went to get some gear for Luke. It was time to drop some blow.

Luke sat down on an enormous, custom-made Dalmatian spotted, leather Chesterfield settee. It was positioned diagonally across from the wooden table in the kitchen and an eye-popping reminder of the vulgarities of modern excess.

Luke examined the detailed proposal carefully and took his time to weigh up the variables. Godwin was moving around with his supersized tureen of frou frou soup; wafts of fresh lime chilies and seasoned meat hung in the air.

"Hello there, Luke," he grinned.

"Hi, Godwin, how are you keeping?" asked Luke thoughtfully. He thought Godwin was a sweet old man and felt sorry that he was forced into domestic servitude at T's at his time in life, but Godwin liked it at T's. He enjoyed feeling useful and liked the nightly comings and goings of all the people who visited.

"Oh, can't complain, can't complain. I'm going to Jamaica before Easter, y'ar know, and catch up there. Tony's getting me an early birthday present so I gets to see some family and ting."

"Oh, that's good," enthused Luke.

"You want some soup? It settles the stomach, you know."

"No, not for me, not just yet," replied Luke, touched by the old man's kindness.

As he pored over the minutiae of the business plan, he noticed the sound of the television volume getting louder. *Sky News* was reporting that a group of pro hunt lobbyists had just stormed parliament, brandishing banners and paint bombs. The funniest part of this extraordinary sight was that the intruders were being chased around the Member's area by the aptly named "Sergeant in Arms" a Dickensian looking character who ordinarily, rolls around in knickerbockers and black stockings. *What could be more surreal,* thought Luke. *Here I am at a drug dealer's flat in the middle of London on a rainy Wednesday, watching some upper class oiks being chased around Parliament by a bloke straight out of "Barnaby Rudge."* Janey and Sarah started to laugh uncontrollably at the television screen as the Sergeant in Arms wrestled one of the protestors to the ground. It was pure pantomime.

Eventually T came back with the gear; it had been spiked with baby powder and cut for easy consumption. By this time, Luke had inwardly committed himself to a slice of the action on the veggie cap deal and told Bernie as much. He was impressed with the idea and knew it could work. He told Bernie he would have his old man draw up the papers and set up a meeting pronto.

Before he left, Tony explained that the way the pill was cultivated and harvested (in the Far East) gave it amazing medicinal as well as euphoric properties. It was a *wonder* drug. Luke was convinced of its marketability because it was 100% legal, easily available in Europe and America, and most important of all had no large-scale distribution network in London. Tony was the **only** supplier.

"It's a good 'un, completely kosher," chimed Bernie.

Tony went on:

"All the regulars have put in orders for the veggie caps and those that don't do drugs, which means it covers everyone. It also comes in liquid form, tea, a balm, and as a concentrated elixir. Different potencies affect different ailments and different levels of sensation." *It's a fucking miracle,* thought Luke contentedly. He needed no further encouragement, shook hands with T, then packed up his gear and promised he'd call him later that day.

Bernie turned briskly to T.

"Once that guy's sold the idea to his old man, we'll have enough dosh to send someone to go get that fucking capsule maker." T smiled, offered the girls more blow and they spliffed the day away with Janice Joplin ease.

Chapter 19

As Richard made his way back to his offices at Snow Hill, right next door to the Serious Fraud Office, he smiled to himself thinking of all those number drones at their desks. *What would they think if they knew lawyers like him were right on their doorstep?* It was that "*wasp*" mentality (white Anglo Saxon pricks), that saved him from detection. They always picked on immigrants and people with foreign-sounding names much more than their own kind. His mobile phone kept bleeping. He had already missed twenty-seven calls. *Could it be work related?* The number looked familiar.

He checked his messages. Some of them were from his uncle Marvin who owned a gold shop in Hatton Garden not far from where he worked. He dialled the number wearily. (He would respond to the other messages afterwards; they were all from the same demanding wealthy client Seymour of Deer Hurst).

"Hi, Uncle Marvin. It's me, Richie," but it was his aunt who answered the phone.

"Oh Ritchie Bubblie, come over come over now, we've been robbed!"

"Don't worry I'll be round straight away."

The thief had escaped with some of his personal items,

including a gold Rolex watch and an envelope with his name on it. Richard's heart missed one two three beats. *Fuck the gold Rolli. That isn't fucking important,* he thought. He immediately called Eva at the office and told her he would be back late. Then he called his uncle again and told him not to report the theft to the "old bill," at least not the loss of his items anyway.

Marvin was sceptical the insurance wouldn't cough up the money to replace the stock if the theft wasn't reported and he couldn't afford to lose such a huge amount of money. Anyway, he had already reported most of the items to the police, but not Richard's. They were kept separately in a smaller safe deposit box. Richard sighed; at least the "the old bill" had no idea of what was missing. He had to make some urgent calls and find Poncho Khan's missing key and paper note with the encrypted figures or else they were all for the chop.

After speaking with his uncle, Richard called Seymour back, and put on a confident professional voice to reassure him that his legal work would be done. Ashen-faced and trembling with his skin tags more visible than ever, he hailed a black cab for the short ride to Hatton Garden. This was bad, very bad. His knees were buckling under him. *What the fuck was he going to do*? The cab driver was irritatingly chatty. He had dozens and dozens of pictures of his two children in the car and was talking about golf, and how bad Man City was doing. *Why put so many* shots of *your children in a* cab, thought Richard. Stuck in groaning lunchtime traffic, the car inched along like a crawling centipede stuck in a mud pool. He had moved twenty feet in as many minutes. He stopped the cab driver,

"Listen mate can I get out?"

"What we'll be there soon now I'll have to turn around

now," Snarked, the cabbie.

"No you won't just stop and pull up here you always hog up bus lanes and yellow lines anyway," groused Richie under his breath.

Reluctantly the cab driver parked up and Richie paid him, then began walking the rest of the distance to his uncle's shop. After about ten minutes, he arrived, greeted by his aunt Esther, a sprightly woman of around sixty-five, accompanied by one of her daughters, Rebecca. They looked tired and worn out like a heap of un-ironed washing. Esther potted around, making tea. She asked Rebecca to go and get some salt beef sandwiches from the Nosherie down the road. Richard tried to protest at this blitz of food, weighed down with more urgent things, but Rebecca was sent anyway.

Marvin, was a short, well fed, typically Semitic looking man, with an Israeli tan and a mass of thick unruly hair that he half covered under his yarmulke. To complete the look he wore a gold signet ring and chunky curve bracelet on his podgy hand. He stared angrily at Richard as if he were the cause of all his mishap.

"Come upstairs, Ritchie, come on let's talk upstairs" He shook his head: "Gold Breitling, John Lobb shoes, Kilgur shirt top of the range shmutter, you certainly look the part, Ritchie."

Richard dragged his feet up the stairs like two blocks of concrete. He knew that surly, flat tone, used dozens of times before when Uncle Marvin had to bail him out of trouble over and over again; he always used that same cranky voice. He was noticeably uneasy and took a long, deep breath before entering the small office.

"Now, Ritchie," continued his uncle, "I'm your father's brother and when he died I became responsible for you as if you were my own boy. So, tell me what this shit is about. Who have you been messing around with this time, Ritchie?"

Richard was out of his depth with his uncle who was a straight shooter and spoke bluntly without unnecessary sentiment. He never fucked about with small talk.

"Look, Uncle Marvin I'm really sorry about what's happened, but I swear to you, I don't know who's behind this. You'll have to trust me, Uncle, what's important now is I get those documents and that key back, that's all that matters now"

"Twenty years this shop has been here, twenty years never any trouble. No one around here has ever been robbed. You're keeping something from me, Ritchie. We'll have to leave this one to the "old bill," they can sort it out. It's too dangerous for you to get involved in. You're a solicitor, for fuck's sake."

"No, Uncle Marvin, don't involve the police any more than you have to. They'll just nose around, file and bin it anyway. End of. Some faceless bird in blue will have us spewing out all the details, filling in the forms, then they'll start nosing around 'cause they 'avent got anything better t' do and they'll find something for sure, like dodgy stock or some crap," Richard continued, "All I want is for you to forget you ever saw those papers or even had them in your shop. Just forget about it."

Marvin stared hard at Richard. It was the face of disappointment and worry. Esther came into the room with a tray of sandwiches and pot of hot tea.

"There we are, dears. Here, get something inside you." Richard looked up and half smiled at his aunt while Marvin shooed her out of the room with a broad sweep of his hand.

"For God's sake, Esther, can't you see we're talking? Please just leave that on the side there."

Esther nonchalantly did as she was told but gave Richard a comforting look anyway as she walked slowly down the stairs.

Richard, now desperate to leave, turned to his uncle to assure him that everything would be all right. He apologized once more and nervously hugged him while Marvin forced a wad of fifty's and twenty's into his hand. "There's only a monkey there, but it will get you through the weekend," he said generously. Richard, embarrassed by the gesture, took the cash anyway. He made his way back to Hatton Garden and walked around towards the Holborn Viaduct.

As his pace quickened, he became acutely aware of the pressure on him to find the stolen bond. *How the fuck was he going to get out of this one*? The "old bill" would love to know about the "salubrious" Poncho Khan, on the surface a wholesome respectable Property Tycoon, Investment Banker, and Bollywood Film Financer, but in reality one of the most wanted and ruthless drug barons in the world. How exactly was Richard going to tell Poncho that he had lost his Bearer Bond and a Swiss safety deposit key that allowed his client access to millions of pounds?

Sweating profusely with severe heart palpitations, Richard decided to stop by The Old Monk pub. He needed a drink to settle his nerves and make him lucid. He decided on a double Vodka and Red Bull. The bar tender, a pretty, blonde Australian in her early twenties, was someone Richard would ordinarily chat up, but now everything seemed futile and all he could think of was the long list of criminal charges Poncho had been indicted for in his former South East Asian homeland: extortion, racketeering blackmail, unlawful killing, robbery, the list went on, false imprisonment, even threats to administer poison. Richard wished he had done a more detailed investigation of Poncho's background before he took him on as a client, but by then it was too late, and anyway, Poncho always had an excuse, a plausible explanation citing political ill will and corruption as just two of the reasons for what he claimed were bogus charges. He had a string of aliases that all checked out, too, and was able to travel freely almost anywhere in the world. How could Richard possibly know what he was really like?

By the time Richard had discovered his unsavoury past, his law firm was being paid a handsome retainer of one hundred thousand per month and he himself was creaming off a further thirty thousand a month for unrelated, "private," work that never showed up on the firm's accounts. Besides, Poncho was not a man to whom you could say no or even maybe to, you always said *yes* to Poncho.

Chapter 20

Two Croatian twins had joined T's payroll, they had all the qualifications they needed to make excellent debt collectors. They could cross their legs a la Sharon Stone, wear six-inch stilettos without falling over, and most importantly, could pout on demand. Fresh from a daring raid on one of Europe's most luxurious department stores the two had been acquitted of robbery because of the magic of their matching DNA. Now notorious and trading on their celebrity tag they were the perfect cover up for T's expanding bizzo. Recruited to collect debts from property owners, private debtors and assigned company losses, Bernie however, didn't like *them* or trust them he wanted *them* off the scene.

With their platinum blond hair and Jean Harlow smiles they had the perfect cool façade to dupe everyone into thinking they were playing fair; but the twins were hatching a swindle of their own. As part of an Eastern European crime gang they were using T's contacts to target on line betting businesses, squeezing them for cash by threatening them with cyber attacks if they refused to pay up. "blackmail by internet" was their hustle.

Bernie sent them off to Hatton Garden to make a visit on an elderly accountant who was five months in the red with a personal debt. Christina spoke first she was diva cool wearing sequins and black leather with a fake fur wrap. Her hair was "bed head" loose and she wore heavy kohl eyeliner and pink blush.

"Hello Mr. Davis, Bernie has sent us."

"I see," he looked at them with a dead lust in his eye.

"Well, I- I'll have to go to the bank I don't keep money here," he stammered.

"That's fine Mr. Davis we'll wait," replied Nadja her twin, they wore identical clothes and both spoke with the same dominatrix strum.

"We can't leave without some payment," Christina replied.

"Please, both of you, can you please – both of you – can you wait outside?" He pleaded.

"No,"

They answered together.

"To be honest and perfectly frank I- I don't want my clients seeing you you're dressed in very revealing, quite inappropriate clothes and my wife will be meeting me here for lunch – please I, I need some time just give me an hour or two?"

"I'm sorry Mr. Davies – perhaps you can put us in a waiting room or somewhere a little more discreet until you've seen your wife and your clients but we can't leave without payment, you owe us money." asserted Nadja.

Mr. Davis was a middle class tremble of a man worried about an unseemly display and his *Jerry Springer* moment. He was cash stumped; all his assets in hock and on the trading floor. He had borrowed £10,000 from a private lender and the debt had now been assigned to T for collection. He was being hammered with interest and unable to keep up with the payments due to the elaborate lie he was leading, faking respectability and financial security. Bernie knew he had a joint bank account with his wife and that he could get his hands on money fast but was refusing to cough up so the twins were piling on the pressure. Bernie was banking on his middle class veneration and artifice to choke it out of him.

"I- I'd like to renegotiate the terms of the loan," he blustered.

"You have to deal with Bernie for that, but today is very simple we take some money and then we leave."

Their presence in the office was like a smothering wind ready to strangle the prayers out of him. It was sordid.

"What time is your wife expected," asked Christine with cold scorn.

"Not long, look I'm writing a cheque now I'll be back in twenty minutes," he answered with crumbling fatigue. He looked at them again this time with pure hate, the kind of boiled hate that wolfs a man from inside forcing him to kill all that is good and all that is right.

Spooked they waited for him to return in silence.

While the twins were out of the way, Bernie had time to do some in house sleuthing of his own. He went to the room they shared and started rifling through their belongings and contact numbers. He found a small lap top hidden underneath some clothes in a wall drawer. He started it up. Once the code had been hacked, he found several internet businesses and what appeared to be a cyclostyle blackmail threat that had been sent to all of them. This was high-risk crime something Bernie felt would put T and the crew under intense police scrutiny. Then he found the "smoking gun" to get rid of the girls for good. They were planning a cyber hit on one of T's regulars a family owned betting shop that had recently started trading on line. Bernie would put the kibosh on their slippery scheme and throw them out. He waited for them to return from the Davis drop.

"Christina, Nadja come here- you were hired to do a job."

"Yah," they looked blankly at each other and then at him.

"I thought you could be trusted."

"Yah," they answered in unison.

"I want you to leave. You're not good for bizzo and I can't have you creating rifts with people we do business with."

"What?" Asked Nadja

"Blackmailing bookies on line is just like stealing from the boss when you know, that bookie is one we have agreements with now get your stuff and clear off you're fucking trouble and double the trouble just ain't worth it." Bernie was impressed by his put down line and felt vindicated by asking them to leave but gave them £1000 out of what they collected anyway. He never cheated "family."

Chapter 21

The sound of a muzzled clock could be heard ticking in Christian's head. It was like the freezing hum of an egg timer: the same tedious beat scoring his soul. He felt trapped and paralyzed in a coke bubble. He was losing it. His only piece of blue sky was Estevez the guy he had been seeing without realizing Bernie knew all about it. When Christian first popped up on the London party scene, he was alive with ideas and the pulse of excitement. He had baby faced ambition and a head of cool:

I would wake everyday and think of my moment out there on stage with a real band and hordes of fans waiting to hear me sing I used to have a wake up and get the world feeling now after nine weeks as a coke joke all I have is a flake out – no hope feeling.

He couldn't shake it; he was on the head start to nowhere. In his real life, away from the acid vibrations of the drug infused world he occupied, he had a family who cared about him. They lived on the Gold coast of Australia and owned plots of land. They were country people, simple decent- no frills- kind of people. They never knew about the dope, or the cheap sex he traded for rent money. All they knew was that Christian could sing that he was a placid, good boy. A proper son, who called home every week, gave them extra cash when they needed it and remembered their birthdays, anniversaries, and Christmas. He did it all. Now, Christian was slapped up on coke and close to giving up. He needed to start over.

Chapter 22

Bernie was chalking up money from clubs, bars, strip joints, hair shops, beauty parlours and a whole string of moneymaking enterprises including betting rings telephone card scams and adult chat lines. One of the most lucrative areas in which they had diversified however, was fly posting. This was how some major Record companies and big businesses would advertise their events; promote bands and record releases, forking out huge chunks of change to T for their posters to fly on wall space and empty buildings. Bernie had tied up all of West End Central and had used up most of the vacant buildings and BT phone booths in the area. It was easy promotion, big money for T with hardly any risk.

Bernie had billed five leading record companies and two high rolling corporate concerns. In effect, under the Planning Regulations 1992 fly posting was a criminal offence but Bernie had it sussed knowing how to avoid prosecution and charge. Later that night one of the MD's (managing directors) of a heavy-duty record label who they were fly posting for, ordered some gear for his promo bash.

"Awright Bernie- it's Jez from Soopa Records. I need an ounce for the party it's at the Sanderson. Get your guy to meet me at the Long Bar. I've got a blonde razor cut, and am wearing a Kingfisher blue Armani suit" He spoke with a Mockney twang.

"Okay, I'll send Tim along for the drop."

"Who's Tim?"

"You know Tim - really "safe ordinary looking" bald head, looks exactly like Larry David from *Curb Your Enthusiasm*. He's wearing a beige raincoat, blue stripped shirt and plain black trousers, what time do you need it?"

"About 8.00.pm"

"Long Bar at 8:00pm."

"Yeah inside the Sanderson I'll be standing by the purple baize pool table."

Bernie got off his mobile.

Tim was a retired money trader from suburban Weybridge. He was approaching sixty-five years of age and now heavily addicted to cocaine. He had taken to living in the upstairs annex of Tony's flat after being thrown out of his home by his long-suffering wife who had discovered him in their marital bed with their former French nanny and housekeeper. He was extremely effective in collecting bad debts, as he was utterly inconspicuous, always polite, civil, and highly persuasive.

"Tim, you have to do a drop for Jez from Soopa Records he's got a big promo party tonight. Make sure you're not late; you have to meet 'im inside the Sanderson Hotel – the Long Bar. He's got on a blue suit and has short blonde hair. You'll find him by the purple baize pool table oh and Tim it's raining so be careful."

Tim was for the main part, reliable and easy to deal with. He set off around 7.15pm to make the drop.

The night was just as important for T and the crew because it would introduce a lot of new money and clientele to the business and generate interest in the fledgling herbal pill venture. These punters were a signature clique of power suits and moneymen, they had the wherewithal to use drugs and experiment with other recreational substances without falling into debt, psychosis, and oblivion. This was a big- league night for everyone. Drugs were just as ordinary to these people as having a cup of Earl Grey tea and they were the sterling demographic Bernie wanted hooked on *natural highs*.

8.20pm:

"Where's your man, Bernie? The party's kicking off and it's a friggin' disaster. Everyone's mooching around with long faces and wooden expressions it's whack we need some yayo to get things rocking." Jez said "yayo" as if he were doing an impersonation of Al Pacino as Tony Montano in:*"Scarface."* It got on Bernie's nerves but he stayed composed.

"He left over thirty minutes ago- hang tight, I'll call him now."

Bernie was surprised Tim was late for the drop.

"Tim where the fuck are you Jez is waiting for you and needs the stuff now."

There was a short pause.

"Um I've had a bit of an altercation," Tim replied, in a ruffled voice.

"What where?"

"Yah someone – has attacked me in a road rage incident he drives a white van and is in a very foul mood."

"Tim, where the fuck are you?" Repeated Bernie clearly rankled.

"I'm about five minutes away and I simply will not allow and will not tolerate such mindless rudeness I..."

"Tim listen to me – we don't want to draw attention to ourselves, now do we? Let's just be rational and end this nonsense now Tim – Tim?"

Bernie got on the other line and called Jez.

"Jez, hi he, er, seems to have run into a bit of bother mate, says he's outside the hotel... I mean if you could possibly just step outside and... Jez?"

Bernie was peeved. On one side he was dealing with a man who was about as street wise as Alicia Silverstone in *Clueless* and on the other a home counties twit. Tim failed to appreciate that he was a drug runner for the evening and not a respected member of mainstream society free to engage in altercations and bust ups without fear of police intervention.

Jez called back:

"Bernie what the fuck is going on here? Your chap is having a very public brawl outside the hotel. Look, I can't be seen to be involved in something like this. It's fucking extreme man yeah, there's no way I can get involved not this not here."

"Sorry Jez can you explain what's happening?"

"What's happening? This is a fucking joke is what's happening: your guy is having a full on one- to- one street fight with some van driver and... oh fuck he's floored him. The van driver is now on the ground, this is loco man yeah it's seriously fucked up. The van man is up now... And he's just bashed your chap on the head Yeah – look I can't be involved in such a ruckus I just can't."

Tim had gone from Larry David to Christopher Walken in *True Romance* after one crazy minute.

"Tim –Tim pick up the phone it's Bernie."

Tim had been knocked to the ground, sliding around in a dirty puddle, cut, and battered, with his quintessential British stoicism still intact.

"Er Jez, could you please meet him outside?" Asked Bernie still on the line.

"Yeah okay I'll make out I'm a helpful stranger- I'll give him the money and take the blow anyway."

Jez walked over to Tim and reluctantly helped him to his feet, while the driver of the white van sped off into the evening traffic.

"You must be?"

"Jez."

"Yes, well, here it is." Tim offered up a soggy wet package smudged with road grease, rain spots, and street debris.

"Are you serious – look at it – this is soaking wet, it's wet right through!"

"Um it should be okay if you er dry it under a hand dryer for a while," volunteered Tim.

"Are you completely stupid – you want me to stick this bag of coke under a fucking hand dryer? Look just go okay- just leave, here's the money for this crap and tell Bernie I'll be in touch fucking clown."

Jez handed over the cash and escaped to the wealth of his hotel. He got straight on the phone to Bernie:

"This is bollocks Bernie! All of the gear is ruined – that dumb fucktard you sent has ruined everything it's all wet, it's fucked useless! He told me to stick it under a hand dryer a friggin' hand dryer I mean what the ...."

"Don't worry Jez, just chill okay it's all taken care of. I've sent Sheila with another batch and she'll be with you before this call has ended."

Sheila, a leather clad Doc' Martin wearing courier chick arrived with package intact and delivered it without any further drama.

Chapter 23

Chewing on beetle nuts and downing large glasses of neat whiskey had become a routine part of Poncho's day. He was a big muscle bound man built on Ghee (clarified Indian butter) and Creatine : a lethal combination. He had large, fat hands that resembled two loaves of Hovis Brown, the sort of hands that could swipe and punch with "deadly precision." He was saturated with overstated bling. On his right index finger he wore a finely cut two carat diamond ring, and on his left hand a twenty two carat solid gold link chain bracelet. He was covered in rough coarse chest hair and worse several heavyset gold neck chains all at the same time, each one at least nineteen inches in length.

Poncho's clothes were an unsettling mix of Elvis circa 1975 (the Vegas years) mixed with Mid West USA business exec. They made an obvious and distinctive statement, and seemed to hiss: "If you're looking for trouble, I'm looking for you." He wore his hair slicked back and greased down, parted to the side, taming his wild oversized curls into teeny ringlets which gave him a rubensque quality.

Poncho was furious. The only reason he had arranged for the bearer bond to go missing was to hook Richard in deeper. He wanted to use him for other projects with the bearer bond lost;

Richard would be indebted to him and could easily be persuaded to play a bigger role in heavier crime deals and corruption rackets. He wanted to link him to the real power chain. He knew that Richard still had colossal gambling losses to settle and was deeply dependent on cocaine and alcohol, but nonetheless his legal brilliance was undisputed.

Right now Poncho was "untouchable," he had premium level contacts everywhere and wasn't about to get stung by some jumped up two-bit crook from the East End. He would teach that bastard Bessie some respect, teach him to hold out on him and learn how to play the game Indian style He should have delivered the Bond to him days ago but was trying to be too clever by half.

Poncho's consignment of decorative packaging ribbon had come through, sent by air courier from Mumbai to Paris to his French lawyers:

"Ello, Monsieur Denoir." Poncho spoke with a goofy French accent mimicking the caller with his oafish parroting.

"Good morning Mr. Khan zere (there) has been a delivery for you."

"Yes I was expecting ze (the) delivery Monsieur."

"Would you like us to send it to you; I will arrange everything for you?"

"Yes have it sent to ze address I gave you."

"It will be with you in three hours," Answered the French man affably.

"Very good," Replied Poncho.

The package was processed by customs but no doubts were raised over its contents as the drugs that Poncho had packed in there were tightly wrapped and hidden around gaudy ribbon and tinsel spools. The spools were concealing around one thousand grams of heroin with an estimated street value of thirty thousand pounds. By midnight, it would be accessible to the public and by dawn, their brains would be blasted with tar and toxins. Poncho was unrepentant, as one of the biggest heroin distributors in the West he had singlehandedly contributed to the spiralling number of deaths and suicides caused by heroin addiction but:

If druggies were unable to control their need that was their fault. He reflected.

Each to his own why should he play judge – if it wasn't heroin, it would be something else. The world was ***his*** *playground and* ***he*** *made the rules.*

Chapter 24

Mishaque was causing bother, a stoutly blend of Irish "Shrek" mixed with scary Jafakain his front was dealing luxury cars. T had set up a meeting to try his gear on spec. He had heard the product was good but then when he had distributed it, locals complained of the after effects saying it made them feel sick and nauseous. It turned out the blow was studded with heroin: ingestion could have been deadly. T refused to pay for the sample and on principle refused to talk to Mishaque. He sourced another dealer but Mishaque wouldn't let up and felt like he had been disrespected.

T's phone rang:

"T my house thirty minutes," he spoke as if he were a cardboard cliché of a hard nut.

"On my way," replied T indifferently.

When he got there, T found Mishaque surrounded by his Albanian posse of gang members and hustlers. A gimpy outfit of amateurs and half-wits, who were faking the gangster life and playing at being tough.

Mishaque was dressed in baggy knee length shorts; his portly rolls of fat hanging over the top of his stomach like a jelly barrel. His skin was pale and stippled with pigmentation spots.

T was boxed in. Mishaque clicked his fingers signalling to one of his "boys" to put on Sound *Murderer* a drumming Ragga tune. When the opening lyrics started, he began waving a gun in T's face tracing it up and down his body, across his face and up his nose, all the while doing a freakish dance. He was half-singing – half-talking:

"If you don't pay man you won't see another day man."

He thought he was Drexel a white Rasta pimp played to perfection by Gary Oldman in *True Romance* but the comic gun slinging made him look more like Phoebe in *Friends* when she was pretending to like Chandler. It was embarrassing and grotesque. Anyone could see Mishaque was jammed on coke. Tony stayed cool and never flinched. When the track was over and Mishaque had stopped his jumbled rant T made a break for the door:

"So I'll see you tomorrow T wif all mi money bwouy!"

T knew this was all bravado the gun was probably not loaded but Mishaque was bad news, unclean, trying to mix two dangerous drugs together was not right. He was banana crazy to try such a move. It could lead to multiple deaths and injury, something T wanted no hand in.

2:00 am the following morning:

As Mishaque was leaving his house, he opened the front door and was shot twice in both legs.

No more dancey prance for you, Thought T when he heard.

Chapter 25

Tim, still smarting from his sodden encounter with Jez the voguish moron with choppy hair whom he resented, because he had treated him as a prize chump, decided to fuck the night away with a "coke" slut.

3:00am: there was no one around except Tim who was prowling the neighbourhood looking for sex.

He pulled up in Inverness Road Camden. Undercover police were on the lookout for punters and street action. Tim rolled down his car window and approached a familiar working girl she was skinny with blonde hair and bug eyes. The police moved in:

"Hello miss how have you been?"

"Yeah okay," she replied with feral monotony.

"Been a bit hungry- that's all," she sniffed.

Yeah she was hungry -hungry for coke she was starving for coke, she needed coke to crack her longing she would have begged me for it. Tim thought.

"Can I have a quick word with you Miss?"

"Yeah?"

"I'm letting you go with a warning tonight okay?"

The policeman turned his attention to Tim:

"Hello there Sir."

Tim stared ahead without acknowledging him.

"What's gone on here is that I spotted you approaching a known prostitute and..."

Before he could finish Tim blurted out:

"We're all prostitutes officer we're all selling ourselves for something there is a pleasing candour to what I was about to do. I was going to be an MP (Member of Parliament) an MP..."

"Yes sir, do you understand what you're being arrested for and that the arrest is by way of summons and that you must turn up to court to answer those summons?"

"If I hadn't had that silly affair I would be on track to the House of Commons officer, do *you* understand that?"

The police officer continued filling his forms in and Tim bluffed his contact details.

"The summons will be sent to the address you've just provided sir and it's likely you'll be facing a fine, I now have to ask you sir to kindly leave the area."

Tim skulked off into the shadows muttering:

Morality is nothing but freedom; with money, you can create your own morality.

Chapter 26

Bernie was waiting to be paid. He had joined "Dodgy Dave" at the Limelight club in Shaftesbury Avenue. "Dodgy Dave" was a former gangster, turned tabloid celebrity and club promoter who had made a fortune selling his memoirs and hosting club nights on the continental rave scene.

He was creaming the dream with a steady flow of cash and instant respectability. Dave greeted him with a superstar grin and a diamond earring, he wore an all white suit, and CJ's Lucchese Cowboy boots.

"Bernie 'ow you been?"

"Yeah good."

"Shall we get some drinks then have a chat?"

"Yeah sounds good mate – got a "drop by" later someone owes me some cash so she should be here soon."

"Yeah that won't be any problem mate."

They got a table at the side of the bar and sat down.

The Limelight was a converted church that had re-invented itself as a nightclub venue. There were bars on every floor and secret alcoves and open balconies. Bernie had asked a regular punter to meet him there to pay her debt for the coke she had scored from him.

"I want in on the natural high pill bizzo; I spoke to T about it the other week" Explained Dave.

"Yeah how much can you front asked Bernie"

Although he never knew Dave that well, he appreciated the fact that Dave had managed to make a good living out of his criminal past and that took guts, hard work, and numerous contacts.

Who says crime doesn't pay Thought Bernie.

"I was thinking of maybe £10, or 15,000."

"Sounds good."

As they rolled on with their business talk Suzie, a shameless coke chick came by. She was vamped up "Goth" style with a tongue piercing and a ripped top that exposed her cleavage. A mix of Courtney Love and Winona Ryder. She was smutty cool and yet, fragile like a broken doll. Bernie was of course indifferent to her magnetic hook.

"Hi Bernie - I know I owe you lots of cash," she rippled with buttercup seduction.

"I was thinking, we could, perhaps come to an arrangement and that I could, well pay you off in kind." She had climbed onto the bar table sliding her legs in front of her, leaning down so that her breasts were on show- her voice trailing to a whisper. Bernie pushed his face out of her shirt.

"I can't reach you- a physical impossibility...so I suggest you pay up- you've got one hour now tramp off I'm doing business."

She pressed her lips close to his and gave him a stud ring kiss.

"Okay, but you're missing out on something really special."

She sauntered over to the bar and spying an easy mark lured him away to a dark corridor, her back pressed up against the wall holding his head while he tongued her as she looked on at Dave and Bernie with a *fuck you* smirk.

What a delicious slut I am she thought to herself.

After fleecing the guy for cash and drinks, she returned to pay her debt.

Bernie asked her to wash her hands before she parted with the cash.

Dave was amused by the whole spectacle, ordered more drinks, and proceeded to get "butchered" on Es and dope he was in the *zone* looking for an orgasmic rush.

Bernie took his money and left.

Chapter 27

Richard was on standby for Bernie's call who wanted to talk to him urgently about Rabbi Romberg, one of Uncle Marvin's closest friends. Richard had heard that the distinguished Rabbi had disintegrated into a downward spiral of drink and drugs after the death of his dear wife Lottie. Now he was a key player in the criminal glitterati. He kept it secret from his uncle but had no idea why Bernie was on to him.

T had found out that Rabbi Romberg was doing much more than simply organizing cocaine soirees. The Rabbi had started dealing. It was unacceptable. He had crossed the line. T had supplied him with five hundred grams, just two days ago believing it was all for private consumption and then discovered he was slanging his turf. This may have been okay if he had paid his way for a seat at the table but now Bernie was forced to eliminate the competition for the sake of "natural highs" and gangland respect.

"Yeah Bernie it's Ritch."

"We had an understanding with your illustrious Rabbi Romberg- now we hear he's upped his game taking much more than a pie slice."

Richard remained tight-lipped. Bernie went on:

"We agreed to rent him the flat so he could get his rocks off, have his parties and get fucked on snow not so he had a safe place to deal and cut us out of the jam. In the beginning we agreed to supply because he was a safe mark – now he's become a threat, taking the very food from our table. He must be dealt with."

"What?"

"Ritchie – you know how it is, your Rabbi has been a very naughty, greedy greedy boy, he's eating our profits, stealing our bizzo and I want it sorted today."

"Look I'll try speaking to him okay, he'll bow out."

T knew the best way to eliminate this kind of competition would be a simple hook up with a "bent copper" off the record of course. A tip off like this would make everyone smile – the old bill for netting such a heavy-duty dealer, the lawyers for raking in their legal fees and T knowing his profits would be safe. Richard had no time to waste on niceties to spare Uncle Marvin's blushes he told it to him straight:

"Uncle Marvin it's Ritchie I"

"What is it come on?"

"It's about Rabbi Romberg uncle he's um in serious trouble. I um think he might be dealing cocaine."

"Ritchie are you mad boy? Have you taken leave of your senses? That's the phrase isn't it, they use for people like you who've gone a bit loopy loo? Are you off with the fairies boy? Perhaps *you're* on something. You can't be disrespecting the Rabbi like that, he's a servant of God Ritchie and is it too much to ask for just a little bit of deference and consideration for a man who sacrifices for others, Ritchie how can you say these things I just don't know first the robbery and now ..."

"Uncle please, please just stop I have it from a good source – a reliable source that Rabbi Romberg is dealing drugs. I think we should go to his flat tonight, the one he rents in Brittan Street and I think..."

"Okay Ritchie enough of this you're giving me blood pressure please we'll go okay but don't go shooting your mouth off. You can't make such outrageous allegations on a hunch or a source the man deserves our respect!"

Later, that evening around 8pm Ritchie and his uncle took the short cut to Brittan Street.

Outside the flat, there were three police cars and two Alsatian sniffer dogs. It was clear to anyone they were on a drugs bust. Ritchie made his uncle duck down as they fled the scene. The Police were on a roll:

"Rabbi Romberg this is the police please open the door." They knocked louder with their batons.

"Rabbi Romberg open up now it's the police, we have a warrant to search these premises please open the door now." The door was locked from inside but the police could hear drunken laughter and loud music.

"Rabbi Romberg open this door now or we will be forced to knock it down"

"One two three!" They charged at the door with a ramming baton forcing it to cave in and break off in fractured pieces.

The eminent Rabbi, coked to the stars, was found wearing nothing but boxer shorts, a spotted bow tie around his bare neck, and striped woollen socks. A naked prostitute gyrating in front of him to the sound of George Michael's: "I want your Sex."

"Get some clothes on" demanded the police officer to the bewildered floozy.

"Rabbi, we have reason to suspect there are illegal drugs in this house and we have a warrant to search these premises"

Within seconds, they found kilo wraps of cocaine and thirty thousand pounds in cash. A further three shoeboxes of cocaine were hidden in a secret panel in a desk drawer.

"Get dressed Rabbi Romberg you're coming in; we're arresting you based on what we've found at this property." The Rabbi was dazed, and unresponsive as the officer read out the standard caution to him he listened but had no idea of what was happening all he could see was "marmalade skies and tangerine highs." He was in a coke slump and nothing could free him from it. The Rabbi's drug scandal was wall-to-wall news all over the globe and now it would be up to Ritchie to save him from prison and penury.

Chapter 28

T and the guys were playing War craft III. Whoever got the lowest score had to arrange a visiting order for T's cousin currently on remand at Pentonville Prison. T hadn't been in contact with Dixon, for over ten years but the other day received a letter from him requesting new trainers and a mixed bag of contraband. Pentonville was one of the most infamous of all the English gaols forever immortalized in song, poetry, and death. With a bloody and morbid history, it was a Victorian swine pit built in 1842 standing on the scruffy end of London's Caledonian Road. It fell on Tim to do the necessaries:

"It's always me that gets chosen for the profusely vile, the most unpleasant, and degrading of tasks," he sighed.

"I don't know why you're complaining Tim you're always saying how you want to express your artistic side and now finally a chance" Said Bernie with a caustic smirk.

"Yes- think of it – think of it as Performance Art" Scoot, added playfully adopting a fake upper crust accent a la Prince Charles. Richard was hovering in the background like a bad mood waiting to happen but soon eased up on hearing of Tim's plight. He had a massive gloat on and readily admitted to bouts of schadenfreude.

"Oh Tim this is perfect for you it's a real opportunity for you to finally embrace your art – be an artist. Look who's been there Pete Doherty (Babyshambles), Boy George, Hugh Cornwell (The Stranglers) John Alton and of course, the big cheese himself Oscar Wilde!" He twittered clapping his hands.

"I don't think Oscar Wilde would appreciate being referred to as a "big cheese" and who might I ask is John Alford?" Retorted Tim with mild distaste.

"John Alford is an actor – a thespian an artist," Exclaimed Richard with a taunting grin.

"I bet you had to "Google" him" sulked Tim.

"I absolutely did not," argued Ritch impatiently.

"Name me one film/ TV show/theatre production he's appeared in then?"

"Look Tim the point is all the best have been to Pentonville and soon, dear boy it will be your turn. They all "suffered" for their art Tim and that's what makes them truly great!" Agreed Bernie, needling him.

"Yeah you always said your one ambition was to create great art magnificent art that your one unfulfilled dream was to create now here's your chance your very own art- fuck moment this is it the spotlight is on you it's *your* time baby!" Ritchie squelched.

"Shut up Richard you sound like a fucking moron."

"Says the man who's going to shove cannabis wraps up his anal passage and smuggle them into her majesty's pleasure Pentonville!" Cracked Richard, with demented laughter.

"Take no notice of slick dick he *is* a moron. It is art- it's risqué, anti- establishment dangerous and fucking mental," Cried Bernie excitedly.

"It's such a trip man- best piece of performance art ever it will give you such a wicked buzz. I mean you must have heard of the Italian artist who sealed dozens of tins with his own crap inside then labelled it then sold it. You know Piero Munzoni. The Tate Gallery only went and bought the crap for squillions of pounds. They paid for a tin with excrement inside that's the truth," Scoot explained informatively.

"Yes but didn't they later find out that the tins weren't full of shit after all?" queried Tim desperate for a way out.

"Look the fact is, an artist filled up some cans with crap and sold that shit and the public bought it and the galleries bought it and who gives a fuck at the end of the day art into shit – shit into art it's all relative man you have to push the boundaries" Scoot continued extending his arms forward as he spoke.

"You'll have to go in disguise as a priest a catholic priest," Said T resolutely.

"You'll be taking in more than dope rammed up your backside; you'll have to take cigarettes, phone cards and some money. He explained.

"I haven't agreed to all of this yet," Warned Tim.

"No, but you will you're an art fuck – you love all this crap and it will be something to tell all your stiff suit friends at your local wine bar," encouraged Scoot.

"What's the worst that can happen to me you know if I um get caught?"

"Ritchie!" hollered T

"Tell im what will happen."

"Well there is a down side of course if you do get caught you're looking at a charge of trafficking."

"What will they do with me – will they keep me there locked up?" Asked Tim anxiously.

"In a nut shell this is how it works," replied Ritchie with his most reassuring legal voice:

"You go to the prison and give your visitor's card over they seat you in the right place if they have reason to suspect you have any contraband they'll search you pat you down nothing major unless they ask you to undergo an intimate body search. Then if they find the gear, all they will do is confiscate it and take you back to the police station where they charge you and at that point, you should call me."

Tim's face had developed a ghastly yellow sheen he was sick with worry.

"Don't stress it's unlikely they'll be interested in a white man of the cloth they're hardly going to suspect you're carrying besides you've got the trainers as a diversion tactic."

"I don't know bringing in cash, ciggies, phone cards, and trainers are one thing but the dope..."

"Come on Tim *Non est ad astra mollis e terris via*" Bernie's Latin phrases annoyed Tim. He reflected:

"Bonus quod bene fit haud perit."

"Yes and we are all good here Tim, come on you're an Etonian I'm sure you had some fagging and hazing to deal with this is easy for you." Bernie snipped.

One week later:

The physical impracticalities of inserting a cellophane block of cannabis into Tim's rectum were proving cumbersome. Stripped to his waist with only a small hand towel covering his modesty Tim stood upright in the bath appealing for help:

T looked at Bernie who looked at Scoot who looked at Bessie while Sabatini sat in a haze not understanding a word.

"Just push it up there none of us can put it in there for you Tim you know you just have to do it pretend it's a TV role you're auditioning for and just push," coaxed Bernie with unstoppable laughter.

"Very fucking funny you half devil you spore of evil."

"Yeah okay Tim the devil references aren't cool very witty half devil indeed," remarked Bernie drily.

"Have you covered it in coffee granules and is it securely packed in cling film," yelled Scoot.

"Yes – everything's done it's just inserting it that's tricky everything else is covered."

"Go nice and easy, slow take it slow you'll be okay Tim," urged T.

Finally, an hour later Tim came out of the bathroom in a Roman Collar and black shoes crab stepping gingerly to the waiting rabble in front of him.

"Tim you good?" Asked T with honest concern. He knew that Dickson had only written to him because he was under extreme strain. He may have had his life threatened and was feeling the heat from inside – they were definitely leaning on him, he was under their control and it was highly likely that the Prison guards, admin staff, patrol, and security were all on the take. Whoever was tightening the screws on Dickson T knew he couldn't let him down and had no option but to help.

"You have to walk normal man you can't be seen walking as if you got a jelly roll up your Butti fool."

"This is torture," winced Tim

“You only have to keep it up for a couple of hours more just fucking relax now let’s go” Grumbled Bernie.

At around 4.30 in the afternoon, Tim emerged from the impervious doors of Pentonville and, just like rock “royalty” and writing nobility before him had conquered his artistic dream. T gave him £5,000 for his trouble and an expensive Norwegian Escort for the evening.

Chapter 29

Poncho's poker face revealed nothing but blazing arrogance and a money streak. He was turning tables at the Crockford Casino situated in the timeless elegance of Curzon Street. Blinged up and suited he had razzle dazzle charm and cash to burn. With him *Big Phil from Notting Hill* an old "face" from the sixties a pin up gangster with a "mars bar" weal scraping his left cheek and of course two "wag" slags in tow trussed up like French Poodles with "Bratz" babe stares and Gucci Handbags.

"Hello Mr. Khan, so nice to see you sir." Poncho was greeted with that Dom Perignon hospitality, the kind reserved for the privileged few who are always "comped," take Conde' Nast holidays, binge diet on Beluga caviar and don't pay their taxes.

"Very well thank you," Replied Poncho with pleasing pomposity.

"And how many are you in your party Sir?"

"We are four," he continued with exaggerated grandeur.

"And will there be anyone else joining you tonight Sir?"

"Possibly," answered Poncho with a hint of mystery.

The doorman was spiffed up in Edwardian splendour with a top hat and tails.

"These days we have to ask for proof of identification from your guests Sir," He said discreetly.

"No problem" he responded with reciprocal courtesy.

Ahead of them, a situation was developing between the security personnel and a Pakistani blue blood she was arguing with them about her attire she was primped up in French lace and blue denim:

"Madam it is a strict policy of Crockford Casino that nobody be allowed in wearing jeans."

"I'm not wearing jeans I'm wearing my choori dhar (leggings) which is my National Dress with this "Dupata" (long scarf). This is Middle Eastern dress please don't insult me by comparing me to a 'cow girl,'" she implored with a wounded sulk.

The security staff conferred between them as Poncho looked on:

"Mmmmm we don't really want a scene we should let her in after all her family owns the equivalent of a small country," A suited official murmured softly.

"Okay Madam that's fine please go through."

Poncho was impressed with her smart reply and fiery riposte. He waited for her to sit down. She took her place next to Mrs. Calibresi who was there to ask her family for funding to stabilize her debts. She had been a close family ally and their professional advisor for many years and now it was her turn to seek help. Mrs. Calibresi always triumphed it was a given trait. On the side of their table was a tray of sandwiches, finger food, coffee, and signature chocolates in a pink velvet box with gold lettering and tassels. Mrs.Calibresi was regally decked out in black silk and vintage jewellery. Poncho eyed her curiously for a few minutes and insisted she become his talisman for the evening.

"Hello dear lady, I insist you be my lucky charm for the night, please bless these chips and say something lucky if I win I'll give you 10%."

Mrs. Calibresi was well acquainted with oddballs and familiar strangers she took the chips in the palm of her hand, pressed them together and gave them back to him.

"Now please go Sir – whoever you are, I can't place you but I've seen you somewhere before always remember evil deeds yield no happiness for anyone," she said these last words with a telling look.

"What do you know?" Asked Poncho bluntly .

"I don't know *you* personally Sir, I just say what comes naturally, and sometimes it comes to pass. Stay lucky."

Poncho had reserved a table for dinner in the opulent dining room and leaving the two women there, he trounced off with Phil to wreak havoc on the gaming tables. The subtle hauteur of Crockford's was at odds with the showy vulgarity of the Vegas strip, where Poncho and the rest of the gambling elite could indulge themselves at will. Five times, he bet and five times, he asked for Mrs. Calibresi's blessing then crunch time at the Roulette table he put it all on "red" as Mrs. Calibresi instructed:

"Bets Please," The croupier announced with routine indifference.

Poncho placed his chips on red 3 (one hundred and twenty thousand pounds) in a double or nothing bet. He drank his whisky neat the tension in the room building like a hanging at the gallows: round and round the wheel spun then a pin drop silence: the ball landed on red 3. Poncho had doubled his "net worth" he was oozing money.

They had struck two other casinos that night and at each one had consecutive wins of over two hundred thousand pounds. The casinos were haemorrhaging losses as Poncho had a string of other players stationed in the smaller gaming clubs all on a supremely lucky winning spin. He cashed in his chips and gave Mrs. Calibresi her dues. He tipped the wait staff, the front, the croupier the back room girls and the valet and door staff. Then Big Phil and the rest of his group made their way to *Annabel's* for some bourgeois chic and "dirty dancing."

Chapter 30

Bernie, T and Tim were in the Square House listening to Barrington Levy and sweet Marley on repeat trying to scribe a vibe to write a track for their record label and publishing outfit.

"Gimme a brew man chah."

"What do you want- Red Stripe or Stellar?"

"Rude bwoy I is Jamaican I want Red Stripe."

"Don't you have any Rioja?" Whined Tim.

The others just ignored him singing:

"Mr. Leroy let it roll rap and ting."

"Didn't you hear me Bernie I asked for some Rioja?"

"Do your Russian Cossack Dance and shut the fuck up!"

"Not until you get me my wine."

"Send Sabbatini to Mr. Rashid's down the road for Tim's poncey drink so fucking ridiculous we're trying to create here."

"I just want a glass of red to take the edge off- can we listen to *Desperado*."

"No we fucking can't this isn't some LA Country rock jam reminiscing on the psychotropic pot pansies of Haight Asbury. This is the soot and smut of London mate."

"That fucking *Desperado* song should come with a warning attached to it forbidding any middle- aged alchies or manic depressives to listen to it yes we get it, outlaws make fuck up decisions and die alone"

Tony avoided them both and cued up House of Pain's *Jump Around*. He got up and began his lyrical assault:

"Pack it up pack it in let me begin..."

Tim folded his arms, on the kick of the beat, knelt down, and started his Russian Folk dance. It was 2am and the office lights of Saffron Hill were flickering on and off like flashing glow sticks.

"We could get Zhy to cut the track."

"Yeah if we write the words and put it out on our label we net the publishing so let's think up some words she's got a few humping tunes we could use and then add her vocal."

"Tim, you're an educated man come up with something." Urged T.

"What do you want the song to be about?"

"Anything, nothing doesn't matter just needs to bite, if there's a rap beat it will be much easier to do the track it's a simple one two rhythm."

"What about this: I'm hot and I'm cool I break all the rules I'm white and I'm high my body can fly."

"Stop stop nuff of that crap man we're not gonna 'ave a hit with your stupid sixth form college boy lyrics I'm hot and I'm cool I break all the rules what's the name of your fucking universe Tim that's shit it's just shit."

"Well it doesn't really matter if the hook and chorus work, and you get a cool lop down." Countered Bernie, with a knowing air.

"The what down?"

"The lop down you know it goes intro' verse – chorus lop-lop verse chorus and the lop down can be repeated in any one of those formulas so you've got: dum dum dum cha-cha-boom chachaboom then something a little different then back to verse chorus."

"You're such a fool sometimes Bernie."

"Yeah why?"

"That lop down shit is the middle eight fool everyone knows that."

"I call it the lop down."

"Yeah fool."

"Now both of you come up with some radical lyrics no one wants to hear that crap they want to listen to boozed – up lyrics rammed with bling and pussy control even from a chick."

"They'll listen to any shit if the thump and bump flows get mi?"

"Yeah a musical journey."

"Well Zhy's tunes are wicked."

"Yeah we should try cueing the track and then adding some effects and then the lyrics."

T started adding multi effects to Zhy's instrumental, a sound technician popped his head through the door.

"Hey T, do you guys need me for anything?"

"No man just mixing tings up doing a little shake and bake for Zhy."

"Cool yeah well I'll be in the back if you want me."

The volume levels on the monitor were being moved around by Tim, who was now using a mike stand as a prop for a substitute female.

"Would you care to trip the light fantastic with me my dear?" He charmed.

"She's not responding," he sighed. Bernie flinched.

"Will you stop that it's shady weird."

"I find this whole experience a trifle shady" Retorted Tim.

"Look Tim it's not fucking rocket science it's join the dots simple all you have to do is come up with some song words for a record that's got no enduring value except it's catchy hook when it's forced onto a bunch of club nuts cranked out of their brains."

"Did you sort that situation out with DJ snizzy B?" Asked T

"Yeah."

"What did you do?"

"Took 'im off the scene he's at Don March's country house."

"You bein' serious?"

"Yup that's where he's at safe and sound until the money's all paid up."

"And Don March?"

"Don March loves having him round he's more than okay about it real headline DJ."

"I got nuff effects now we can call Zhy in if Tim's come up with some lyrics she can record the vocal and we can start bizzo."

"Tim you come up with anything half decent?"

"I've done a sort of social comment number."

"How's it go?"

"Like this..."

"Ain't no justice in this world if you're a black boy or a poor girl. Ain't no dream to keep alive when you're mum's a crack whore. Blowing to get high there are seven million stories all the same. Only one gets money and all the fame so now you need to

make a change make a change and set yourself free, make a change for you for me."

"Not bad man."

"Do you not think it's bit race on race and rich man poor girl?"

"Nah the colour chart exists it's real, and so does inequality between those who gotta lot and those who have nothing, it's about now what's going on now as Marvin would say."

"Zhy will kill the track man kill it, liccle bit of controversy makes the world a better place."

"I like the pathos there was a definite tenderness to it a sort of Rolling Stones edge."

"Yeah you're tripping Tim it was about as tender as a sledgehammer on a block of ice."

"Bernie how many people want to use the studio tomorrow?"

"There's at least eight acts booked man."

"Good keep those package deals flying in and why not price up the recording time from one hundred pounds an hour to one hundred and twenty five pounds."

"Yeah why not."

"And have you got all the stock equipment checked?"

"Yeah dats, cdrs, tape ampex all stocked, all ready to sell this bizzo pays for itself."

"There's zero botheration with it."

"Safe well let's book Zhy in tomorrow for some recording time so she can get the vocal down."

"We should go see Richie about making him a Director for the publishing company."

"Yeah 'I'll get on it straight up."

They were spliffed out, everything was Jimi Hendrix cool and as the nine to fivers plodded into town, the sepia- toned tint of city smog heralded the start of a new day.

Chapter 31

"What's the fuzz doing outside?" Richie asked as he entered the Firm.

"Your office has been ransacked – papers are all over the place, files missing and some of Mr Wiesel's personal items have disappeared as well as a little petty cash." Responded Eva with a know- it- all pretence.

She really is a gossip troll Reflected Richard.

"So – basically we've been robbed." He concluded sharply.

"Yes Mr Wiesel wants to see you immediately."

Mr fuckwit Wiesel pronounced Weeeezel was a plumping Boss Hogg look alike from the 80's comedy The *Dukes of Hazard*. His suits, always cling film tight stretched the length and breadth of his short body. His trousers, skimming his ankles revealing a vast expanse of pink flesh and old-fashioned sock garters.

"Come in" He spittled his voice: a fluster buster of Welsh Hills and North London street twack.

"Oh yes Richie come here, come on boy."

He waggled him over; his hands, like two bunches of over ripe bananas thick and wide set. The room was typical of most lawyers, stacks of files, a large solid wooden bookcase with a pretty cherry glaze finish, that stored dozens of legal journals books and case precedents, and of course the ubiquitous green Banker's lamp, the replica version, which every law firm from London to Las Vegas seemed intent on keeping like some badge of honour. Richie hated it and on principle, refused to have one in his room. In the centre of the office hung an imposing and solemn ecclesiastical tapestry, woven in 1890: The *Adoration of the Magi* was a Morris and Co depiction of: The Birth of Christ. Richard found its Victorian colour hue, most comforting and saw a promise of future goodness in all.

Wiesel arched his left eyebrow at Richie and flapped him closer.

"You see the fuzz are here boy, keep that window open go on check its open I might have to use it – be quick off the block understand?"

He wasn't joking John Wiesel had a pit bull Lebanese mistress after him and a money grabbing- bitch of a wife who was constantly in need. This caused him to leave the offices under clandestine cover of the window. It wasn't as extreme as it sounded as his room was situated on the ground floor and made for a simple get away. His crease –grease shirt was stained with the salty remains of his favourite English dish Toad in the Hole that he had gobbled away in secret in the privacy of his room. He was sweating like Red Rum on Derby Day. His nostrils flaring in and out as he troughed:

"Give me that elastic makes me think right."

"Yes Sir."

Richie went to his desk with the rubber band.

"Now watch this boy – brilliant for focusing the mind."

Richie stared in curious fascination as he took hold of the elastic and spread it across the balding part of his crown it was a

Monty *Python* moment. Richard had to jab his fingers in his palms to stop himself from howling with laughter. He had often wondered what the reason was for this peculiar custom but his mind was concentrated on the approaching police presence outside the room.

"Now Richie when they come in I want you to herd them out and keep them in your office and I don't want them here with me for too long see."

"Yes Sir."

"They've already asked me a couple of questions and I told them you'd be able to help them as it was your office not mine."

"Yes Sir."

"Well Richie what's it about then boy why was your office done over?"

"I honestly don't know Sir." Shrugged Richie.

"What you mean you don't know don't talk rubbish Richie did you check the client log any dodgy names that spring to mind – people who can't be trusted ?"

"We have as you know taken on a very dynamic and substantial client Sir a Poncho Khan."

"Oh yes the Indian Financier – the Bollywood chap."

"Yes Sir he has many different kinds of business."

"Don't mind the Indians – lots of money they're very enterprising people good for the economy Richie but some of our more traditional clients might not like seeing them around the building understand?"

"Er yes Sir" Richard blushed, he wasn't comfortable with this pre-war British rhetoric but remained quiet about it.

"Well if that's the only new client make sure they're gone quick I don't want them sticking their beaks in chasing good clients away so make something up that will satisfy them and let them be on their way."

His cheeks were like dimpled balls of hardened lard mixed with scarlet veins they got larger and larger as he puffed his orders out like a Sergeant- Major in the Royal Guards.

Richie still couldn't quite believe he was having to obey a man of nearly seventy sporting an elastic band around his forehead and sock clips around his ankles it was Steve Martin zany!

"Richie, Richie go get me a glass of Jack."

"Do you think you should with the er Police just being outside?"

"Listen boy yours is not to think understand just fetch me my whiskey."

"Yes Sir."

When he returned the Old Bill were seated just outside Mr. Wiesel's room. They glanced at the empty glass and whisky bottle Richard had in his hands then gave him a disapproving headshake.

"Afraid, It's all been a bit of shock officers," he blathered trying to conceal the bottle under his jacket.

"Indeed," replied one with all the sincerity of Wile E Coyote trying to entrap Road Runner.

He closed the door firmly behind him.

"They're waiting outside," he half- whispered.

"Come here come here." Wiesel rattled back lurching forward for the whiskey.

"Ahhhhh that's better," he gulped and tore off the elastic band.

"They're waiting for you so go out and see to them in the Conference room and get rid of them. Don't tell them anything about anyone or anything about anything got that?"

"Yes Sir."

Richie hurriedly smoothed his hair and straightened his tie it was barely eleven o'clock but already he felt like he had been through five rounds with Mike Tyson and was about to take some more.

"Morning again gentleman – my name's Richard Davey, it was actually my office that was the site of the burglary- please come this way."

They followed him through to a large oval shaped room that was a watered down shade of bland; it possessed a death – like conformity with eight swivel chairs all the same. In the middle of the table, an assortment of biros and pens and one solitary pencil. The beige safety of the walls camouflaging the rotting stench of corruption and avarice.

"Please, sit down officers."

"We just need some information; any details we can get may help us with our enquiries."

Only one of the two spoke with a familiar android precision.

"Can you let me know if you've had any new clients Sir?" He went on.

"Well officer you know that I can't really reveal any names of any clients new or old as the rule of confidentiality puts me in a very awkward situation."

"Yes Sir, but I'm sure there are exceptions."

"I don't know I'd have to check it out with Ethics and Guidance."

"You're a lawyer Sir, can't you decide yourself?"

"Not really no, not when it comes to a matter of Professional Ethics I need to seek Expert Guidance from my own professional body." Recounted Richie, with textbook smugness.

"I see Sir we're only trying to find out who may have been behind this robbery."

"Yes I understand and when I have a clearer understanding of what I'm permitted and not permitted to divulge you will be advised. Now have you um checked the scene for fingerprints."

"I'm afraid there's too many, it would be extremely difficult to isolate the perpetrator's prints for definite and identify those prints which were innocent and those that were not the office is public and open to all."

"Yes I see your point officer."

"That's why it would be helpful if you could identify anyone yourself Sir."

"I'm sorry Officer I wouldn't want to compromise client confidentiality."

"No Sir, could you perhaps think of any clients former or current who may have a grudge against you at all Sir, or who may have a requirement for the papers that were stolen from your office Sir?"

"I'm sorry I can't really assist with that officer and in any event it's not just my client files in this room there are other associates files in here too."

"Yes Sir, have you recently, or in the past refused to hand over any client files or papers or any documents of a sensitive nature?"

"Once again Officer – the doctrine of client privilege would apply and we have over two thousand clients the majority of whom are corporate so it's a big headache to go through everyones' files and see where we are exactly, as we 've yet to establish whose papers have been stolen."

"I see Sir yes do you have any internal security in the building, cctv monitors, any other type of internal surveillance?"

"No officer, we used to have a camera outside which was regrettably vandalised so the—"

"Well," interrupted the Police officer.

"We can tell you all about outside; the old camera was destroyed and covered up."

"I don't know anything about that officer."

"Is this the only way in and out of the office Mr. Davey through the main entrance and then the voice intercom?"

"Yes."

"Who has the keys to the inside rooms?"

"Well the partners all have keys, let me think the Landlord has a spare set of keys, and his agents as they're doing structural repairs – actually I have a card you can call the Landlord on that number." Pointed Richard helpfully.

"Thank you Sir, who else might have keys to the offices inside?"

"Well the concierge and the cleaner both have sets of keys to my office but I can't really imagine they would be implicated in this."

"Well as you know Sir we can't rule anyone out of our enquiries, now we would be obliged if you could perhaps call your Ethics and Guidance Team at the Law Society and see if you can answer some of those earlier questions Sir."

"Yes no problem Officer, I'll have my clerk do it immediately excuse me a moment."

Richard walked out of the room and left them there he made a brisk call to the Law Society and dashed back.

"If you were dealing with any important cases you could have the equivalent of a Watergate affair." One of the officers remarked.

"Well some of our clients do have a strong public profile and there are sensitive issues."

"Yes Sir, we understand did you manage to find out if you were at liberty to answer some of our more immediate questions Sir?"

"Yes officer as far as client privilege is concerned it's sacrosanct and its' importance can't be overstressed I could end up in deep trouble if I were to divulge anything about a client and be liable to prosecution myself."

"I understand Sir when you were out Sir, our supervisor advised us you could seek a client waiver and then we have a list of clients and can work on it that way."

"I'll definitely look into it officer" Richard replied through clenched teeth now annoyed by their relentless quest to secure the contact details of the Firms' clients.

"Most obliged Sir those who give you a waiver – you can release their files and information."

"Correct."

Just then the conference room telephone rang, it was an internal call from Mr. Wiesel.

"Are they still with you?"

"Um yes."

"Why can't you shake them off get rid of them now hear me?"

"It's not so easy" Gritted Richie adopting the skill of a ventriloquist smiling at the officers and speaking under his breath into the phone.

"Well start walking out with them wrap it up understand, close the meeting tell them most of the cash float is safe and don't tell them anything else, say nothing of consequence was taken from me now get rid of them boy!"

"Sorry about that officers, the Senior Partner was just wondering if you'd like to join him for lunch at The Bleeding Hart?"

"No we're on duty."

"Right well I'm due in court in a few minutes so if there's nothing more then here's my card the direct line and the mobile is on there failing which you can always leave a message for me with Eva my secretary."

"Okay right um we may ask you to come down to the office if any of those client waivers materialize."

"Yes very good officers I'll wait to hear from you good day."

"Goodbye for now Mr. Davey."

When they had finally left, Mr Wiesel badgered his way into the conference room.

"Don't like the fuzz here Richie they bring your reputation down."

As if you have a reputation thought Richard sourly.

"Well have they gone for good?"

"I'm not sure Sir they wanted me to get waiver forms for client release."

"Humph we'll see about that must get on now Richie too much time wasted, if my wife calls I'm at a meeting if my mistress calls I'm with the wife!"

"Yes Sir and er where will you *actually* be you know, in case of an emergency or—"

"Improvise dear boy I'll be betting on the horses at my club."

"Yes Sir"

"And Richie..."

"Yes Sir,

"Keep 'em peeled."

Chapter 32

Bernie and T were chilling in the kitchen. T was puffing on a Cohiba cigar and Bernie was engaging in some online chat about social unrest in deprived areas of London. They were waiting for Tim to check in he had volunteered to go to Liverpool with some of the gang on a lorry heist. They had teamed up with one of the country's most powerful crime families to break them in and take their share of this prized black-market booty. Back in the day, old school gangsters would steal from cash van vehicles but now technology had forced them to rethink their game and the new sting of choice was swiping luxury merchandise from freight trucks. It was low –risk with guaranteed return. If this one went down well T was thinking of making it a regular gig. T

The Mersey Side mob had expanded their network all over the country and for them a reliable firm down South would increase productivity and enhance their distribution chain. Bernie had done extensive research on the Liverpool Posse he knew that they had a team of insiders on their payroll and that they knew exactly which Lorries to target as well as all of the travel routes, rest stops, and lay bys to do the job properly. Today's little expedition hoped to net them at least twenty-five percent of goods with a retail value of £1000, 000 pounds or more. They were, in effect stolen to order, and already deals were in place to offload the goods, which included coveted gaming devices and the latest XBOX.

T had agreed that Tim should be used as the front decoy for the heist. He was to pose as a Government Vehicle Inspector from VOSA (Vehicle and Operator Services Agency). Tim was smartly dressed wearing a blue cap and tweed jacket over checked flannel trousers and hush puppies. On top of his jacket he wore, an official looking fluorescent yellow VOSA regulation vest this gave him authority and an air of bureaucracy.

He was with Dipsy La La and two others: Lance and Wayne from the Mersey side Mob.

Once the truck was in sight, they began tailgating it and flashing their lights motioning the truck to stop. Dipsy was at the wheel, he indicated green while Tim tried to flag the lorry driver down.

They all wore VOSA vests and their faces were slightly obscured by their hats.

Tim wound down his window and politely asked:

"Pull over Sir; I'm from VOSA I 'm doing a spot check on random trucks today."

They parked diagonally in front of the lorry blocking its path then Tim and Lala got out.

"Hello Sir, I'm from VOSA," he flashed a bogus name badge at the driver who looked on in a bewildered fog.

"I need to do a vehicle registration check on your lorry sir and examine your cargo sir."

The lorry driver was confused worried he may have broken some rule or upset the authorities. He was a French national and his English limited:

"I 'ave my license here monsieur."

"Mais Oui," replied Tim with loathsome affectation. He spoke a curious mix of "frangalis"; schoolboy french that was well past it's sell by date. The Mersey Side Gang didn't appreciate this cosy tete a tete they didn't want Tim getting too friendly with this man. They were there to do a job not play a game of dominoes for Christ sake!

"Move on Tim!" Lance shouted gruffly.

"Er yes okay," answered Tim briskly reluctant to upset anyone especially the Mersey Side duo.

"Can you please look at these papers they are in several languages?" He asked with tidy brevity as if he were a civil servant.

As the lorry driver bent over to study the paperwork in front of him Dipsy, La La, and the others moved to the passenger side of the truck and jumped in. Tim slammed the driver door shut and took up the rear while the Mersey Side mob flashed a Glok at the terrified lorry driver.

"Remain calm and drive."

Wayne snarled with a nasal slur, sounding like Ringo Star from the Beatles.

"Where- what's going on please don't hurt me," the driver sobbed white with fear. He was a large beer bellied man with greasy hair and heavily tattooed arms.

"Shut up and drive," Snarled Lance.

"Where where you want me to go please?" He whimpered.

"Just follow your usual route, just stick to the same way then you'll be alright," responded Wayne. Tim and the Liverpool mob were equipped with satellite navigation systems, haulage trucks and their own team of operators who drove behind the truck ready for the next phase.

Dipsy seized the driver's phone and wallet and slung them to the back of the wagon. The driver's hands were clamming up, beads of sweat forming on his brow and upper lip. He had seen better days.

"Right there should be a lay by just about ten minutes away from the truck stop," announced Lance.

"When I tell you, listen to me when I tell you pull up to the kerb," commanded Wayne with impatience.

"Yes – yes okay."

"One wrong move – any fancy footwork and you're over mate do you understand?" menaced Wayne with slimy intent.

"Oui yes Oui," answered the driver feebly his hands quivering.

Behind them keeping a safe distance, was Tim in the Range Rover and another truck behind him. When they got to the lay by they got out of the truck and unloaded the freight into the lorry waiting for them. The Mersey side mob drove it away while Dipsy and La la remained with the driver. They forced him to drive another fifty miles to a secure location where the Mersey Side gang and Tim were on watch.

"Now easy step out carefully and release the wagon," instructed Lala.

"I don't know – I don't know what to do," bawled the driver.

"Do as I fucking say," barked La La.

Fumbling with the lock, the driver finally managed to undo it. The others started their getaway as Dipsy warned:

“Don’t look this way, don’t call anyone or raise the alarm for twenty minutes. We’ll be close by, we can see you, understand there’s fifty quid twenty minutes,” he repeated signalling the number with his hands.

Tim called T:

“It’s done I’ll be back in a few hours with our cut."

Chapter 33

Christian was coked up to the eyeballs. He had a music audition that day that was being aired on some reality television show. Bernie pulled him close and stuck a Frenchie bang on his lips, but it made Christian gag slightly and he couldn't hide it.

"Sorry, I'm just really nervous. Pass me those mints please, hun," cooed Christian.

"I'd better get off now, facial and manicure, I want to look my best for later." Bernie was glad he had already paid a visit to Dr. Johnson, supposedly a genuine witch doctor originally from Haiti now living in leafy Finsbury Park in North London. As a supremely superstitious man with an appetite for black magic, the occult, and dark forces; Bernie had acquired loads of information about this kind of stuff. The man he met, Renee Baptiste Johnson, had several clients and Bernie found him listed under "*witch doctor*" in the local phone book.

Bernie had confided to Dr. Johnson that he wanted to teach his lover a lesson and that he knew his lover was cheating on him and he wanted him to stop but still loved him so didn't want him hurt. He had described all of Christian's personal traits, including his weight, height, and body fat index.

He had given him a recent photograph and brought an item of his clothing so that Dr. Johnson could "ju ju" it so that Christian would never stray again. He had given Bernie an incantation to read and told him to place three raw chicken livers in a pair of Christian's shoes at exactly 2:00 p.m., precisely when Christian's audition would start. Then Dr. Johnson promised that Christian would succumb to the power of the magic and be taught a lesson he would never forget.

Later on, Bernie cautiously recited the incantation and exactly at 2:00 p.m. laid out some of Christian's shoes and squashed the sinewy pieces of meat inside them, first with his hands, then with his feet, squeezing the squelchy gloop into a well-worn, handcrafted Churchill's brogue. Afterwards, he started labelling different pieces of Christian's body—eyes, legs, arms, etc.—with yellow post-it notes around both shoes. It was like a scene out of some Mike Meyers movie. Then he started piercing Christian's Gap Tee shirt with short, thick pins; deeper and deeper he gouged until the shirt was ripped to shreds. He sat back, satisfied with his efforts, certain that this bizarre ritual would work.

Chapter 34

Kamilla was retching again. She had vomited at least five times and it was only mid morning. It made her eggshell shaky but at least she would lose five pounds. She was casually dressed in "Sweaty Betty" track pants and an Abercrombie knitted tank. Her long, dark hair, neatly tied in a "Juicy" hair band and her face free of makeup. She had the news on and was browsing through the day's papers. Some "morality merchant" featured on the BBC was waxing lyrical on how the government was planning a campaign to teach young people about the hazards of too much sex, drugs, and alcohol. Blah, blah, blah, but how was some faceless government think tank ever going to curb the youthful curiosity of the "Now Generation?"

Most of Kamilla's friends had been clubbing, fucking, and doing blow since the age of sixteen. It was a known fact that "society" whores were always up to some bad gal tricks somewhere. Rich kids were like any other kids except they had a safety cushion of cash that allowed them not to give a fuck, as well as a Harley Street doctor on speed dial. She let out a dark, throaty giggle as she thought back to Shepherd's Market where she and one of her best friends, Georgie, were playing tongue twister together. "French kissing" one another slowly as if they were on show in an Amsterdam brothel and then smiling for the cameras as they licked coke off each other, then snogging some more while press photographers continued to snap away. She checked the diary entries of her Smythson; it was candy pink leather with grosgrain-gilded pages.

There was a charity ball in Grosvenor Square; of course, she'd been invited. It seems her trashy sex kinks had pushed her up the popularity scale, but, on the down side, some tight "cunt" had also sent the pictures to Scotland Yard Crime Squad, who were "investigating" the allegations of illicit drug abuse and lewd behaviour at the private party.

She changed into a simple black wrap dress by Diane Von Furstenberg and some exceptionally high Manolo Blahnik's. She opted for a Cartier day watch and an Erikson Beamon pendant flecked with crimson sapphires and rubies. She was sexy cool. There were at least ten daily newspapers strewn on the glass table in front of her. It was all over the "red tops" and even the broadsheets, pictures of Kamilla and Georgie, two rich bitches being bad, really bad, A1 bad. She called her father's lawyer, Richard. He'd sort it out and know what to do.

"Hey, Ritch, sweetie it's Kami."

"Kami?"

"Yes, Kamilla Verity Moore Taylor," she said flatly with an air of affected arrogance.

"Oh, she of the 'drug fuelled orgy' at Shepherd's Market?"

Richard enquired flippantly.

"Don't fuck around, Richard. Some of these papers are alleging that the police are investigating reports of illicit drug use and lewd conduct or some shit."

Richard muffled a laugh. "Look, I'll find out what the score is, okay?"

"Yeah, I'd appreciate that because I've got a Venetian themed charity ball to attend in Grosvenor Square soon and I don't want PC Plod coming around harassing me. Then I've got to do a model shoot later for a new glossy with Scarlett Wright, as in Brazilianaire Scarlett Wright." After her conversation with Richard, she called one of her art school fashionista friends, Estevez, and told him to rustle up a very elegant come- do- me in the bedroom not on the kitchen floor type creation for a society charity dinner. She assured him his outfit would be clocked by millions of people worldwide and, more significantly, a loyal coterie of heavy weights in the know, at all the key fashion houses in Europe, the US, and the Far East. Estevez was understandably excited and set about drawing, sketching, and pattern cutting.

Despite his obvious talent for dressmaking, he was often annoyingly clichéd in his self-parody of himself and had a deliberate and obvious way of talking that most straight people associated with gay men. He would frequently insert the word "dahling" in nearly every sentence that came out of his mouth. It was more than a stereotype; it was "loser" dumb. Kamilla was unsure about having him with her at the ball for the whole time. He had spiky, in-your-face hair reminiscent of David Bowie in his *Ashes to Ashes* phase, far too many tattoos, and was always clunking around in silver "antique jewellery."

He also had a firm, fit navel with a belly ring that Kamilla was fond of blowing kisses on. She agreed to meet him later that evening for a fitting to explain why he should only stay for twenty minutes or so. She hoped he would bring his new boyfriend, Christian.

"Hi Kamilla—Richard here. The boys in blue aren't taking

any action yet, but they're keeping their line of enquiry open. Everything's cool for now."

Trouble was, thought Richard *people like them (officialdom and authority types) loved making examples of people like Kamilla Verity Moore Taylor: over-rich, overfed, over-confident. They loved making them squirm as if they had something over them.*

"Thanks, Ritch, want to go to that charity ball? It's for a good cause. I mentioned it before."

"Thanks, but I'm busy," sighed Richard.

Miserable wretch, thought Kamilla *He was making loads of money off her and her family, yet he was so fucking rude. She faked sweetness into the phone.*

Chapter 35

As good as his word, Luke had invited Tony up to his ancestral home in Deer Hurst Gloucester. The family home was an impressive, stately manor that had been fully renovated and lay in the glorious English countryside overlooking the Cotswold's and not far from Cirencester. Tony would get there by train, taking an intercity link to Cheltenham and then a short half hour taxi ride to Gloucester.

Deer Hurst was once renowned for housing every kind of exotic flower and plant known to man in their lush horticultural conservatory and gardens, but a creature of an altogether different type had now decamped to its illustrious confines.

Tony sat chewing a piece of dry breaded chicken, a favourite staple of most Jamaicans. This particular piece of chicken had already travelled a cool thirty-six miles and would be savoured to the very last bite. Fast food outlets were rare in the sleepy village of Deer Hurst and Tony relished these taboo munchies, guarding them like a Pinscher dog does a rare bone. He was talking in between mouthfuls to a small television screen playing the latest music videos.

Tony liked satellite television stations and did not realize that, because Deer Hurst was originally built in the 1800s on a historic plot that formerly housed a monastery and still stood on a remote, isolated land site, it had a restrictive channel selection and weak satellite connections. He picked up his mobile phone whilst chomping contentedly on the soft white meat.

"Yo, bro," he chuckled loudly. "Deer Hurst's only got the five channels, d'ya get mi?" He then made a distinct chah sound by pursing his lips together in the shape of a long vowel sound. It was a typical form of Jamaican patois. The chah phrase had now filtered down into the mainstream of inner city London youth but had never been heard in the hallowed walls of Deer Hurst.

He continued talking. "Okay, bro, see you in thirty minutes." Tony also had to physically get up and change the television channels, another chore he soon tired of and was not accustomed to.

He reluctantly stood up, his round, burly frame slowly rising. Cleaning his hands with a small, sanitized lemon-scented napkin, he proceeded to change channels. To his right were a set of two original sixteenth-century Italian walnut wood tables, now faded, worn, and etched with markings.

A magnificent hand crafted Knole sofa exquisitely upholstered in fuchsine red lay in the centre of the room while to his left there was a large freestanding solid mahogany, Chippendale clock. A small fifteen-inch television set was gingerly balanced on a multifunctional IKEA- style shelf unit that now stored other concessions to modern life like three pin plugs, adaptors, cable leads, and a portable fax machine and telephone unit. The walls in the room were a subtle mix of ivory and pearl they gave the impression of deep-seated affluence, generational wealth that can't be bought on the back of a gangster rap record or a footballer's "signing on fee."

Tony had immediately noticed the calming texture of the walls; despite his obvious "rough and ready" hue, he had a natural artistic eye, which encouraged him to explore beyond the realms of his own world. He hovered anxiously by the television set, wondering if his channel tuning would result in a better program choice. He had spied several boxed sets of DVD films and noticed that the television had a built-in DVD player. He wanted to watch one of his favourite Brit flicks, *Lock Stock, and Two Smoking Barrels*.

It was a Guy Ritchie creation and Tony was sure he had met most if not all the supporting cast who featured in the movie. He couldn't be sure, though. He laughed out loud and sat back down, ready to immerse himself in the action unfolding on the screen. Once snugly ensconced on the intensely comfortable camel back chair, he raised the volume of the television set and took out a packet of Wrigley's Extra, nonchalantly chewing. He resembled an overgrown child: chocolate button eyes and Buddha blubber.

He had a round, cute face dimpled with cherubic naughtiness. Some said Tony was a "loveable rogue." As he concentrated on the images before him, Tony grew drowsy. All of the fried potatoes he'd polished off with his chicken were now taking their toll and slowly he began to doze off; his eyelids grew heavier and heavier until he could no longer keep awake. He was only asleep for a few moments, however, when the still country air was punctured by the shrill metallic hum of an outside drill.

He looked up out of a long bay window and saw a tall, dark figure drilling the side of a wall. To the left of the courtyard ahead of him was a wide, open lake across the fields. It shone like mirrored glass in the afternoon sunlight. He turned away and carried on watching the movie. There were often random workers scattered around the Estate, all engaged in normal every day activities. He glanced at the clock in front of him: quarter to four. He wondered how long Bernie would be.

The owner and proprietor of Deer Hurst was a dapper, mercurial fellow, a welcome and eccentric anti-establishment figure with aristocratic lineage and an enviable vitality. His long hair was streaked with grey, and fashionably cut in thick, blunt layers. He looked like a Dutch master from the 1920s. He was a "true blue" and had a cultivated and benevolent air about him. Now he had become an unlikely ally of Tony's in his bid to corner the market in the manufacture of new age herbal pills. He was extremely well- read with a brilliant and engaging mind and counted Oxford dons and Yale professors as his friends and counterparts. He had a well-publicized distaste of The Hapsburg Empire and saw the current Royals safely settled on the English Throne as nothing more than lucky opportunists. Of course, apart from his noted disdain for the current Monarchy, Seymour received a great deal of attention for living with an assortment of South East Asian and Japanese women. He was not married to any of them but treated them all as wives regardless. It was a further eccentricity that grated on the English Establishment. Milo, a companion of Seymour's whom he had met on a recent trip to Tokyo, had entered the room where Tony sat. She was a slight, diminutive-looking woman with gentle features and a soft, cherry blossom smile.

She greeted Tony with a customary bow and then asked him if "everything is all right." He got up and went to hug her but instead she politely stretched out her small, dainty hand, which he gladly shook. Milo looked about the room: a salty, dry aroma hung loosely in the closed space and she instinctively went to the window to allow the freshness of the day to free the musty air.

"Er I'm waiting for Bernie and Seymour," Tony explained.

"It's all right, Mister Tony, it is fine, Seymour is expecting you." She spoke with a kind, lyrical delicacy that reminded Tony of a dove cooing. She was simply dressed in a long blue gown with a pale cream sash and tiny rose -coloured ballerina slippers. He watched her with mild curiosity and then turned his attention back to the screen. She padded around the room adjusting things: moving books, reorganizing flowers, and politely engaging Tony in small talk that was easy and friendly. Tony had no idea why Seymour had taken such a liking to him but was grateful for the opportunity to get involved in a proper business venture. He wanted to "do good."

"Seymour will be coming down shortly, Mr. Tony," bleated Milo. "Can I get you anything?"

"No, no, thank you," responded Tony. In the Louis Vuitton monogrammed duffle bag (the genuine article) Tony had stashed forty veggie caps and a sample gift box for Seymour's attention. He had been talking up his idea for some time and was relying on Bernie to explain the business concept to Seymour. But Seymour, after hearing the nuts and bolts from Luke, had only wanted Tony to "sell" it to him.

"Ah, Tony, so lovely to see you." Wearing a brightly coloured pink shirt and navy virgin wool trousers with tan, suede loafers, he was the epitome of sartorial cool. No brash logos, no labels, just Brit swish. He had a deep, resonant voice that was at odds with his long, unruly hair. He greeted Milo warmly with a gentle kiss on her cheek and spoke to her in a scholarly mix of ancient Ainu and modern Japanese. She bustled out of the room, leaving him alone with Tony.

The media reports of Seymour were patently untrue. By all accounts, Seymour was a shrewd and wily business man. Since his inheritance of the family coffers, he had successfully generated a cool two million in just under six months by embarking on a series of highly lucrative and exciting sponsor tie ups. He had signed up to be the key sponsor for the annual Estate Air races in conjunction with Zip cola, a famous beverage company, and was hosting monthly online casino competitions with a major leisure retailer. In addition, there were the usual daily paid tours for the public, corporate and private hospitality events, as well as location monies from film companies and record studios that featured Deer Hurst in their various projects. His sparky entrepreneurial spirit, combined with his brash "can do" attitude, had netted him some of the most sought after and exclusive media contracts in the business.

It hadn't taken Seymour long to do a rough computation on the massive potential of an alternative 100 percent natural veggie cap business. The possibilities were endless. He had already agreed to the idea after being presented with the plan by Luke. He decided he wanted to take a risk and pledged his commitment for venture capital right there and then. Tony was bowled over, his face beaming like a huge pug. He didn't think it would be that easy and was a little surprised. He immediately called Bernie to give him the good news.

Seymour then went on to explain that a company would have to be set up and shares issued. He would instruct his lawyers to firm up the deal. Naturally, it would be off shore to take advantage of tax breaks and banking benefits. Tony would be the majority shareholder and Luke and Scoot would have equal shares with Seymour. This was all a bit daunting for Tony, who was struggling with the enormity of the project but understood that in order for his plans to succeed the operational aspects of his idea needed to work and would have to be freed from the confines of his West London basement. This confidence in his concept made him feel as if he was finally on the edge of success; it gave him dignity, peace of mind, and a raging hard-on. Ultimately, it was acceptance.

After the initial shock of joining forces with one of London's most beloved drug dealers, Seymour explained that once the "legals" had all been signed off, they could start moving the nuts and bolts of his manufacturing plant to the East Side Barn situated on its own in a large four-thousand-acre gated paddock, until a more suitable venue was found. The barn would work well as a temporary production point for the fledgling business. As soon as the company was formed, the start-up capital of over £400,000 would be transferred to the company bank account and they could begin making "loads a money."

Seymour knew this type of new age, clean green ethos would appeal to the US health market and he was going to pitch the idea to some American hedge funders who would be keen to invest in the scheme; he was sure of it.

Tony and Bernie stayed for dinner. They had home-smoked venison with dauphinoise potatoes and chocolate and chestnut cake with fig and caramel sauce. Then they left for London.

Seymour had left messages on Richard's office phone, private mobile, office mobile, and pager. Richard called him immediately. Seymour wanted him to set up an off shore company bank account and source some prestige London premises for a new start up. He said it was urgent and he expected everything to be done no later than close of play Monday. Richard was irritated by his tone but dutifully scribbled some notes down and remained pale and quiet when he was given details of the shareholder's names. He had already made the connection and was not relishing the thought of an André Breton style, face-to-face in the conference room, with his old school friend-now-drug-dealer turned entrepreneur. It was a "Mickey Mouse" moment and belonged to the land of make believe. *Fucking ridiculous*.

Chapter 36

There were no more easy days for Richard now. He knew he was in deep. He was sinking fast and it made him queasy. He had already smoked around twenty-five Marlboro lights, and it wasn't even 10:00 a.m. His throat was dry as straw and spiked with bile. He was nursing a mouth abscess and had a piercing headache. It made no difference that he was smoking "lite." His tobacco- stained teeth still carried a brown tinge even though he regularly power bleached them every ten months. They were beginning to hurt him, a dull, thudding ache that moved around his mouth and settled at the back of his throat.

He must have made at least a dozen calls with no leads. Nobody seemed to know anything about Uncle Marvin's robbery or his office and if they did they weren't letting on. Finally Richard decided there was nothing for it but to call Tony. Now with a prime business portfolio, and of course direct access to the criminal network. He could feign interest in his start up and tap him for information.

Richard was certain he would know something about the snatch. He hated calling him because Tony had at least seventeen different numbers, which meant leaving at least seventeen messages all the same. As most of T's work was done at night, he was unlikely to be up before noon, another annoying trait of the "career criminal."

Finally, Richard managed to track T down.

"T, hi, man. Congratulations on your start up. I hear you got Seymour to fund it for you?"

"Ritchie, how did you know? We only sorted out the deal the other day."

"I'm the lawyer for the project, man."

"Ah, yeah right.

Means I can wind down that other bizzo, d'ya get mi?"

"Yeah, man, I understand but I need to see you about some other business. Look, I can't talk on the phone Can we meet up at Café Boehme around 8:00 p.m.?"

"Yeah, okay, but I'm looking to get out of that other game, Ritch."

"Yeah, whatever," he answered.

You knew you were in a *Jean Luc Goddard* type quagmire when your dealer was talking retirement, off shore accounts, and Grand Cayman tax havens. Welcome to the decade of free enterprise, equality, and esprit de corps. Richard had an open mind on all this new age natural stuff, though; after all, with big name brands like Zip cola diverting into healthier lines, perhaps this scheme wasn't so improbable after all.

Chapter 37

Bernie was on line trying to set up a lottery scam. He had joined up with a Spanish syndicate who would send out bulk emails to persuade random surf heads to part with their private information on the false pretext that they had won gazillions of pounds and were subject to a one off tax payment upfront to release their winnings.

"How does it work precisely?" Enquired Dipsy.

"Well the email is nearly always the same, in the subject line it reads Spanish Lottery Sweeps then it goes on to tell the lucky recipient how much they have won usually over a million."

"And then?"

"Well here's the tie –up it's really quite cool to lock them in we don't give out hardly any info' about us at all. There's a link within the body of the email that's sent out the punter clicks on that link and they get directed to a dummy site which doesn't even exist."

"So how do they part with their money?"

"Well once they get directed to the site we just download this special key- logging soft ware onto that person's computer which allows us to get all of their private info' that's all required to burn their plastic. As soon as we get the details we hit their plastic. It's quite an easy ride so far I've had fifty two bites and we split the profits with our Spanish Amigos it's all easy pickings there's plenty of gormless kevins out there who are greedy enough to take the bait."

"Hmm I don't really get it."

"Luckily for us you don't need to – the download key is activated as soon as the individual clicks on the link then their info' is immediately accessible to us we can gate their passwords, secret questions and all that stuff before you know it you have all of their personal data ready to use. All I need to do is send the info' to the techie guys in Spain and for everyone we hook in we get fifty percent of sales from the mugs who buy into the con."

"Don't you feel bad it could be your mum or your grandma?"

"Very unlikely as both of them have passed onto pastures new as they say they're seven feet under ground anyway it's just a game no one forces them to buy into it just like any other probability hustle and just as bad as selling non- existent shares to people or making them join and pay for a Ponzi scheme."

"Point taken" Replied La la analytically.

"Bernie!" Shouted Godwin

"Yeah what's wrong man you sound vexed."

"It's Tim he's gone mad man he says he's been stopped outside The Church of somethin' man?"

"What?"

"The church of science something mi can't make it out"

"What?"

"Here you talk to him I can't understand." Godwin shoved the handset to Bernie.

Tim's comical blue stocking voice now loud and large on speakerphone:

"Who's that? Was it you Bernie did you section me?" Tim thundered.

"What?" Yelped Bernie, with equal aggression.

"Did you- try –to- section- me under the Mental Health Act?" He screamed in a staccato beat.

"No what the fuck are you goin' on about?" Asked Bernie clearly miffed.

"I've been stopped from doing the drop near Tottenham Court Road."

"Why?"

"Because apparently there's a Restraining Order against me and I can't do anything within three hundred yards of the Church of Humanology so basically this blow is gonna get wasted by me."

"Don't you fucking dare Tim you come back to the flat right now with the gear and any paperwork you got, do you understand I'm not fucking joking Tim."

"Someone's tried to fucking section me they said I streaked down Oxford Circus and that I have a history of psychotic illnesses and I've been banned from the Charing Cross End to the Marylebone end!"

"This is fucking mental Tim come back to the flat now you can explain when you get here."

"What happen to Tim?" Asked Godwin

"Fuck knows he'll be here soon."

After about twenty minutes a huffing- puffing Tim appeared at the door looking like Larry David after a round with Susie Green. Bernie, Godwin and the others made him sit down.

"Godwin go get him a brew."

Godwin trotted off to get his pint.

"Okay Tim let's hear it then best start from the top."

"Well I was minding my own business trying to do the drop off at that new bar everything was fine until someone from outside of the Church or someone near the church asks me my name."

"Why d'ya give them your real name you've got at least ten aliases." Reasoned Bernie

"Oh thanks Godwin." He took a swig from the can.

"Who asked for your name?"

"I don't know she was very cagey and seemed to know me"

"What did she say?"

"She said might I ask who you are and what you're doing here."

"I said I'm not doing anything my name's Tim I'm here to deliver something."

"But why d'ya have to go that way?" Interrupted Bernie

"That's the normal way anyway so I said my name's Tim and even before I could give her my surname she calls her Security Guards on me and they threaten me with the old bill."

"I'm not getting this Tim what the fuck were you doing outside the Church of Scientology?"

"Not the church of scientology – the church of humanology."

"Whatever, what the fuck were you doing there."

"Nothing I was merely on my way to deliver the coke."

"Always a fucking drama some bullshit goes down it's a fucking joke now you're loitering outside people's premises itching to get nicked, I mean what the fuck Tim."

"I didn't do a thing I swear the next thing I know the scheming blonde is pointing at me and talking to the security guys and then the paramedics and a doctor turn up and they ask me the same question."

"Yeah."

"And I say Tim, and they 're like on such and such a day you were seen outside Kentucky Fried Chicken 71 Tottenham Court Road running naked down the street."

"Right." The others looked on blankly.

"They said If I don't leave the area they would have no option but to restrain me."

"So."

"I fucking left I'm gonna find out who did this to me."

"Oh Jesus Tim it's obvious your ex must 'ave done this stitched you up like a fish in a net." Cried Bernie, shaking with laughter.

"You got threatened with a restraining order I've never heard anything so funny." He spluttered.

The others were rolling around the floor Godwin clutching his sides; he needed La la to steady him.

"Yeah you think this is fucking funny."

"Come on Tim where's your sense of humour and come to think of it where's the nose snow?" Sniggered Bernie.

"Here –!" He threw it on the table.

"Careful Timothy we don't want to send you off on one! Here give me those documents we'll make Richie kiss it buh bye."

"I'd appreciate it."

Chapter 38

Kara was a promotions mix and mingle girl she worked part time at one of T's quasi-legitimate -outfits. Clients booked her to sex- up corporate events and launch parties.

If the punters were game she also provided extras, supplying them with T's gear. Her cut was a respectable twenty percent on every sale she scored plus a discretionary commission for her own use. She was on late shift tonight and turned up looking like an internee of the Priory a well-known rehab clinic.

"Jesus fucking Christ what we got here then is it Marge Simpson's twin sister Patty, or Amy Winehouse, or a mix of the two?" Gawped Bernie.

"Talk about fucking bad hair day this is like scarecrow ugly you can't go out like that!"

"Yeah thanks there's just too much shit going on with me but I need this gig."

"Right so what's with the Halloween get up?"

"You know I just don't wanna be doing this crap over and over."

"Why not? Pay's good."

"I end up moving from face to face and place to place it's not healthy man- I end up nowhere and back where I started from."

"Yeah, well whose fucking fault is that we gave you a chance Kara you can sing but you're a fuck up."

"I know Bernie I agree it is what it is I'm a fuck up I just hate doin' this shit sometimes."

"I can't put you in the studio Kara not again we gave you like three no it was four try outs and remember what happened each time."

"Yeah I know, I know."

"You fucked up, T was left with a bill the size of J-Lo's arse and you were a no show."

"I Know Bernie I just don't wanna be greasing old guys until I'm fucked up and forty."

"I don't need your fucking life story darlin' tonight Kara we're gonna be busy so let's just get through the night."

"Yeah okay where do I need to be?" She groaned.

"Listen Kara if I hear of anything."

"Yeah you'll let me know."

"Yeah now go make pretty – fix up look smart- and do something with that hair there's a Zip cola promo tonight at the Met Bar. Usual suspects: A- Z listers, here take an ounce knowing that lot you might need more if you do just bell me."

"Safe."

"Stay in touch yeah, and fucking lighten up everything is everything and nothing is well...I can't think of the rest but stick a smile on your gob please you don't want to scare the punters d'ya?"

"What the crap!" She half smiled.

"Mazel tov!"

It was around eleven the same evening when Kara got to there.

The Met Bar, part of the Metropolitan Hotel was a bump and grind affair, sleek wooden floor space, cushy armchairs, and haute couture stools. The place was popular with champagne hipsters, media sluts, showbiz types and scene kids. Part bar, part gentleman's club and rave dive it also drew glamour chicks and money pricks who liked to coke it up and get laid. After some killer cocktails and a wrap or two anything could happen.

DJ Alan Beeby was on the turntables the crowd was popping beer and getting high on dirty break-beats and dub step. Amid the crash and peal of the music and the exaggerated grate of the club berries, an *Abercrombie and Fitch* guy waved Kara over. She looked him up and down as if he were on the examining table in a biology lab.

"How much d'ya want?" she lipped.

"Just a couple of Gs." He crisped back; his voice was all Hugh Laurie and Piers Brosnan.

"Meet me outside yeah; meet me near the men's loo in Trader Vics."

"Yah, okay sure." He replied grateful he'd passed the initial test.

Kara was savvy enough to know who were actual customers and who were rival dealers or undercover police. She left the jump and thump of the bar and clocked the guy in Trader Vics.

"One hundred pounds please."

"Here you go darlin'. "

She slipped him the wrap.

"Nice doing bizzo with you" she spiralled.

"Yeah see you."

"Bye."

Kara didn't feel like a dial and go coke pusher but she was a supremely good hustler. She took out a strawberry flavoured chuppa chup and went back to the Met Bar where she continued to mingle. As she worked the room, she noticed a group of circle heads dicking around one of them was a goofy little shithead with a chin- strap beard. He was bitching off at a smartly dressed black man who was waiting for service at the bar.

"What the fuck are you looking at nig?" he cooned with ignorant malice.

"What did you say?" the man asked in a low voice.

"I said what the fuck you looking at nig short for nigger."

His voice, ripped with crack and booze. He reminded Kara of a handbag sized chucky doll. He was ugly as fuck.

"Okay that's enough." She interjected signalling to the black guy that this fool wasn't worth it.

"Enough? I'll tell you when I've had enough and when enough's enough." The creep slurred back.

Kara threw him a look of disgust.

"I'm warning you one more word and..."

"And what biach?" he crowed in a fake Jamaican accent.

Kara called security from her two-way radio.

"There's a big mouthed racist cunt in here who needs a quick lesson in respect and racial harmony."

Within seconds, two muscle heads had lifted the toad out of his seat and escorted him off the premises.

Minutes later Kara caught up with him and grilled him about his neo- fascist views.

"Why did you say those things back there?" She asked.

"Why are you so fucked up with hate?" She continued.

"Listen biach if you come any closer I'll..."

It was over before it had even started. Kara was a yellow belt in Jujitsu, with a pet hate for racists and liars she left him in Hyde Park spitting blood and nasal hairs.

Kara finished her shift at the Met around three and profit-fucked the dawn away with a wealthy Arab businessman; she was slut-bomb cool.

Chapter 39

Poncho was feeling raw and sexed up. He had been artfully screwing a Danish call girl for over one hour now. He forced her down in front of him and slowly wrapped his arms around her tall athletic frame. Now his breath was on her face. She could feel the heavy warmth of his body all over her. She leaned back into him as he fucked her from behind until he found it hard to catch his breath. Release: he stared into her half-closed eyes as she let go.

"Take it easy," Poncho whispered. He'd use this girl again.

After a long, hot shower, Poncho put on his soft cotton robe and open-toed Nike rubber sliders. He had calls to make, people to deal with, and, more importantly, people to deal with. He strode into the large opal-shaped room hung with contemporary artwork and minimalist furniture. It was tastefully decorated and had a clean post- modern edge.

"Get me that weasel Richard dog breath on the phone, and don't take any bull crap from his half wit of a secretary. I want to speak to that ugly Chihuahua now."

Poncho threw this order into the air. It wasn't directed at anybody in particular but already a chorus of: "Yes sir, Mr Khan" and "right on it, Mr Khan," was heard. Meanwhile, at least two random individuals, nervous and for the most part, faceless, scurried around eager to please in the task they'd been given. It was Mack, the part-Mexican, part-Scottish employee, who had brought Richard to the phone. Their conversation: direct and simple:

"Mr Khan is very anxious to speak with you. Please do not annoy him."

"Well, put him on the phone then," replied Richard tartly. He knew he had something to do with both break ins but was too chicken to raise it directly with him.

"No, you will have to wait until he picks up the other phone, I suggest you continue holding," explained the worried underling. Richard abhorred these thugs. They spoke with an impotent power, the power of another person behind them. It was sordid; he wished he could kill this ugly pretence. Why didn't these minion men get real jobs? He was worried now and hadn't been able to meet with Tony yet, despite making arrangements to do so. He was itching his face, and had come up in a weird skin rash: all blisters and zits. It was quite unpalatable and made him look like an extra from *Shaun of the Dead*. Time was running out. He had been putting Poncho off for days now and was acutely aware of what he was capable of doing. Still, he was a lawyer. Perhaps he could outplay this slime bucket yet. Now, he had no choice.

"Richard here."

"I know it's you. Why do you announce yourself as if you were someone of consequence?" demanded Poncho. He was clearly irritated by Richard's phony accent. It smacked of colonial arrogance. That is why he had hired Richard in the first place. He enjoyed the idea of hiring a white "boy" to do his bidding because he liked turning the tables of colonial rule on Richard. It empowered him. It gave him a kick to think that Richard was pent up with fear, dreading what was going to happen next. Poncho knew it all. He had arranged both the theft in Hatton Garden and at Richard's office and knew Richard was stonewalling him.

He wasn't in the least bit panicked, that the bond was still missing, as he also knew that *everyone* had their price and no one was out of reach.

He laughed aloud a big, dry chuckle tinged with sour inflection. "Any news about my matter, Richard? The interest continues to grow as the days go by. I know you appreciate that, being a lawyer."

Richard felt the onslaught of an allergy attack, but in a calm, matter of fact voice replied, "As we speak, Mr Khan, I'm looking into some possible leads that should yield positive results. I will have a more detailed idea of the situation in a week or so."

"Expect me at your office in seven days," came the terse reply.

Richard attempted a stab at normality by talking of schedules and dates to avoid; he heard the faint sound of an audible sneer, then an abrupt silence as the phone clicked off.

His eyes were watering and he could feel them weep and sting; his nose was running and now he had an inflamed forearm and dry mouth on top of the already ghastly skin rash.

"Atishoo.... Atishoo."

He couldn't stop sneezing. *Christ, why couldn't he stop sneezing just for one minute*?

He just needed some time to think for one fucking minute, that's all, think his way out of the mess. This was like some Noel Fielding creation, except the joke was that it was all real all happening right now to him; it was not some other alternate state of conscious or the result of too many ecstasy tabs on a rainy Sunday afternoon. His reality wasn't dressed up in grainy "electric cool aid" acid drops.

Chapter 40

Kara and Christian met back stage at Bagleys Kings Cross for their audition. They had an easy and comfortable conversation before she hit the stage for her two-minute solo.

"So you're up for this band thingy, too, are you? It's by Whizz Management. I hear they're really good?"

"Yeah, a friend of mine does their accounts," explained Christian helpfully.

"What track are you going to do for your solo I mean?"

"Not sure yet, something uncomplicated, perhaps a *Take That* number."

"Unless you go completely a cappella, they should have a backing track," volunteered Kara authoritatively. She had plenty of experience searching for the big fucking dream. Yeah, all those years of star search had made her what she was today: a burnt out, used up serial slut who had flipped her soul over to the carnivores of pop "muzak." All she ever wanted was to be a singer in a band. After the euphoric victory of a talent competition six years ago, she had begun to perform as if she were a zombie checking in and out of a graveyard. Her dance moves were laboured and forced, her spirit broken and her "talent" watered down and factory packed. She had been callously exploited and subject to a world of artifice and vanilla coated banality. Now, finally she had a real chance to make it.

"It's you and me for the duet, we've been put together for that song," she beamed.

"Yeah, but look at the title track, Marvin Gaye and Diana Ross—my voice won't cut it. I'll destroy that song, be like fingers-scratching-on-a-blackboard painful with those high notes," laughed Christian nervously.

"You'll just have to down some Jack Daniels and think of the misery of your life." She replied wistfully.

"Think of Otis, think of James Brown or Miles Davis..."

Her name was called out and she hurried on to the stage.

"Wish me luck," she whispered.

"Good luck," Christian shouted back.

The Panel was made up of three "industry" executives: a label manager, a talent scout, and a marketing dame. All of them eyed her lasciviously as if she were a slab of prime rib. It was highly distasteful. She studied the judges intently: one looked like a cross between Eve Pollard in drag and a Rottweiler; another resembled a disturbed ferret with screwed up wrinkly eyes and a wincing high-pitched voice. The third and final Judge reminded Kara of aging plaster. He had particularly obvious red veins that scored the left side of his face and humdrum neutrality reflected in his beige clothes and tofu-coloured hair. He appeared devoid of real emotion.

Kara thought him the worst; he had somehow managed to hoodwink as many as twenty-five television networks and probably just as many millions of people in the world that he could really "recognize musical talent," but Kara knew all he recognized was T and A on a string and he was nothing more than a sleazy puppeteer. So long as there were souls for sale, he was there to buy them. Kara needed this gig; she was tired of her dead end, no hope day jobs, all of which zapped her creative energy and made her feel useless. Pushing twenty-eight, she looked older but felt younger. Kara had once believed she would be someone, someone more than no one, someone who mattered more than no one. She knew she had it; she just had to make *them* believe it.

As she sang her heart out, you could feel the fragile vulnerability in her tender voice. It was raw, naked, and rhythmically beautiful. The panel were impressed.

"How was it, Christian?" she asked breathlessly, all smiles less than ten minutes later. "Christian, you best get..." She turned to face him.

"Oh, my God! Oh No! Oh, please, would somebody help me, please, Christian, how- oh my God!" Someone had shot Christian clean in the head, a silent shooter with a deadly aim. The blast had torn out a hunk of his brain, which lay splattered on the floor in a warm bloody pool.

"Please, please, someone come, he was meant to sing the duet with me, oh my God, Christian." Kara sat cross-legged on the floor, trying to hold his shorn-off head in place, shivering with hysteria while other contestants and the film crew on site gathered round.

"It's Christian, he... he was going to sing with me," she stammered.

The police and ambulance services were on their way. There was nothing they could do. An officer at the scene tried to calm Kara down. She was shaking uncontrollably and her jeans and black shirt were saturated in his blood.

"It's probably unlikely that he felt anything. The blast

would have knocked him out cold," he said gently and with authority. The story was the lead item on every single news channel and made the press the next morning.

Bernie was inconsolable. Tony had a bad feeling about all this. Things were getting complicated. Now that the reality TV show had turned into a crime scene the "old bill" were swarming around, trying to solve the mystery of a murdered Rent boy, who also happened to be a successful underwear model and former member of one of Britain's most popular boy bands, they knew they had to keep their heads down. It wouldn't take long to find out that Christian was Bernie's coke bitch and that would prove uncomfortable for everyone.

Chapter 41

Richie had been sent on a continuing professional development CPD course. It was a stipulation of the Law Society that all qualified Solicitors had to continue their training after their qualification to enhance their skills and refresh their knowledge. Richie saw it as a royal excuse to get pissed and laid on the Firm's time and money.

They had deliberately booked him into a local guesthouse in moth eaten Rugby at least twenty miles from the nearest town.

"Yes Sir do you have a reservation?" Fluttered a nibble and fribble receptionist with a hot- shag hair do and ink blue eyelashes. She had honeydew lips and a come- get- me shirt on.

"I should bloody well hope so." Heaved Richard from his short walk there.

"If you could just give me your name Sir?"

"Richard Davey."

"Yes Sir, here is the key to your room you're staying with us for two nights I believe?"

"They told me there was a *Holiday Inn* around here?" clipped Richard in a fuck -you tone.

"Yes Sir I can give you directions." Replied the hotel clerk.

Richard had been shafted by tight-fisted Mary the Firm's book –keeper. Knowing his propensity for jollying it up on the Firm's budget they had deliberately booked him into the smallest guest inn they could find more Basil Fawlty than Ian Schrager.

"Do you need help with your luggage Sir?"

"What, do you actually have anyone who could assist me with these then?"

"Yes Sir."

"Don't bother I'll carry them up myself," he bristled.

"Yes Sir," she simmered.

Richard thought she was RTF (ready to fuck) but skipped the invitation she was too easy. The room was a basic no frills-clean but dour affair. There was a small window and an old -fashioned bath tub with a shower attachment.

We'll see who gets the last laugh he groused to himself as he laid out his clothes on the bed, it was shop worn and hard with a sagging mattress. *So they thought it was really funny sticking him in some humpbacked flophouse well if he couldn't go to the party the party would come to him!* He decided.

"Yeah I want to make some calls can you hook up the line please."

"No problem Sir the line is now open." He dialled the number of directory services and instead got the hotel switchboard.

"Fucking hell what is this fuckery why do I keep getting you?" He stormed.

"What number do you want Sir?"

"I'd like Escort Services please a list of Escort Services." He snapped.

"You'd like the telephone number of which service?" she clucked with puritanical displeasure.

"Escort Services, you know call girls, prostitutes, women who honestly fuck for money." The phone went dead.

Richie was gonna get his shoop shoop de lang a lang one way or another and no one, especially some grizzly old telephone operator was getting in the way !

The office was calling him he diverted it to voice mail. It was Eva something about Poncho and advance funds for a transaction. He called Mungle right away.

"Um hello it's..."

"Richard," snaked Mungle in his Mumbai lisp.

"Yes what can I do for you?"

"I have another delivery it's urgent."

"I see I'm not at the office"

"I know you're in RRRRRugby" he rolled.

"Yes how did..."

"Mr Khan has his eyes and ears on all of his connections"

"Um I see." He writhed.

"We will arrange to have the suitcase delivered to your guest house."

"What here?" he panicked, not sure, how the desk staff would react to the arrival of a leather attaché case rammed with cash.

"Don't worry I will be very discreet a black Bentley will pull up outside in one hour. Be at the front entrance thank you."

Great just what this day needed some catch 22 criminality.

He had a quick shower, and shave then gelled back his hair. He looked like a Sears Catalogue Model, albeit a chubby one still he was satisfied with his efforts and convinced he would pull tonight even if it was one of the hotel staff. He waited in the lobby cum bar area and ordered his usual Jack and coke. With a case full of scrilla he could leave that road house dive and groove onto the *Holiday Inn* their sanitised simplicity a welcome reprieve from the fleabag pit he was in now.

An hour later he caught sight of the Bentley flashing onto the gravel drive way. He approached it with a healthy deference and secretly enjoyed the stealthy immorality of the visit despite knowing that Poncho was on his tail.

Mungle opened the passenger side of the car.

"Pleasssse come in RRRichard," he sputtered.

"Thank you Mr..."

"What is it with your English niceties we've already been through this please just call me Mungle artificial formality is a bore," he interrupted with a wave of his hand.

"Yes quite," peeved Richard he'd never faced an allegation of boredom before and it rankled him.

"Here's the money there's two hundred and fifty thousand in there just like the last occasion."

"Okay."

"When can Mr Khan expect it back?"

"Should take the same as last time seven to fourteen days but I had a call from him a couple of days ago and he said he would be visiting in person."

"Exxxxcellent, what a strange little town this is what are you here for?" Continued Mungle ignoring the info' on Poncho, his eyes stalking around like beady antennas.

"Oh the Firm sent me here on a training course it's um a professional requirement and mandatory for all solicitors."

"Hmm don't they do the same courses in London?" Asked Mungle.

"No it's um cheaper for the er course providers to run them out of London all lawyers have to do them." The truth was penny pinching Mary could have got a fucking course tutor and provided him with an in house training session at the Firm but in a wilful attempt to cut costs had settled for the provincial choice. Now Richie had to explain all this to a man whose boss owned half the world and wanted him dead. *What a fucking embarrassment*! He cringed.

"Would you like a ride back to London?"

"Um no I have to er complete the training."

Of course he'd like a lift back to fucking London or anywhere that was half civilised what was he going to do all night long in that pisshole of a town.

"Very well Mr. Richie see you again soon."

Once the Bentley had gone and Richard was left alone with the cash, he zeroed in on the scene before him; sullen pockets of industrial gloom fractured the horizon with chain coloured buildings and sour little office suites. Richie felt he was drowning in parochial purgatory it was too safe for hell. He needed to go let it out let in - get shit faced and fucked to the max. Then and only then, could he escape – free himself from that stifling plain- Jane nausea.

He walked back to his room choosing the stairs instead of the run down elevator. Inside he spread out on the bed and dropped the briefcase to the floor. He called switchboard for some local taxi numbers and found the nearest pub. He opened the case and took out a grand then placed it under the bed. If he was going to get wrecked he couldn't risk taking the money with him. It was such a bitty, isolated motel, no one would ever guess that sort of cash was lying around. He changed again. Tonight he wanted to lose control and bring the noise.

At around two am Richard staggered back to the motel with three wiggle and giggle chicks and two other straight clowns one of whom had a peach fuzz head of hair. The other was vampire hard with a blue box of memories to offload on everyone. They were arguing with each other talking horse -shit. “That’s not right it can’t be that small” Jibbered Peach fuzz.

"Yeah double means double the size,” jabbered vampire. One of the women started undressing, using her hands and her mouth to get closer to Richard. She was stripper dirty and RTF.

“What are you doin,” Belched Richie.

“Just getting friendly,” she nuzzled in a sling-back whisper.

“Stay over there.” He ordered.

“No one asked you to get *friendly* you’ve been paid to hang around not try to screw me so stay over there where I can see you. You ain’t nothing you’re a sleaze and tease know your place." He slammed.

“I get violent when I’m fucked up I get silent when I’m drugged up.” He started singing *Clash* songs, as she continued peeling off her clothes then draped herself on the settee like an Aldo Palazzo print ;a scorching poem of erotica. He flung a look of revulsion her way.

“You know what you are?” He leered.

“What’s that?” She pulsed with swelling desire.

“You, my dear are a lay and pay that’s all you are. Now get the fuck out of my room!” He cracked. Richie was a power-player in his head. He needed people around him he could dominate and control. Ever since he was a child and had witnessed the shameful suicide of his father, he had been forced to do as everyone had told him. At work, he was on lock down to Wiesel and now with Poncho on his nuts he felt he was losing the game. Then everything went cookie- crumble.

"What you doing?" He bawled.

"Leaving." She crisped back.

"What without your clothes?"

"Yep."

The others just gaped as she sailed out of the room and waited for the lift stark naked: "Aurevoir." She giggled.

Some hotel guests were waiting nearby, riveted by the shenanigans they looked on in amazement."

What's the matter she stirruped

"Haven't you ever seen a naked woman before ?"

"Not one like you – not for a long time and might I say you look simply lovely, quite quite lovely" gushed an elderly gentleman.

She clambered out of the lift careful not to stub her toe with Richie sprinting behind her: "Put this on now – there you go it's cold," he shoved a coat and her party dress at her. Reluctantly she got dressed.

Richie's little night of excess cost the Firm more than a heavy pay out to the hotel. The Police and Environmental Agencies were called by concerned onlookers, fearful the hotel was organising illicit orgies or worse. Richard had to placate them and reassure the hotel he would pay for the inconvenience. He faked illness the next morning blew his CPD course and zoomed back to London twenty thousand pounds better off courtesy of the dreaded Poncho Khan.

Chapter 42

Tony and the guys had decided to keep a low profile since the news of Christian. They had sent their condolences to his devastated parents and marked his passing with a silent prayer and a round of Laphroaig, the world's finest single malt whiskey.

Bernie was unnaturally quiet. It worried Scooter, who thought he would do something he might later regret. They tunnelled their energies into the capsule venture and set about buying consumables and office gadgets for the start up. Tony wanted to hire some new work jockeys and Bernie agreed they should stick some desk clerks on the payroll for the smooth administration of their business. First, though, they needed to collect some debts and Tony wanted to send Bernie with Tim to chase a payment.

Before they set off, Bernie asked their designated porch monkey Sabatini, a homeless Portuguese "artist" who had been "adopted" by T and was now living there, to go get some mince and onion pies. After they had eaten their snack, they would head off and make the money run. Almost an hour passed with still no sign of him. Eventually Sabatini returned with a packet of fresh mints, one onion, and a cherry pie.

Bernie flipped and started screaming and shouting at him.

"I'll slap you up, bitch, are you being fucking funny? We're hungry here. I gave you twenty quid for some mince and onion pies and you come back with these?"

"Let's have a drink and calm down." Tony looked at Bernie, who was sheepish and sullen after his vicious outburst. Scoot looked at Tim who was trying to pacify a stunned and subdued Sabatini and then all of them began laughing and relaying the events to a bemused Godwin who had returned from lunchtime gambling at the bookies.

"We'll pick something up at a Petrol station en route," Bernie said impatiently.

"Come on Tim let's roll."

"Bye, guys," replied Tim to the group, who nodded and waved back at them. Even though the monies for the start up were drawn in, it wasn't possible to simply stop the drug business. Just like any other cash rich enterprise, there were bills to collect on, stock to offload, and a distribution and source network to inform about Tony's retirement plans. He might have to start looking for a replacement, someone who could fill his shoes and be just as much of a success. In the meantime, business would tick over as usual.

Chapter 43

Scoot was in limbo. Should he knock the relationship on the head entirely with Madrilène, or try to stall her mad mother? For weeks now, he had been seeing a wealthy Russian socialite, Madrilène Radanovich, but it was her mother Olga, she had been stalking him for days. Now she was outside the flat demanding that he speak to her! It was embarrassing and uncomfortable. She had sent him some supremely extravagant 18-carat yellow gold and diamond cufflinks by Fozieri, a Mont Blanc pen, and handmade dark chocolate truffles by Knipschildt. He had tried to refuse the items but she wouldn't listen. She was a potent blend of blonde Afghan hound and Donatella Versace always ready for confrontation. She had threatened to kill herself, tell her daughter that she loved him, and generally behaved like a deluded maniac. She called him at least ten times a day and had promised him a million-dollar lifestyle. Dressed in a white dinner coat with ornate, gold stitching, she wore wrap around Gucci shades and a poisonous frown. Even the derma fillers injected into her smooth veneer couldn't mask her over dramatic angst.

"Open ze door, Scooter! Open ze door now. I can't wait any longer!"

"Tony, tell Godwin not to let her in. She's a Royal nut. I

mean she's absolutely barking. Please, Tony, do something," Scoot pleaded.

Tony couldn't help laughing. He peered out the window. "You know, she's not all that bad, brov', what is she, like fifty, fifty-five maybe?"

"She's in her late forties, man, don't be so gross."

"All I'm saying is she looks quite fit, y' nar."

"Yeah, for a mature Russian witch." Tony called Godwin, who was sent outside to politely, get rid of the menacing Olga, now shouting the neighbourhood down. "I vant you, I need you, Scoot please come out."

"Ugghh, so weird," Scoot complained. After being confronted with an unwashed and unshaved Godwin, Olga seemed startled and highly irate. She returned to her taxi and removed a small "duck egg" blue gift- wrapped box from the inside of the car. Thrusting it into the palm of a bemused Godwin with her gloved hand, she sped off.

"Don't bring it in!" shouted Scoot from downstairs, but it was too late. Godwin was already carrying the noxious smelling package into the flat door when Scoot rushed towards him and threw it out of the nearest window.

"She left me a text message saying she's sent me a pile of shit because that's how I made her feel. Eeeeuh, it's real shit! The crazy bitch wrapped up some shit and delivered it to me. What kind of psycho bitch does that?"

Outside the contents of the elegantly wrapped gift box lay stuck and smeared to the pavement in ugly brown splatter.

"I has to go wash miself in carbolic soap or someting."

"Yeah, you and me both," sighed Scoot.

"This is fuckery, man. I've got a meeting with Luke later

today, Scoot, go home, get cleaned up, put a suit on. You have to come to the meeting, too."

"Yeah no probs, brov. She's fucking scary, man." They called Addison Lee, their local cab firm, and Scoot went off to get ready while Godwin got washed up and T made more preparations.

Chapter 44

Richard was still looking for answers. He needed to speak to Tony alone without any of the usual interruptions. He would try his phone again later. He decided to clear out his UK bank accounts anyway and keep some easy readies on him, putting the rest away in a deposit account in Jersey. At least then he'd have a little bit of security if he needed to get away in a hurry. He would give Eva a week off and make his contingency plans then. He headed straight for his local, The Griffin to get drunk. He would while away a few hours there until it was time for the offices to close. Then he could start moving money and transferring his assets without interference or the choking quagmire of his work in- tray. In The Griffin, a regular punter was boozing, an ex-con who had been inside for at least fifteen, of his thirty years. He was drinking a pint glass of whiskey with two shots of tonic and had just completed a ten-mile run. He claimed that he always went running now to take the psychological edge off his time in prison.

"I love it speeding along roads just me and the fresh air. Inside you'd be locked up like a battery hen, except you weren't a hen, you were a real person, and now I run every day to get those fucking memories out of my head. I hated it inside, you come out worse then when you go in and they send you down for petty stuff you know pub fights and all that, it's bollocks."

"Must have been pretty bad for you."

"Pretty bad? Yeah, I should fucking say so, locked up in a five- foot manhole wif someone who don't care whether they're alive or dead. It's criminal that."

The irony wasn't lost on Richard.

"Ere you're that brief, in't ya? The one that got famous for getting Keggsy off that robbery charge?"

"That was some time ago when I just entered the profession, mate," Richard replied, smiling at the ceiling with a Vodka in his hand.

He took a deep breath and went on:

"I was a real lawyer then wanted to save the world, fight injustice and keep the door to truth open."

"Yeah, well happens to us all gov' life comes along, pisses right on you then you just 'ave to do what you can you know to *survive*, is it true you're looking for a piece of business?"

"What do you mean?"

"Come wiv' me, Gov."

Richard finally realized that about three months ago he had asked T if he knew of anyone who could get him a "shooter." Tony wasn't really into supplying stolen arms or weapons but managed to trace an old mate of his in Camberwell who had the contact details of someone who could help. Now a chance meeting in their local boozer had netted a result for both Richard and Tommy the ex con who would make at least a grand for setting up the deal if Richard bought the weapon off him. Richard was dubious, though. Was this a chance meeting or was this guy put there by Poncho or, worse, the "Old Bill?" His head was a mess. Should he go to the East End lock up with this Tommy person or should he make him go and get it first? He chose to wait it out in the bar. The afternoon strip show was on and if Tommy was serious, he would get it off him when he came back. Why should he put himself at further risk?

"Listen, mate, I don't know where you got that info' from, but as it happens, I wouldn't mind paying a reasonable sum for a cheap 'Glock' just to keep me safe at night."

"I'll make some calls, Gov. You stoppin' 'ere then?"

"Yep, tasty little floor show on now and I've still got loads of booze to get through," replied Richard, putting on his best "mockney accent." Tommy made the call. The Glock was for Richard all right. Poncho would see that Richard got the Glock.

Chapter 45

As a Portuguese citizen, Sabatini was free to live, work and most importantly of all get married in the UK. Earlier that morning T had received a phone call from a Yardie operative looking for a favor he needed to find a bridegroom for a three o' clock wedding. Their original sap had backed out of the bogus ceremony. If a suitable replacement wasn't found, there was a real danger that Keisha his Jamaican princess would be deported. T could get as much as £10,000 for this tidy little job. It was a polished operation: the ring, the morning suite two fake witnesses, the reception, the photographer, and even a one-night honeymoon were all part of the scam.

"You got to be at Marylebone Registry Office in three hours, bring your passport and a copy of your birth certificate," Bernie told Sabatini casually.

"Why?" He asked suspiciously.

"Well, T needs you to help him out with a small indulgence – nothing major; he needs you to help the family with a minor task if you will" Replied Bernie. "

"What, don't understand - what I have to do – yes am good artist I help T how?"

"You just have to turn up at the Registry office enjoy the party possibly some jiggy wiggy then you come back home tomorrow its' simple."

"But what I have to do?" Persisted Sabatini.

Well, it's like this, you know you use a lot of drugs and that costs the crew money but you say you need them to do art, painting well T has he ever asked you to pay even once?"

"No." Sabatini blinked.

"And you stay here rent free has anyone ever asked you to pay even once?"

"No." Sabatini responded.

"And T buys you all your canvasses and paint, clothes, you always get good food here and money to go out, has anyone ever asked you to pay?"

"No" He repeated.

"You see Sabatini you're given everything you need here, you're looked after and taken care of and you're part of the family. Now T wants you to help the family by agreeing to do a minor gesture and turn up at the right time and do as T says it's simple."

T gave Bernie a dark look signalling him not to say anything further. The last thing they wanted was a deranged Sabatini on their hands. With a bit of luck he wouldn't catch on until it was too late.

"Here's fifty quid go get a haircut and shave we're going to a party!"

"Yes party," Sabatini agreed with a broad smile.

The proprietor, of the Duke of Wellington pub was typically used to office trade from the BBC, "yummy mummies" out for an afternoon tipple, well-heeled locals on the go, up market shoppers and moneyed tourists looking for a traditional English Pub. Then, twice a month he would host the Jamaican wedding party: turning the tasteful charm of the Duke of Wellington into a riot of colour and West Indian pizzazz.

He made around £7,000 behind the bar and the celebrations would go on all night long. The Landlord appreciated the bizzo with pubs shutting down at an alarming rate and wine bars and gastro eateries opening up all around him he was only too glad he could facilitate the service.

With his "Soho" haircut and naturally sun burnt complexion Sabatini was Di Caprio cool. His angel eyes melting with innocence. Keisha was Beyoncé lush, she had a strong wholesome figure olive toned skin, wavy chestnut hair and an over stressed Jamaican accent.

They met in the pub shortly before the ceremony, for a thirty-minute briefing. Sabatini had a vague idea that what he was about to do was not lawful but he was coked to the nines and wanted to stay with T. He appreciated what T had done for him and respected him; so would do exactly what was asked of him.

Keisha was more theatrical with her role and obviously overjoyed. If things went okay she could stay in England with her Yardie boyfriend. She was gussied up like a Mardi Gras Queen sticking with tradition in white silk bordered with beads and glitter but beneath her veil was a bursting bust line aching to be let loose and long blue garters that skimmed her thighs.

"Ello darling my you is a pretty boy mmm ooh wee you got competition man he is fine oh bwouy so fine." She went and sat on his knee giving him a hot red one on the lips.

"We is gonna have fun tonight boy oh man you look good." She simmered.

"Ere what mi say Sabatini now you just 'ave to say, I do, and that's that, nobody gonna ask you anything and Keisha turn it down a little bit and no drinking before the ceremony okay?" warned T.

Sabatini nodded. The briefing over, they crossed the road to the Registry office and everyone got into place. They entered the building. Keisha's chitter breaking the solemn dignity of the room, Sabatini looking at her as if he were observing the tail end of a David Lynch epic. The Registrar was a cheerful looking man in his late forties, he had no reason to suspect the "happy couple" after all this was the same Registry office where Patsy Kensit and Liam Gallagher tied the knot why should it be any different for Keisha Leticia McKenzie and Paulo, Agostino Sabatini?

"Now repeat after me please Mr. Sabatini I call upon these persons present here to witness that I, Paulo Augstino Sabatini do take you, Keisha Leticia McKenzie to be my lawful wedded wife." Sabatini repeated the lines as if he were a hook-billed macaw, but Keisha said her vows with radiant aplomb. After twenty minutes, Mr. and Mrs. Sabatini and their guests returned to the Duke of York Pub for a carnival celebration:

"Get the drinks here's three grand to get mash up and blow down."

"Thanks Tone your business is always appreciated."

"Now ere what mi say the boys are bringing in their own sound system. The tracks you got on the juke box Bonnie Tyler Michel Bubble, all that kind of stuff is not going to work for the dancehall vibe and we got speeches, toasts to the bride, toasts to the groom this is going to be one, heavy session man."

"Ere what everyone make yourselves comfy the bar's open yeah he's got Red Stripe, Rum cocktails, Krug, champagne, it's all here." Beamed one of the gang.

T's Yardie friends were filling the pub. A bemused crowd of regulars watched in silence as the normally quiet bar was ram jammed with Jamaican Ska beats, gallons of Rum and plates of curried goat, Jerk chicken, Calalloo, spicy patties and yam.

"We'll need Yellowman, Billy Boyo, Massive Dread, Bunny Wailer and Shabbah, all our boomlick tunes and we want it loud," someone shouted.

"Everton and Leroy have gone to bring the sound system in it's massive man" Replied T.

Sabatini was in a coke daze he couldn't quite get his head around the scene. The quiet, Catholic born artist had definitely married a woman today and would leave her tomorrow but for now he was in the right mood to get mashed.

Letita let her cleavage do the talking as she started a booty grind for her "real" boyfriend and then tried to get Sabatini to join in the fun but he couldn't shake it so she gave up on him pumping him with more Red Stripe instead.

Next came the best man speeches. Sabatini was surprised to see a man he had never met before regaling the guests with stories from his childhood as if he were his best friend, charming them with frothy anecdotes from his teen years and approaching manhood. It was a Jean Michel Basquiat moment and Sabatini was pleased everyone was so happy. He got tanked up on more beer joining the elders at the card table and playing domino games. The drunken jamboree lasted until dawn. Sabatini had paid his debt, and was reunited with T and the crew by noon.

Chapter 46

Mondays, to Wednesdays were generally quiet for Tony. A drug dealer's diary usually gets busy from Thursday to Sunday morning so he tended to do all his personal business at the start of the week. Christian's death had affected them all and he wanted to spend some family time with the crew.

Bernie and Tim were watching a local news channel on ITV it was a prime time show.

"What a pile of piss this is" Grumbled Bernie

"Yeah, I've nick- named them Munty and Bunty, I mean they're meant to be covering serious news items and Munty 's all squeals and giggles like a house pup who needs to be neutered, I mean look at her she's wearing a pinafore on national tv she looks like she's ready to do some painting or decorating."

"Yeah I mean it's actually a pinafore what were they thinking in wardrobe oh let's just stick her in this she's supposed to be highlighting the core topics of the day not telling us about DIY."

"Yeah haven't they seen proper news channels CNN for example slick- glossed up news kittens with loads of va va voom elegance and just enough suit power to make you believe what you hear."

"Yeah if Munty and Bunty ever say anything it would be delivered with such shelf – stacking banality you probably wouldn't believe it anyway."

"Yeah when it's breaking news on CNN you know it's something serious."

"If you two have stopped dissing the local news chiefs can we like make a move?"

"Yeah alright – not like we're on a time line or anything."

"I wanna get there for the first one."

"Doesn't matter each movie is around two hours thirty minutes and we're gonna watch them all."

"I like to get good seats – big tub of popcorn, king size Pepsi Haggen *Daz*, it's all about the movie experience man"

"Yeah whatever."

"Come on let's fly."

"Yeah like we're in Brooklyn as if we're in the hood –let's fly chah."

"We are in the hood this is *our* neighbourhood."

"What we going to see?"

"Meet the Parents."

"Are we going to the *Empire*?"

"Serious blood best place to catch a movie."

"And..."

"Yeah?"

"It's right near Pizza Hut."

"Yes Pizza Hut." Dragged Tim, with a long, weary sigh.

"What you complain' about it's got a salad bar and you can 'ave pasta for ponces like you."

"I'm not strictly complaining it's just well Pizza Hut- hardly gastro nosh is it?"

“We don’t want that we want good wholesome regular junk nuff of your complain' let’s just go.”

“Three adults for *Meet the Parents* please”

The cinema usher was a scrappy non-conformist a cross between Marilyn Manson and Kurt Cobain:

“Where would you gentleman like to sit?”

“At the back high up” Answered T

“First Row Second Row?”

“Oooh let’s have a look at the seating plan.” Tim asked getting a little carried away.

“Look we’re gonna watch a movie, not book a fucking flight to Japan” Complained Bernie.

“Yeah you go and get the munchings Pepsi for everyone sweets, popcorn ice cream and Nachos if they do them here’s a nifty fifty should do the trick” Smiled T.

“Yeah cos Nacho’s and all that other crap is really gonna heighten the experience.”

“Stop your whinging man you’re killing our buzz you know what you are Tim?”

“No doubt you’ll let me know.”

“Yeah a whinopath ha ha a fucking whinopath- you just go on and on now get in the queue for our scooby snacks.”

“Okay then that’s three adults for *Meet The Parents* back row."

"Great your tickets and your change – enjoy the movie.”

“Thanks.”

“Hurry up Tim.”

“I’m in the queue can’t go any faster.”

Bernie pulled a face and followed T inside.

After the movie, they headed across the square to Pizza Hut.

T liked homely family themed eateries they reminded him of where he came from and gave him a comforting nostalgia. He was a big fan of what he termed "ghetto food" and Pizza Hut was a noted favourite as he used to go there when he was a kid.

They took a table for four although there were only three of them.

"What I absolutely detest about these places is that clinking din of cutlery it reminds me of an airport galley oh and that piped chart music that filters around the background like you're jammed in a lift somewhere wretched like Scunthorpe."

"Tim you're such a fucking snob we're here now and they do good Pizza."

"And garlic bread."

"Yeah and garlic bread."

"And salad bar," grinned Bernie.

"Yeah you can eat all you like from the salad bar."

"We're just chilling man having some down time we don't need no poncey wait staff over priced house red, or a Napoli inspired wall hanging to make our lunch authentic," yawned Bernie lolling around in the booth and stretching out.

A fit and flirt waitress armed with a neat little jotting pad and biro sidled up to the table.

"Hi there my name's Lisa I'll be your waitress today what can I get you all?" She glowed.

"Yeah hi Lisa we'll have..."Started T.

"I want the ice cream factory," butted in Bernie

"Ssssh man hold on okay – the ice cream factory's later." Lisa grinned with franchised repetition the kind of grin that says I'm so glad I'm out of here come 5 o clock in the evening.

"Right shhup blood we'll have four portions of cheese topped garlic bread, chicken strips."

"Would you like one portion or two?"

"How many you get in a portion?"

"Erm about five or six strips."

"So we'll take two of those and two portions of wings."

"Could I get some olives?" chipped Tim

"Yes of course Sir."

"And we need three plates for the salad bar."

"No problem salad station – three do you want large or small on those?"

"Large."

"Okay, and what about your Pizzas?"

"Well I'll have the meat feast, vegetable supreme and hot 'n' spicy."

"All three pizzas just for you Sir?"

"Better believe it!"

"And for you?" She looked over at Tim.

"I'll just have a margarita classic nothing else."

"Okay."

"Bernie?"

"Yeah I'll have a hot 'n' spicy with extra jalapenos and black olives please."

"Okay."

"Now what can I get you for drinks?"

"Yeah, large cokes."

"I'll just have table water," sniffed Tim

"Oh I'll just have table water," mimicked Bernie as the waitress went to deal with their order.

"Tim you're such a bambaclat!" Roared T.

The restaurant was packed with after school families leaving the office treadmill for some cheap branded entertainment.

Sitting on the table opposite, was a traditional family of four. A mother harried and torn with stress lines and crows feet misting her eyes, her lips chafed and thin. The last traces of lipstick feathering the corners of her mouth, and outlining her hidden anguish. She was cock-a doodle do happy on the outside, focusing all of her attention on an auburn haired child of around twelve.

"Stop staring Hannah that's rude." She scolded with an apologetic smile to T and the others.

"Mummy why's that man's hair blue can I have blue hair?"

"It's just the way he likes it and no you can't have blue hair not yet. "She replied impatiently.

"He's trying to be different," interrupted the gangly teen sitting next to her. He was all zits and *Munster* tresses as if he were part of the *Adams Family* without the alabaster skin and marble freeze eyes.

Tim gave them a polite nod the mother returned with a friendly acknowledgment but the little girl poked her tongue back at him with a petulant grin.

"Stop annoying that family Tim." Rebuked T as he tucked into his pizza.

Bernie was getting irritated.

"Oi Tim can you go fill my salad bowl please?" Asked T

"Oh very well." Tim grumbled.

"Yeah make sure you overload on sweet corn and potato salad no vinaigrette blue cheese dressing and no shrubbery"

The little girl was in a crotchety mood she kept kicking the side of Bernie's chair and making rude faces at him.

"I've had enough of this," he huffed and threw a burnt piece of buffalo wing at the table. The father, a long angular man, whippet thin with bony elbows and a receding hairline was yakking on his mobile phone and spoke in overstressed sentences as if he were talking to someone who couldn't understand English. T and the others were kidding around having fun. Then it struck, a big slice of half- eaten pizza came flying onto their table slapping Tim on his head. Bernie and T were cracking up snorting in between mouthfuls of food. Bernie piled up a plate of used up garlic bread and everyone's leftovers then emptied the entire contents on the family's table flicking bits of gloopy cheese onto the little girl.

"Ha! That will teach you for shoving my chair!" He growled.

"Bernie behave she's only like seven!" T teased.

"Yeah well she should know better than to throw food at our table" He swiped.

"Bernie easy now."

"Do something," the startled mother at the table shrieked to her husband.

Then, looking directly at Bernie:

"How dare you?"

Their raised voices alerting the management, there was a loud commotion going on. From nowhere food was pelted all over their table, T's table and now, other people were caught in the cross- fire. Bernie, and the teenage greebo being the prime culprits. The father took cover at the back of the restaurant leaving his wife and children to fend for themselves.

Sticky balls of glutinous cheese, fizzy drinks and jalapeno peppers lay stuck to the heavy carpeted floors and walls. Other diners were leaving in disgust.

"I really don't think this is appropriate behaviour Bernie you're completely to blame, this is most unedifying" chided Tim

"She started it" Bernie retorted defensively.

"I think Tony should go and apologise before the management get all nervy and ring up the old bill"

"Tim's right for once chah all I wanted to do was have a bit of pizza and chill and now we got little children crying, a man scared half to death, and the Pizza people all stressed chah this is bullshit man- serious it's fucking crazy."

At that moment after much coaxing by his staff and fellow eaters the manger appeared. He was nothing more than a pimple of a man with lanky dark hair and an unfortunate stutter.

"I – I must ask you to leave sir" He trembled.

"No problem bro' sorry about all this chah y'ar no need to look so vex up man we ain't gonna to pillage or nothin' we like Pizza Hut don't we boys ?"

"Yeah, we're sorry we love Pizza it's sweet man."

"If you'll just leave now then," stammered the manager.

"Here's a monkey for the damage." Soothed T generously.

"Oh that's very kind of you it will help with the staff's overtime."

Bernie made the bird sign to the family as Tim hurried them out of there. It was the *Blues Brothers* dinner skit only in real time.

Chapter 47

Poncho was a rampant illegal film copier. He had a heart-warming enthusiasm for the industry but was singlehandedly responsible for at least two thirds of Mumbai's video piracy that had a knock on effect on the global film trade. With a network of small Indian run stores based all over the world he was able to produce and replicate Hindi and Western movies taking them from cinema to rental shop in days sometimes even hours. One of his largest shops was located in Tooting South London. It was a drab and dismal Tuesday, the sluggishness of Winter curdling the afternoon sky.

Piles of recording equipment Dvd burners, and blank discs were clacking noisily at full speed. Outside there was a steady ebb and flow of people milling around in the gold shops, sweetmeat centres and Tandoori houses. The area was famous in England for Indian goods and homemade exotic fare. It was known locally as Little India. Inside the store customers were jostling around as Dvds were being rented, returned, bought and sold. Same old same old until a van pulled up outside and behind it a police car. A group of officials barged their way in. The Police officer entered first:

“Excuse me Sir I’m from the Met office are you the owner of these premises Sir?” He flashed his warrant card. One of the people behind the till answered him.

“Owner not here.” He surmised in stilted English with a Punjabi accent.

“Yes well we will continue with our search, who are you Sir?”

“I am Sanjay.”

"Right yes um Sanjay we believe you are selling and producing pirate films here.”

“No no no! We are not pirates we are not pirating.” Rebutted Sanjay.

“Well would you like to remain on the premises Sir while we take these items away?”

“No! No these machines not for sale we don’t make them for sale this is our own private machines no you can’t have.”

“Yes Sir we understand that but we’re investigating an allegation of video piracy.”

“What? We don’t have pirates here all good copy look, English not that good request translator need interpreter interpretation no search until Landlord comes back and bring Punjabi speaking interpreter." He insisted.

“Where is the landlord?” Asked the officer with growing irritation.

“He’s gone say prayers.” Answered Sanjay folding his arms.

“Can we telephone him? The shop is being investigated for video piracy following intelligence from FACT the Federation against Copyright Theft and we must be allowed to conduct a full examination of the premises.”

“No can’t telephone he is praying, understand Landlord in temple making Pooja - mobile off no no can’t make contact with him.”

"Right Sir, well you run the shop in his absence don’t you? You’re in charge here”

“No no,” countered Sanjay smiling.

“Landlord don’t pay me enough to be in charge Landlord in temple will be praying and ringing bells of temple.” He folded his hands as if to pray saying :

“He make Pooja.”

"I understand Sir perhaps it would be easier if you would just accompany us around the store as we are going to execute this search.”

"No then to court search not proper if Landlord not here me not proper man to caution about search.” He protested knowingly.

“And how are you so informed about the technical requirements to effect the search Sir?" Asked the Police officer with a look of cynicism streaked across his face.

“Oh because of previous raid not here – but in Billy’s shop across the street- lots of raids here like traffic warden and stop and searching all goes on here all the time- can’t raid shop if no Landlord not the right person to raid please leave machines officer they are for personal use.”

“Look Sir if you attempt to obstruct the lawful execution of this search then I will have no option but to arrest you for obstructing the police from carrying out their duties.”

“No officer not right I am standing away from you how am I obstructing all I ask is for Interpreter, eh officer you must make notes need them in court.”

"We're making a list of items we're taking with us Sir and we leave you a copy of that with you so you know exactly what's been taken and what remains on the premises. Now if the Landlord wants to know what happened he can call me on this number okay Sir?"

"No – wait please officer can you speak to lawyer?" Enquired Sanjay.

"Very well Sir if you want to get your lawyer on the phone I'll be only too happy to speak with him but the warrant stands." Sanjay got out a card from his top shirt pocket and made a call to Richie's office."

"Hellloooo Sanjay here calling from Doc Khan Sahib need to speak with Mr Richie."

"Oh I'm sorry er Mr Sanjay Richard, er Mr. Davey is on another call can I take a message?"Sanjay put the receiver down most dissatisfied.

"No lawyer not available."

"Well here's my number Sir your lawyer, or your Landlord or both can get in touch with me on that number directly."

Sanjay immediately notified Poncho himself of the raid who rung Richie to sort it:

"Richie"

"Mr Khan"

"You're needed in a video piracy case- the address is 123 Tooting High Street London."

"What's happened?"

"The police have raided the shop and seized some Dvds, blank Dvds, recording equipment a camcorder that sort of thing but I think the search was technically unlawful or improper as the Landlord wasn't present on the premises."

"Hmmm I see," there was an undercurrent of rising tension between them but they remained professional and aloof as they discussed the legal ramifications of the search.

"I'll send Sanjay along to see you today so you can sort this mess out I don't want any comeback on me. From what I understand from Sanjay, acting on a tip off from FACT the premises were raided but oddly enough FACT did more than just assist the Police Sanjay says they were instrumental in the search and were grilling other staff about Dvds and firing questions to them when the police were taking the goods away. I'm no lawyer Richie but FACT have a clear bias in this potential prosecution and allowing FACT employees to take equipment can't be proper."

"Leave it with me Mr. Khan I'll deal with it right away." Richie had no previous experience handling this kind of investigation but he knew there was unlikely to be a criminal charge if the evidence didn't stack up and of course with Poncho squeezing him he needed to do what he could. Some days later after the original raid the police decided there wasn't enough to prosecute and the shop continued to trade. Poncho sent Richie a £10,000 pound bonus a reminder he would see him soon and a bottle of Remy Martin Cognac.

Chapter 48

Tim and Bernie were in the flat Bernie was eBay scamming.

"I just hit this seller with a claim for a lost pair of shoes."

"Yeah like you could get any shoes to even fit you on the mass market." Jeered Tim

"Fuck off is that the best you can do?"

"Well it's early give me time."

"So how does it kick then?"

"Well I press the negative button and then I send a letter of complaint to the seller. Richie would have been most impressed with my note I've quoted the law, threatened legal action and generally been an annoying cunt."

"What does that entitle you to?" Asked Tim drearily.

"It's simple really all of the sellers on eBay need positive not negative feedback from the buyer. We hit sellers from all over, they don't tend to bother with guaranteed post or anything like that to ensure the goods are delivered, and because Pay Pal works with them we can target the sellers most likely to send out goods which could have gone missing."

"Easy as piss."

"It's a simple sting and there's no mess no bother."

"So long as you don't hit the same seller twice it works."

"Oh such vile gluttony such corruption such..."

"Shut the fuck up Tim when you were trading stocks and shares doing your buy and sell are you telling me there wasn't even a bit of Liam Leeson or dodgy inside trading going on a la BCCI?"

"Absolutely not !"

" Ha don't make me gag you Muppet a bit of change here and there on the old eBay spin and shuffle is hardly going to dent the British Economy now is it ?"

"Play to win Tim no rules."

Bernie hit five more sellers this time claiming that he had purchased two items at the same time and that only part of his delivery had been received. As both items would probably have been sent without any postal security he was free to run the scam again without raising suspicion.

"Yeeeeees!" He signalled with a victory gesture

"Got payback from Pay Pal!"

"Cheat Cheat if you can't win."

"There's another con I do on eBay it really is turning out to be a very healthy revenue stream."

"What's that then?" Asked Tim

"I picked it up from a friend in the States they're wired into it now over there but no one over here really knows about it."

"Well, what is it?"

"Basically all you do is send out an email to all the gimps who lost out on an auction it goes something like this:

"Dear munty and bunty would you like another chance to bid for these goods on the auction you lost out on blar blar fucking blar. As soon as they click the link they come straight to the cookie jar and Bad Bernie steals all their credit card info'."

"I don't get that."

"Fuck of Tim you do get that, *you* of all people know lots and lots about hacking, eyes and ears Tim, eyes and ears Timothy hack hack hack!"

"Anyway this is small fry – baby potatoes if you did this all day 24/7 you could earn over fifty thousand a month from this scam because the site we've created looks exactly the same as the one on eBay. The con is sweet, I know of a kid who notched up all these paid for trips to NYC and rung in about fifty thousand selling non- existent consumables to on line buyers. It's known as the second chance scam and it's been running in the US for a long time, tried and tested Timothy tried and tested."

"Hmmm from what you say it seems to work on the same principle as all computer and technology scams; a numbers hit."

"Yeah that's pretty much right the beauty of eBay is that there are literally hundreds and thousands of users from all over the world, a two to three percent margin is all that's required for it to work."

"You would have thought that e bay would have had the technology to block a scam like that."

"Oh yeah they do, they always try it's a continuous cat and mouse game as soon as the scam is blocked there's always a new way to leapfrog it and net the customer in."

"I suppose it's just another way to get by."

"Yeah Tim we're all scrapping for a living and not everyone can be hired by Goldman Sachs or Merrill Lynch and Yahoo, everyone's on the take may be a cliché but it's true, at least we don't sponge off the State."

"Ah the pains of a broken childhood and self taught computer whizz eh Bernie?"

"Yeah well we got to survive that's how we get on."

"Okay, so show me what to do."

The two of them stuck at it for another two hours roping in around three grand and then went out for a curry.

Chapter 49

Bessie hadn't had much luck with Manju over the Hindi-style hieroglyphics on the small piece of paper that he'd taken from Marvin's, so he had arranged to meet Deepak at the TPA bar 7 Denmark Street. Deepak was a former TV soap star who had been written out of the London-based series to concentrate on bigger projects. Typically, like so many of yesterday's "has beens," he was now down on his luck and out of work. He was currently dressed in Chust Silk Pyjamas and Sherwani traditional Indian garb, doing a spot of driving for his uncle's cab firm. It was called *Hindustani Taxis* and they made the drivers dress up as if they were extras from *Bride and Prejudice*.

"Oh, fuckin' 'ell, mate. What they got you doin' now?" Bessie wore classic cut Seven for All Mankind Jeans, a blue-striped Herbie Frogg shirt, argyle socks, and a John Smedley cashmere sweater. He liked clothes and looking "smart." He was a bit disappointed that Deepak was dressed so shabbily but ignored the stares they got on Denmark Street.

"Look, you even got a name badge, that's cute."

"Fuck off, man. What d'ya want, anyway?"

"Shall we go get a drink? There's a bag of sand in this for ya if you want. Looks like you're in need of the cash."

"I'm in method," Deepak replied indignantly.

"Yeah, and I'm in the fucking Bahamas right now with Kelly Brook, so let's get a drink, shall we?"

They made their way to TPA. They ordered two pints and sat down. Bessie took out the folded piece of paper from a Prada man bag and placed it carefully across the scratched, worn table.

Deepak bent down to get a closer look. "Get me a pen and something to write on."

"What is it?"

They read: "UBS: 1,3,57."

"I think that's worth more than a bag of sand, don't you?" he asked archly. Deepak rewrote all the figures down in sequential order and then they headed off to Yming for the House Special. Now that Bessie had got the coordinates for presumably the Swiss bank account and the key to the deposit box, he felt he could do some real negotiating with Mr Khan. He wasn't about to give up such a sweet deal, as Khan had only paid him £20,000 for the run on Marvin's shop and he was sure the key and coordinates were worth much more. They had arranged to meet up in a few days. For now, he would play it safe and wait it out, but fatally had underestimated Poncho's grip on the criminal wire. News spread quickly; Bessie was now a target.

Chapter 50

Warren, a Sous chef at the Ivy, had invited T and the gang to lunch. Popular with celebrities and famous for its hoity toity door policy it had a yearlong waiting list and fearsome reputation. For months now Warren had been hyping up his role in the kitchen. As a regular punter he would buy gear from T already cut at 50% then chop it up again leaving it at 25% purity. He would then sell it on to friends, associates and kitchen staff. One night crawling back to T's after a mammoth twenty three hour shift they got into a routine conversation: "Ere what mi say you're always at my house, my house is your house but whenever I ask you when I can come eat at *your* house you never sort it out for mi. I want to eat at The Ivy man are you ashamed of me or somethin' ?" T asked with emotional sincerity.

Warren was thrown by this open question and started twitching nervously, leaning on one foot then another. He was tall and skinny ; a cross between Zah Zah Binks and Ronnie Wood. He always had a manic grimace and shifty eye.

"No no that's not right man no you just have to give me a couple of hours notice and then I can deal with it proper. Everyone knows about you man, the bus boys, the wait staff the backroom girls everyone man."

"Chah well just make sure." Answered T.

Warren got a fifteen minute warning at peak time on a Friday night:

"It's T. I'm outside." Warren was wired and edgy. He waited for T to turn up.

After the tipsy "hello" from the door- man fixed up like an extra from the Disney parade with top hat and gold buttons, T and the crew marched over to the front desk. With T was Zhy wearing a PVC mini skirt, gold coloured headband and nylon body stocking that revealed her black bustier underneath, with blue eye shadow and orange lipstick, Bernie and Tim followed.

The standard door bitch greeted them with a haughty stare and catty temper. She was like the Hound of Hell guarding the entrance to Hades:

"Ello darling," said T warmly.

"Name Sir, have you got a booking?" She retorted with acid derision.

"I don't need no booking," T objected.

"I'm afraid you do," she mocked with dried –up animosity. Then looking directly at Zhy she added:

"Burger King's only a few doors away."

Zhy smiled sweetly and purred:

"I'm here to eat steak darling."

"Like I say you need a booking," she insisted.

"Chah, go bring out Warren?" Challenged T.

"Warren who?" She asked.

"Warren Sous Chef," he rebutted.

T then started reeling off names of various staff members and she called for the Maitre D.

"I never turn anyone away from my house now I'm coming to their house and look at how they treat me so shameful."

"Quite unacceptable," added Tim.

At that point, hearing the raised voices the Maitre D bustled out of the dining room to diffuse the stony atmosphere and arrange a table for T pronto.

"There's been a dreadful, misunderstanding hasn't there." He gave a scathing look at the receptionist who remained dour and inattentive.

"I suggest you apologize to the lovely Zhy for that uncalled for remark and to T for causing him such great inconvenience."

"I'm very sorry Zhy, Tony, please accept my apologies for this unfortunate error on my part," she said with inimical antagonism.

"You're going to have free drinks and anything you want to eat on the house," the Maitre D added in a soothing tone.

T was immediately seated without further issue.

They studied the menu. When their waiter came along T asked for:

"Chabliss, to begin with."

"Do you mean Chablis Sir the s is silent?" Asked the waiter with graceless ignorance.

"What I mean is Chabliss and I want the biggest bottle get mi?" Replied T indignantly.

"Yes Sir and what would you like as an appetizer Sir."

"Fois Gras," triumphed T with a procacious grin.

"And you madam?" Asked the waiter.

"Caviar," responded Zhy with glee.

Tim opted for the roast beef salad and Bernie chose the squid. For the main they went for lamb, burgers and liver.

The other diners seemed just as prickly as the reception staff causing T to proclaim in a big voice:

"People here only care about where you're from and who you are not where you're going to which is what counts most."

T got that bluebird feeling everything was going to be just fine.

Chapter 51

"Scoot, I'm sending you to the U.S., man, so you can track down the Capsule machine. There's a guy there, Manny, one of Bessie's contacts who said he could get it at cost price. He's the middle guy for his source in India but the deal's going down in New York. You have to be out of here by Saturday. The guy's flying in from Mumbai on Friday."

"Fucking cool, man. I love New York." "Why the fuck does he get to go to NYC?" said Jimmy Irish. "Because I can fucking trust him to do the job, you get mi?"

He won't be doing no blow, he won't be terrorizing tourists, he won't be messin' any shit up or banging any sorts, he's just goin' to do the deal and get home, right, brov?"

"Right," answered Scoot, lazily swinging his feet in the air. He was relieved to be leaving London, the "Christian" murder, and the psychotic Russians were giving him chronic heartburn. He lost count of how many Gaviscons he had to take and he still felt bad.

"I'm goin' home to pack my bags. When's my flight booked for?"

"Tomorrow, 2.35 p.m., Virgin Atlantic straight into JFK, bro'. Listen, the guy's name is Manny, like I said, and then there's another geezer, Leon, but he may not contact you if Manny gets the goods. Your cab's already booked, there's £5000 cash there, and I even got you some opal fruits, gum, Twix, and Snickers for the airport."

"Thanks, bro."

Chapter 52

Dimple was in the first blush of a celebrity romance. A Bollywood starlet once described in the glitter press as India's answer to Brigitte Bardot, she was currently the main squeeze of debut screenwriter and French heartthrob Andre De Veille. Together they were unquestionably bollylicious, the couple of the moment. Dimple spoke with that strange Mid Atlantic Bollywood drawl, her words curving each syllable like the shape of her boudoir frame.

"I'll have to sort that out with my trainer. I'm only allowed to eat eight grams of carbs a day," she honeyed into the phone. She was wearing a tight emerald green, low cut, bell sleeve silk kimono top. It was embellished, with asymmetric, silver discs and sparkled shamelessly when the light reflected upon it. Dimple was all sequins and smiles. Her unabashed sultriness seducing all who came into contact with her. Today she was meeting an affable and lively tabloid television presenter; more bubblegum kitsch than highbrow intellectual, known on and off the screen as a grotesque flirt, more interested in groping and poking his guests rather than the Q&A sessions now openly slammed as T&A crowd teasers by those in the business.

In the makeup room back stage, Dimple applied her own

heavy kohl eyeliner and dabbed the apples of her cheeks with a blush called "Gilded" by Nars. It was her one and only concession to "real" make up and the only product she ever trusted on her now porcelain face. She had been bleaching her skin for over five years and had finally reached the much-coveted colour of neutral beige: fair enough to cut the East-West Divide. It was, however, very thin and prone to blemish easily from even the slightest irritant. She had agreed to be interviewed by Jerry because his viewing figures were always in the high millions and this was a great chance for her to increase her European fan base and promote her new film. Dimple had other matters on her mind; she was due to attend a celebrity charity ball and was awaiting news of her gown, which had been flown in especially from Paris.

Chapter 53

T had a meet up with Chantal Austin a romantic fortune hunter and general impresario now founder and CEO of *Silver Horse* the only transvestite Escort Agency in the country. T had known Chantal from school days they shared the same history class and when T dropped out Chantal began plaiting her hair, acing her exams and “exploring” her female side. Fast forward to the now and she was one of the biggest names in glamour retail and queen of the trannie circuit. Chantal cut a hot shimmy in body con lycra. She was 6ft tall with a dirty blonde wig, sculpted eyebrows, and cherry red lip-gloss.

She looked like a "Vegas” showgirl in rehab. Today she wore a neon pink jumpsuit and silver kitten heels. She spoke with a RuPaul strut:

“Hi Tonyeeeeeee,” she mewled with an elongated lisp.

“Alright Chantal what’s up?”

“One of my girls got iced.”

“Who?”

“Savannah.” The name was synonymous with shoulder pads and TV shows of the eighties like:

Dallas and *Dynasty* it seemed somewhat out of place in the hardboiled reality of West London.

"She was found with her throat slit and her hands tied. The killer had daubed the walls with her blood and written:

"This is the day of Armageddon when boys will be girls and girls will be boys"

"Ere what come again," T was freaked. He was expecting a link up to high end stolen goods – a deal on party dresses or designer handbags possibly a piece of bizarre prostitution but no here was the first lady of glitz talking murder and blood curses.

"Ere what mi say that's nasty, so evil- it's bad."

"Yeah Tonyeeeee really grossed me out."

"How can I help?" He asked his loyalty to his friend bridging the he- she gap between them.

"Well I need you to put someone on the team full time, I've been working from the inside trying to find out which of our clients could be fucked up enough to do something like this but no leads yet. It could have been a rival from another agency, you know like real women if it was we have to get rid. Someone like that doesn't deserve to live. Savannah was one of the highest earners on my books. Recently, she came into a lot of money when a punter left her everything in his will. The bottom line is I don't feel safe anymore T. I want protection."

"Agreed."

"How much is it gonna cost me?"

"I can fix it for around £3000 a week no one will touch you they'll know you're under my protection."

"That's reasonable T I can pull that."

"So how is bizzo otherwise?" Asked T curiously.

"Yeah we make a lot of money from a specific clientele, upscale, very discreet with limited numbers but loaded to the hilt."

"Yeah all them types, like all that kind of kinky stuff."

"Yes they do honeeeeey."

T was very liberal minded but couldn't bring himself to kiss Chantal when she swooped in for the shot, instead he put his hand out shyly and she shook it warmly with a flash of gratitude.

Chapter 54

Godwin was in a purple fog. He was probably the same age as Tim but had none of his palsy walsy appeal or intelligent swagger. He was however, intensely loyal trustworthy and reliable; qualities he felt Tim was lacking. As he busied himself in the domesticities of the day, he spied him in the bathroom getting laced on T's private stash.

He charged at him like a stampeding elephant.

"What you do that for Tim?" He trumpeted with bullish ferocity.

"What you doing get off me – un handle me now this instant!" Tim mooed.

"What what's that you say ?"

"I said off me."

T had only stepped out for a quick bite to eat he would be back any moment but Godwin wouldn't release Tim forcing him to the ground then grabbing both his arms and legs in an iron grip.

Tim was bashed down, his sickly body, moth eaten and vulnerable as Godwin raised him on his haunches like a butchering carcass.

A small crowd had gathered in the street below to observe the stewing brouhaha.

T returned to find Tim dangling precariously from the open window.

"What the fuck are you fools up to" He groused.

"You can't even be left alone for two minutes this is like bull crap. Godwin bring him down now."

"No Boss he was stealing from you man, he don't pay no rent, he don't pay for the gear and he was taking it man your special reserve selection from your bathroom man I couldn't have him stealing from the boss."

"Please Godwin bring him down there's people watching the window man and soon the old bill will be on their way you want for the boss to go inside – just bring him down."

After leaving him to sweat it out for a few more seconds Godwin pulled him inside.

"Now look you're both pension style age and it's not right to be having these kinds of fights. Godwin don't worry about mi okay ,I know Tim is here and he's good for our bizzo and that's it. You be two fully grown men and I find you like this, trying to mash each other up and cause trouble for mi." Scowled T ,giving them both a black look.

"I was tryin' to help Boss he was takin' your stuff," persisted Godwin, unrepentant and sticking to his guns he felt like he should be the only senior figure of the crew.

"I is the only elder in this village. Boss has saved my life and he tried to ruin it I will not take it Boss he is a bad man."

"It's cool Godwin chill out . Nobody is trying to take your position away Tim is only here to help us that's all." He shook his head and sighed :

"Now you had better behave or I'll throw you both out chah idiots."

He smiled walking over to his phone whilst piping the lyrics to the *Black Eyed Peas* song *Where is the Love.*

It was a bumbling skit shaved with good intentions and unswerving devotion. T felt valued.

The rest of the day fell away with a yawn.

Chapter 55

Tony was needed in New York City to close the contract on the capsule maker, as Manny wanted to be sure that the agreement was solid and T was his primary source of communication. T had hoped that Scoot would be able to deal with the negotiations alone but Manny had sent word that he wanted him there for security. This was the first time T was travelling alone. Bernie was busy firming up deals and managing their other investments and the rest of the crew couldn't be trusted. T Needed a passport and an alias, he made a beeline for the *Bullet and Blade* in Upper Street Islington. You could get almost anything there: guns, passports, counterfeit cash, and a shiny new identity. Tony called the owner from his mobile:

"Yo bro, it's T- listen how are you man? Haven't seen you in a long time y'ar know?"

Big laughs and buoyant chuckles followed.

"Yeah I know – yeah man that was funny man…funny times."

"Yeah so you know what I need? - Yeah what- you want your boy to sing? 'Ere what mi say he sings like a lickle song bird sweet man is you serious?"

Scully the owner, had agreed to supply T with everything he needed: Passport, Driving License National Insurance Number- the lot provided he gave his son a Record Deal with Alex, Bernie's cousin. Tony couldn't refuse.

Once inside the bar, the lights were dimmed and the nervous audience made up of suits, corporate fraud heads, small time mobsters, yardies, coke sluts and tabloid glitterati sat expectantly for Josh, Scully's seventeen-year-old kid to "hit the light fantastic." He was a ginger haired, freckle faced yob, a dead ringer for Ritchie Cunningham on the classic TV show *Happy Days.* When he stepped up to the mike and opened his mouth, it sounded like a rutting cat. First a long sour wail followed by a squally yelp. He kept thrusting his arms forward and prodding the air. The pained expression on his face didn't help either, making him look like a constipated newt. It was klutzy, uncoordinated and slapstick funny. Everyone in the pub squirmed uneasily in their seats trying to fake enthusiasm. After a torturous fifteen minutes of the extended version of "*Yellow*" by Cold Play it finally stopped. Scully spoke with glowing pride:

"Wanna here another Tone? 'Es got another song which he wrote the lyrics to hiself...yeah it's about his pet goldfish Hannibal, ain't it Josh?"

Before Josh could screech out another word, Tony responded with artful diplomacy:

"No no man. That...what he did jus then, the Chris Martin song, that was unique man- you know I've never heard anything like that and he was feeling it man. You could see it in his face.. He was feeling it – the feeling was real man. I never heard nothing like that before man...totally unique."

After Tony started clapping vigorously, everyone else sheepishly followed. A couple of blockheads stood up and wolf-whistled for more Tony put his hand up to silence them.

"I've heard enough for now man- all I need when you got such a different sound y'ar know? What I mean...he should go and rest up that voice of his with a liccle bit of lemon some honey- keep that throat in top condition- the boy's a star man he's fresh. I'll make sure Bernie speaks to Alex about him and Bernie will book him into the studio to lay some tracks down."

"Yeah my boy's a fuckin' star," waxed Scully boozed up on brandy and smack. Tony didn't need any agro' with Scully who called out to Rambo a dreadlocked Rasta to go deal with T's request. Rambo led T downstairs to a closed off basement at the back of the pub. There, he would have his photo taken and fake papers would be drawn up. A digital camera and blue screen was all that was required for the alias to be created.

Tony was charmingly meticulous about his appearance and wanted to make the right impression for his picture. He carefully knelt down to tie his shoelaces, thinking they would be in the shot for the photo.

"You won't see your shoes man- it's just head and shoulders," explained Rambo.

"Cha...head and shoulders...isn't that some dandruff shampoo? Mi not have dandruff you being' facety Rambo bwouy!" asked T jokingly.

"Yeah very funny man- look they don't need your whole self just head and shoulders."

"You got a mirror man?"

"You don't need no mirror T."

"I just need to straighten up mi tie make miself look buff and ting me want to look good for the picture y'ar know."

"All you need to do is stand straight man, look across mi shoulders when I say."

"I want a nice picture man."

"You'll get one don't worry everything will be ju-st fine okay now ready?"

"Yeah man."

Tony pulled a big cheesy grin. It looked like a mug shot from a spoof edition of BBC's *Crimewatch.*

"Hey man that's not natural. Ee'll have to do it again. No smiling, okay? Just be natural...your face has to fit the dimensions for the passport to look genuine. It has to fit exactly so no smiling."

"Cha what you talkin' about man? Mi looks cris, chill y'ar know me looks radical and nice chah."

"Yeah man that's fine but your picture has to fit into a specific space d'ya get mi?"

"Yeah yeah bwouy yu sa facety!"

"Okay so let's try this again- stand up straight and look past mi shoulders when I say okay?"

"Yeah man."

Tony smoothed his hair down with Dax and a tortoiseshell comb, looking directly ahead.

"After three okay?"

"Yeah meh got it okay,"

Well it wasn't *Snappy Snaps* but it was just as good. Eventually, after about twenty minutes, the picture was ready.

"Paperwork will be done in a day or so...send someone to get it yeah?"

"Yeah man thanks."

"No worries bro."

Chapter 56

Richard was being watched and Bessie was being watched. Poncho had more eyes than a red octopus has tentacles. Every second of every day they were getting closer to their wasted tomorrows. Living in purgatorial blindness, soon they would be hit harder than a scale six quake.

Tony, Jimmy Irish, and Vinnie were all playing a computer game, "Grand Theft Auto." It was about stealing cars. Bernie was sulking in a corner by himself reading The Daily Mirror and Godwin was busying himself in the kitchen, preparing the chicken for the afternoon meal.

"The orders are coming in thick and fast for the natural highs, bizzo man. We can't meet demand if we don't get that capsule maker soon," complained Bernie.

"It's sorted. Don't worry. Scoot is meeting wif the main man tomorrow or the day after and then it will take a few more days for the machine to be sent over," replied Tony without looking up from the game. He put his phone on vibrate.

"Luke says the new Kensington offices are ready so we'll have to make arrangements to move everything there soon," went on Bernie.

"Yeah, we don't need to take much, just the computers

and shit."

"Any news on Christian's body?" Tony looked over to Bernie, his head still buried in his paper.

"Nothing, brov, but I 'eard from 'is sister and she says the family want to take him back to Australia sharpish for a proper ceremony and shit."

"I fuckin' miss 'im, man."

"We all do, bro', why don't you go and see Scoot's old dear 'e told me to keep a look out for 'er while 'e was gone."

"Yeah I'll go take 'er some flowers."

"Yeah, you go wiv 'im, man." Tony made a face at Vinnie, who seemed reluctant to accompany Bernie anywhere, especially all the way to Dulwich to see Scooter's mother.

Just then, Bessie called.

"Listen, T, I got something fucking amazing; this is fucking huge, man, fucking A1. I need to talk to you, bro. This is heavy, heavy diamond shit, man."

"Look, brov, I'm gettn' out of this game. I'm winding down. I'm set with a legit business now, the capsule making *Natural Highs*. I'm trying to cut all that other shit out now, brov."

"Listen, T, this is the fuckin' bollocks and will set you, your family, their family, and their family times ten after and beyond for life, man, for fuckin' life. But we got to move quickly, man, we got to jump now."

Tony was more than used to Bessie's histrionic way of talking. Nearly every deal he was involved in was bigger than the BT Tower and he was always going on about how much money he could make. He sounded different this time. There was something urgent in his voice, almost evangelical. Still, Tony was reluctant to get involved with him and his harebrained schemes. He wasn't sure about him, not sure at all. Although T was a drug dealer, you knew where you were with him; he could be trusted.

But Bessie, he was like that snake "Kaa" in the movie *Jungle Book*, always looking for more.

"I'll see you at Tin Pan Alley as soon as but I'm warning you, man, don't fuck with me, Bessie. I ain't makin' no promises."

Chapter 57

Scoot checked into the Bryant Hotel, a study in modern luxury. It was discreet and tastefully furnished. Suitably rock and roll, with a slice of old world elegance thrown in. He ordered a light bar snack and some rum and coke. He held the bartender's eye for a full sixty seconds. She was dressed in a short black skirt with long black boots. Her blouse, white and tight-fitting with just one button concealing her pert, tanned breasts. She had freckles on her nose and across her chest. She looked around twenty-two, probably "studying" to become an actress. Scoot was surprised at just how many New Yorkers were pursuing acting careers.

The women who'd dropped him off at the hotel were at drama school, the door guys at the front of the building were in between jobs for acting assignments, and even the bell boy was taking time out to "method." Scoot thought this was all bollocks. The bartenders, the limo driver, the waitresses, and the club hosts were just that. Why did they always pretend to be something else, something they thought was better?

"Hi, I'm Scooter, British film director..." but he was unable to finish his sentence. The waitress awoke as if from a methadone sleep and squealed: "Oh really, yeah? Loooooove your accent by the way. It's sooooo cute. I'm an actress, my name's Cindy Bartels, and I do just about anything and everything. I can do like classic, modern." Scoot had stopped listening; the glib sales patter had surprised even him. The girl was like a smiling android on bad ketamine. She had probably rehearsed those lines a hundred times a day and now everyone was tired of hearing it.

"What are your plans right now?" he went on.

"Oh, I can leave here in like a few minutes. I can get..." Scoot hated this type of pitiful hypocrisy more than he hated people with acute halitosis or people with unnatural race intolerance. It made him physically sick. He had more respect for working prostitutes who were refreshingly honest and uncomplicated. Disgusted, he moved to a lounge table and failed to spot the slug-like creep who grabbed one opposite him.

Suddenly, everyone's gaze was directed at a large open window. Several patrons of the restaurant had gathered round and there was a general air of commotion and noise. Cindy, freed from the confines of the bar, was boldly resplendent in her oversexed glory. She looked every inch a "Penthouse Pet." For a brief moment, Scoot imagined her without any clothes on, but then the braying squawk choked him back to reality. He moved closer to the open window.

Staring at the crowd, her face white like a Kabuki dancer because of the glare of the helicopter lights overhead, was a completely naked black woman on the roof of the adjacent building. She looked peaceful in a semi-conscious way and was utterly unaware of the high- level security risk she posed to herself and the crowd below her. She swayed precariously in the soft night air, waving her arms above her tall, lithe body:

"It's okay," she kept saying. "I'm only high." Her voice trailed into the distance as an armed police officer lifted her to safety. Scoot felt sorry for her and wished the crowd hadn't been so intrusive. One of the diners muttered something about "typical Afro American behaviour for a Saturday night." *Years of prejudice would be hard to erase*, Scoot thought, and he returned to his table. In the seat nearby, sat Pavlov (the slug).

He appeared to be drinking a pint glass of milk. He looked around him in a sly, furtive manner. He checked his watch and moved slowly to the old style retro Juke Box and pumped the machine with seven quarters: Frank Sinatra, Dean Martin, Elvis, Cole Porter, and Lady Day. It was a choice selection and hit the right note on the bar's sombre atmosphere. Nothing like a bunch of tourists singing along to Sinatra to put everyone in a happy mood.

Dressed in a sports jacket and open-necked Ralph Lauren shirt, he was "casual smart," wearing Diesel Jeans that were ripped at the knee and filled in with denim squares. He still looked like a slug. It was the shape of his head and his unusually tall stature that made him loop like a slug; that and the way his eyes were drawn so close together.

As the songs came on, Pavlov sneaked closer to him.

"Let me buy you a drink. I overheard you talking to the waitress. You're British, aren't you?"

"Thanks, yeah, over here for a couple of days seeing the sights, and what sights there are to see. So what will you have?" "I feel like a Jack and Coke."

"Good choice. If I was a drinker I'd probably choose that." Cindy came by and took their orders.

"I used to live in London a long time ago when I was promoting fighters, boxers."

"Oh right, yeah."

"It would be a personal pleasure to me if you let me show you what the Big Apple has to offer. I had some good times in London and would enjoy taking you round."

This was not unusual in New York. Scoot had already been asked for his number and to do drinks with at least five random strangers in the space of an afternoon. They agreed to meet the next day at Jimmy's Bar on 46th and Broadway.

He checked his messages: two from his mother, one from Tony, and one from Manny. He'd call Manny first.

Chapter 58

Bessi was waiting to be buzzed in when he saw Bernie and Vinnie coming out of the door.

"All right?" he greeted them both.

"Is T expecting you, mate?"

"Yeah, look, I'm runnin' late somewhere else. Could you just make sure he gets this package? I want 'im to look after it for me."

Bessie had remembered he had left his cooker on high, and though he only lived minutes away, he wasn't about to take a risk over a fire. He left the sealed package containing the Bond, the key, and the coordinates with Bernie who trotted upstairs and left it with Godwin while T was in the bath. When T came out he found Piez Lerue there, the former Editor of a "lads mag" and subject of a BBC 2 "fly on the wall documentary."

He was in a punch up mood and wanted to get wasted. Apparently his girlfriend Ellie had publicly humiliated him about his "sexual prowess" or lack thereof on the show; now a ratings winner. The whole country had been transfixed by the low budget programme, entertaining British viewers with inside secrets of their "bedroom" antics. Bosses at the *Beeb* had indicated the show was right for international syndication so now

Lerue would be famous for all the wrong reasons. Piez appeared at the flat prettified in a floral shirt and blue jeans throwing out riff raff phrases as if he were a an East End Rebel. He was "mockney stupid" and sounded dull and clichéd. Around his neck he wore the emblem of hate the distinctive "Iron Cross" of the "Wehrmacht" An obvious expression of Nazi sympathy and not tolerated by anyone in the room.

"What the fuck are you doing here with *that* on your neck you fucking fascist" Bernie screeched with revulsion.

"It's an example of my avant- garde fashion style," he replied with jumped up chutzpah I place no significance on what it represents or what means I just like the way it looks, an expression of my trend spotting taste."

"The fuck it is!" Laughed Bernie.

"Any minute now Markie Mark is rolling by, come to pick up some gear for himself and his new girlfriend Ellie your ex right?"

"What they're coming over here now?" He groaned.

"Yeah Markie Mark, you may recall is 6ft 2 looks like The Incredible Hulk and Tiger Woods: that charismatic blend of he man and sports god then there's you in your fucked up flower blouse and a Nazi necklace. I think you'd better take it off now Nazi cunt."

Bernie was outraged at the spunky nerve of Lerue and his lack of feeling.

"I can wear what the fuck I like" He griped.

"The fuck you can!" exclaimed Bernie.

Just then Markie Mark and Ellie entered the flat staring at Lerue as if he were a croaking dung beetle.

"I'm only going to ask you once to remove that ugly chain

from your crusted neck you brainless gimp" scowled Markie Mark.

"No" Lerue protested.

Markie Mark reached over and held him in a bear lock.

"Take it off him!"

Ellie, centre- fold hot, with a painted smile ripped it off with stylish verve.

They left him blubbering in the corner like rotting bile. Godwin was in a dismal mood convinced that all this negativity had to do with the lay lines of the original site of the flat. According to his "internet research," it was built on the site of a medieval burial ground where victims of smallpox, the bubonic plague and witchcraft had fallen to their deaths.

"This is the house of the devil," he rattled with disillusion it's a fool's paradise.

What you babbling on about now?" asked T wearily.

"The Nazi boy came here and the bad stuff comes because this used to be where witches and small pox and the plague was," he whinged.

"Then there was that schizo who kept making those devil gestures."

"What? Who you talking about now Godwin?" pumped Bernie.

Godwin was new to typically English humour and a few days ago in a coke- stupor a young actor had been imitating a great British Comic, Tommy Cooper. Cooper was a superb stand up who had perfected a trick with a light bulb. He would rummage around in his pocket and bring out a light bulb setting it down on some antique measuring scales "Light bulb" he would announce casually then, bring out another light bulb putting it in the opposite end making the scales rise and fall, "heavy bulb," he would state with deadpan sagacity. Joe Doxon the thespian hanging out at T's never actually had the light bulbs or the scales to demonstrate the trick but attempted it anyway.

Using his hands, to illustrate the "heavy bulb" and "light bulb" he raised and lowered his arms. Godwin was jangled with fright, watching him move his hands up and down in an inspired contortion as if he were an extra from *The Exorcism of Emily Rose*. Godwin suffered hallucinations and alleged visitations from the "six demons" and insisted that Joe was calling the devil to the flat. As the actor had also appeared in the film *"The Mummy"* he was positive the flat was haunted and plagued with evil.

"That man using his hands to call the devil in here puts his arms up as if he's having a demon fit."

"That *Emily Rose* movie is based on a real movie, man about a girl what gets possessed by the devil and that Joe was making all these jagged movements just like she do in the film man it's like a monster. For five days I been thinking of the poses he makes and then comparing it to the signs in the movie and he raise up his arm and lowers his arm just like she do."

"Yeah that's a trick, Godwin a famous joke Tommy Cooper did, he was a well known comic. Joe never had no light bulbs so he put his hand up for "heavy bulb" and his hand down for "light bulb." Reassured Bernie. Not quite believing he was, actually forced to explain this vaudeville classic to Godwin who was hooked on the idea that Joe was raising up evil spirits.

"Look, I know about these things trust me Godwin no demons here." He spoke with certainty.

"What nonsense fool this flat also used to be the former offices of EMI and where you're sitting now they made Beatle records so all your jibber jabber about demons and possession is just bad karma. They had John Paul and Ringo in here to squish out those evil curses and demon crap. *All you need is love love love is all you need,"* fluted T sweetly.

Chapter 59

Outside Mrs. Calibresi's home, one of Poncho's hitters was lurking about, looking for leads. Bernie and Vinnie were pulling up the driveway when they spied "Electrical Harry," so named because he had a way with electrics and explosives. Concerned about Mrs. Calibresi's safety, they immediately called Tony, who told them to "sort it out," but electrical Harry had already entered the house.

"It's about your boy,"

"What about him?"

"He owes me a casino debt and I've come to collect."

He's not here, he's in America. Now get the hell out of my home before I throw you out."

"Now, now, no need to get upset. When will he be back?"

"Get the hell out." He reached over and grabbed her small hand.

"It would be a shame if I had to cut these off," he sneered. Mrs. Calibresi wrenched her hand free and placed it flat on the table.

"That'll make it easier for you. There you are, pick your finger." She spat at him and cursed him in Sicilian. Bernie and Vinnie had snuck through the back door of the conservatory. They crept up behind Harry, who fell and hit his head on the kitchen chair. Mrs. Calibresi, recognizing Bernie and Vinnie, swung forward with a rolling pin in her hand, lashing out at the startled thug now bruised battered and being sworn at by all three.

"All right, okay, I'm leaving. I'm not looking for any trouble I was just trying to collect on an old debt."

"Listen, get the fuck out, and don't come back," snarled Bernie.

"Don't let on the old dear beat me up wif a rolling pin."

"Get out of it, come on out." Bernie and Vinnie escorted him to the door.

"This ain't what you think. It's bigger," he said quietly, then left. Mrs. Calibresi could hold her own; she wasn't scared of anyone, even Poncho.

Chapter 60

"Tony it's Richard. We need to talk, man, it's serious. Look, I screwed up. I'm in some heavy shit and I need your help."

"Meet me at Café Boeheme in five minutes. Your shit has already left a nasty trail and is heading straight for me. I'm not happy about this, Richard. This is BULL SHIT. I'm tryin' to get out of this business and you land this fuckery on my lap. It's not fair Richard. You've known me since I was a fuckin' baby, man. You went your way and I had to go mine. I even said you should stay away from me but it turns out you're in even deeper than me with heavy hard shit."

"I'll explain it all when I see you." Richard had no time for this sentimental mush Tony lived on. At the end of the night, it was black and white: everyone for themselves.

When he got there, Richard scoured the small patisserie: dead souls and shrunken talent is what he saw.

"Let's go upstairs, man."

The nauseating reality of a grimy Thursday evening made his flesh crawl.

"It's better to talk down here," insisted T.

"Fine, look, I need a favour, man. I need you to ask around and find out who did my uncle's place over."

Tony looked at Richard with an icy, disapproving stare.

"Your uncle's place has been done over?" he enquired in disbelief.

"I was holding something for a criminal client. If I don't get it back for him, I'll be in serious trouble."

"I'll see what I can do." They left together in silence.

Chapter 61

Eva had never been to New York before. She had seen it lots of times on television and of course in: *Sex and The City*, the television show that was set in Manhattan, but when Richard had given her a week off, she knew that's where she'd go. Three days there and then maybe LA. She was looking forward to going shopping at Bergdorf Goodman and Bloomingdales and wanted to check out all the bars and clubs, too. She had travelled with her fiancé Serge. They were booked at the Paramount, one of the hippest hotels in the city. She wore open toed, diamond- heeled Jimmy Choo mules and a Temperley dress that draped around her like a second skin, cut in soft waterfall fronds that curved and buffeted her every move.

She waited at the bar for Serge and ordered her first cocktail of the evening: a strawberry Margarita. Serge appeared soon after. He had left the hotel to get some shoe polish. It had cost a hefty fifteen dollars inside, but was only three bucks in the local Duane Reade. Dressed in a Richard James shirt, calfskin leather brogues, and Ermengilda Zena suit, he was supremely dapper with that artless East End charm Eva loved.

Their dinner reservations were for 8:00 p.m., then they were going either to B-lo or 40:40 for some club action. Serge put his hand on Eva's knee; he enjoyed handling her in public. He liked the feeling that she belonged to him and kissed her full on the lips, his tongue caressing the inside of her mouth. Eva drew closer to him until she was almost touching him, their eyes locked as he fingered her beneath the table, his hands gently tugging at her soft, silky G. She felt his hand slide through the material until he felt her warm and sweet, his hand slowly moving back and forth. He loved the taste of Eva. She was a perfect ten.

A group of loud New Yorkers woke them from their erotic daze: six women seated around them, all different and yet all the same. Big smiles, red lipstick, fashionable hairstyles, and fake tans and nails: NYC BARBIE. In fact, they seemed a little scary to Serge; "plastic fantastic," it was the super set of bright whites that did it. Their smiles were definitely bigger than their bodies. Serge looked away quickly.

As Eva and Serge stepped into the starry Manhattan night, Eva wanted to walk a little, even if she was wearing shoes that cost £300. They went straight ahead, then turned left out of the hotel onto Times Square. As they stepped across the lights, Eva caught her shoe heel on a loose paving slab. Scoot coming from the opposite direction near The Rockefeller Centre on 7th Avenue, stopped to see if he could be of any help. Serge managed to get her free and then she tripped again, falling into his arms with Scoot watching by her side confused and bewildered.

She had collapsed into a tiny bundle of blood, glitz and heels.

"What the fuck, Jesus H. Christ, get down, get down," shrieked Serge.

"Everyone get the fuck down."

One solitary gunfire shot had ripped open the Manhattan

skyline and mottled the night air red. It was a horrifying sight to behold, like a Damien Hirst installation without the safety of Perspex. Eva's beautiful corpse lay slumped in Serge's arms, her still warm body drenched with blood and her face contorted with fear. Serge was badly shaken. He started to cry, howling like a whimpering animal, deadening the shock of the crowd that had gathered around him.

"She's not breathing," he bawled. "She's gone, gone."

Scoot got an onlooker to call 911, the emergency services, and then decided to get back to his hotel after making sure Serge was okay. He'd never met him before, but knew he was from Britain and thought he might ask if he needed anything.

"I'm really sorry, mate. Look, she may be all right. You don't know yet wait until the ambulance gets here. Just keep believing. I'm staying at the Bryant hotel, the number's on the back. If you need anything, anything at all just give me a bell," he said warmly.

"Yeah, yeah, thanks, thanks for that," said Serge in between sobs.

As a driving cascade of peach and white petals tumbled to the ground in a *Millais* echo Scoot knew that Eva wouldn't make it through and could only hope that he was wrong. He had no inkling the shot was intended for him.

Chapter 62

Manny had been selling capsule makers for months now all over the world and his best source was the man they called the "chief" from Mumbai. He had the best capsule making machines in the business. Tony had found him through one of Bessie's old connections and he seemed to have the knowledge. He also told Tony that he could get it at cost price so they would be quids in. Tony had given him all of Scooter's contact details in NYC and told him to arrange the deal.

Earlier that day, Manny had a visit from Pavlov, who had asked him to keep him in the loop about the deal, as he was looking out for his boss's interests. Manny agreed. After all, Pavlov had paid him ten thousand bucks. It was a sweet transaction.

"Hi Manny. It's Scoot from London."

"Yo, dude, whassup, how's it hangin?"

"Yeah, good, except I saw someone get fuckin' blasted today, man."

"What the fuck? Are you kiddin', man?"

"No, serious, man. She got shot down right in the middle of Time Square on West 45th."

"Fuck, man. Yo, where you wanna meet up, bro?"

"What about Jimmy's Corner?"

"Cool place, man, that's 140West 44th ride?"

"Yeah, be there around 10:00 p.m."

"See you there. I'll be the one wearing an Ali T shirt."

Scoot made a quick call to Tony, who was glad to hear he was okay and didn't tell him about his mother or Richard but warned him to be extra careful and not to trust anyone. He thought he sounded different, tight and wound up. He spoke briefly to his mother, who wanted to know why a Russian-sounding woman of around forty-five had turned up at the house looking for him and had to be forcibly removed by a neighbour. Scoot cringed. *God, why wouldn't that crazy slapper leave him the fuck alone*? He told his mother not to worry about anything and got ready to meet Manny.

Chapter 63

Bessie was feeling fucking good. He'd been snorting *charlie* all night and most of the day. He was going to show that wanker Poncho that he wasn't anyone's bitch. He was insulted that he thought he could be bought so easily. With Tony and his contacts, they could make that bitch cunt pay for his Bond. If he wanted it back, he'd have to cough up.

He decided to grab a snack before heading over to Tony's place, so he thought he'd swing by the local Burger King. In the queue he asked for a Double Whopper, fries, and onion rings, and after a few moments collected his order. Behind him were throngs of people jostling about. Then he felt it, like a searing burning sensation right under his spine. His eyes clouded over; everything was a blur. The last thing he saw was the startled gaze of a small child as he collapsed in a writhing mess on the floor. People were screaming: "Someone's been knifed, dial 999!" The restaurant was locked down; just another stabbing in Tottenham Court Road.

Chapter 64

T was in a blue mood, his open reflections on the isolation of his life floating like Jazz notes under a pink moon. He needed to take care of some family matters before leaving for New York.

"Mum-it's me." He hollered from the driveway, which was crowded with spring flowers and clusters of herbs. She came to the door quickly, dressed in loungewear with a neat bun and *mumsi* smile.

"Oh Tony dear boy come in – so much is going on is everything alright?"

"I need some advice." He had known Scoot and his family his whole life. Mrs. Calibresi welcomed him as her second son. Along with Richie they were childhood friends.

"Sit down, sit down I'll make you some Vongole with the special sauce you like."

"I'm goin' to New York doin' the deal – I want to get out for good mum, straighten everything out and make things work. I want to take care of everyone mum d'ya get mi?" Tony paused and shot a look of tender devotion at her.

"What's wrong Tony?" She asked softly.

"I need to make sure Amber is safe that she goes to the right school, y'ar know? That she gets a good education and ting. I don't want Amber getting in with troublemakers and rough neck thugs. I don't want her around people....well people like mi, y'ar know? I want to be a good father and I want Amber to grow up nice, like a lady. I need you to get mi the proper schools, boarding schools – the best ones she can go to and I want you to be her legal guardian, y'ar know? Just in case like if anyfing should ever happen to mi, I don't trust that slag bitch mother of hers she's using' Amber to get money out of mi."

Mrs. Calibresi shook her head ruefully.

"But I'm so old now Tony. You need a younger person like one of your more educated friends."

"No mum they're all rotting on cocaine or hammered on drink."

Mrs. Calibresi shrugged her over burdened shoulders feeling the weight of responsibility close in on her like a choking noose.

"I'm physically not up to it T...look, I've got rheumatism, arthritis, bad knees, hypertension. I might not have much time myself."

Tony jumped to his feet and embraced her, shrouding her weakened body.

"You'll always be around mum, forever."

"Nice sentiment T but not one shared by God above," she sighed.

"Who then – who will we get to look after Amber?"

"I'll think about it, someone decent, and someone we can trust Amber won't suffer," Mrs. Calibresi replied calmly.

"I've got £70,000 here I'm leaving it with you for Amber."

He stooped down to get his brown leather attaché case.

"T, this too much money for me to keep here. Where will I put it?"

"Mum I trust you- to keep it for Amber- please just take it I trust you."

"What's brought all this on T what's wrong?"

"I'm flying next week y'ar know it's good to take care of tings."

"Yes you said – you're going to New York for the capsule deal."

"First time mum first time I'll be on mi own just got a feeling a hunch it's nothing mum I just wouldn't want Amber to be ..."

He stopped.

"I just don't want Amber to ever be alone like mi."

Silly boy you're not alone you have me and everyone in this family. I'll make sure she gets looked after properly T best schools and good people around her."

"I'm gonna make Richie put it in a will and stuff so the slag bitch can't cause trouble."

"Okay dear."

"It's all I can ask for mum, all I can hope for, y'ar know? A better life for Amber that she turns out good and has respect for who she is. I never asked for this life I never thought it would be this way ..."

"It's alright T it's okay don't fret now come on and eat your Vongole before it gets cold or then you'll see what kind of life you'll have upsetting me by not finishing your meal! Come on now eat up."

Chapter 65

Poncho was in a red mood slanging with rage and needed to cook himself out of it. Poncho had a whale of an appetite and when he felt stressed he liked to cook and eat and eat some more. Right now, he felt like a homemade Masala chicken that would ease his lashing temper. He set about preparing the dish with maniacal insanity while shoving handfuls of salted peanuts down his gullet and slurping ice cold *Fanta.* He looked like the *Swedish Chef* from the Muppets as he bobbed about the kitchen in a starched white apron. The ingredients for this inviting feast were resting on a sliver side tray divided into little sections each one filled with exotic spices: Garam Masala, crystal sea salt and delicate fronds of pure saffron. He took the breast of chicken from his stainless steel Bosch Fridge.

Thereafter, he started to season the meat with crushed garlic, salt finely chopped chilies olive oil, and spices. He placed them neatly on a baking tray lined with tin foil and put them under a pre- heated grill. As he waited for the meat to cook he paced the room bellowing on his LG mobile, intermittently breaking off the conversation from Urdu to English. He was swearing in both languages waving his hands around like a frenzied crossing guard at a railway station. Then, the ping of the oven timer. The food was ready. Now he would eat. He immediately dropped the call and placed the freshly cooked chicken on a serving plate with some steamed Basmati rice and salty Indian side salad of tomatoes, green chilies fresh onion, and coriander. It was called "katchumber" and one of his favourites.

Poncho was loath to use violence as a way of forcing his hand but understood that the threat alone of brute force was sometimes not enough to make things go his way. He ate noisily with an operatic gusto relishing every bite. With his appetite now satisfied to excess, he took his mobile again and started cussing in Urdu making a fist and clenching his teeth:

"Don't fuck with me you moron fuck- may you be stewed and boiled by a high fever you son of a dog you stupid fuck so when I say fuck off I mean now..." It got worse:

"His *lulla* (dick) is mine you joker his *lulla* is mine." He hurled the phone on the table and shouted for Mack:

"Mack! Mack! Here- now!" He delivered the command with canine authority.

"Yes Sir Mr. Poncho yes Sir." In came Mack frog footed and terrified.

"I want you to take care of this slime donkey; he thinks he can show me a thing or two. I'll now teach him who he's dealing with."

He reached into a drawer pulled on some industrial strength sterile latex gloves then handed him a picture of Richard with a full bio' sheet, a James Noble hunting knife and a Berretta 22. It was gun time and Poncho was on the prowl for dead meat.

Chapter 66

Tony was supremely superstitious. He always entered a room with his right foot first, when he saw a rubbish cart in the street he would treat it as a sign of good luck, he never walked under ladders and had an illogical fear of being haunted by a "jumbie" or a "duppie." In West Indian folklore, this expression was used, to describe ghosts or supernatural beings. He believed strongly in "karma" and didn't like strangers staring at him for too long in case they gave him the "evil eye" Unlike Bernie however, he stayed away from dark forces and the Occult. As he approached the BA Ticket Desk, he was convinced that an old man he had accidentally bumped into earlier had "hexed" him with an evil spell. Tony never knew the man but viewed the whole incident with distrust and kept a watchful eye on the people around him. He was uneasy about the fact that he had no control over his flight, or how long the journey would take. In the departure lounge, he stocked up on sugared sweets and chocolate bars to take his mind off it and waited quietly for his gate number to be called.

Chapter 67

In the world of: *Big Macs, Starbucks* coffee and oversized SUV's, it was business as usual: *snort and go*. Scoot and Manny were sampling the delights of some top- drawer cocaine. It had been delivered to them with the help of digital know how via a text link on a computer terminal giving them elaborate codes for timing, drop off and who would call. It was as if they were ordering Chinese takeout. Coke to go this was cool, A faceless smooth efficient way to do bizzo.

"This is quality this," enthused Scoot. "T would love all this technology but he's getting out of this, now we're going au natural."

"Totally the way forward dude – herbal pills lots of thrills."

"Hey that rhymes."

"I know, what time does Tony's flight get in?"

"Around 6.00 pm I think. The lawyer Fred has sent car service for him."

"Good so he should get here by around 7.30pm. We can go have dinner and spin the wheel then talk all that stuff."

"Sounds like a plan Stan."

"Okay so the rhyming is getting lame."

"No I think it's pretty cool man."

"Hey, in years to come you'll be able to get coke on line – just a friggin' mouse click away."

"Everything's on line now man that's the future right there that's what it's all about you know."

"Yeah here in the US, man in this like techno age, you can live your whole life on line you can shop, eat, date, hell you can even get married and make funeral arrangements on line."

"The land of gateways and firewalls."

"Everyone's switched on man."

Manny and Scoot were waiting for T to land discussing life, the universe, and the size of Jenna Jameson's implants.

They were snowballed – just another Monday commute into orbit.

Chapter 68

Four hours into the flight after ordering three mini sizes of Gordon's Gin and Tonic, Absolut Vodka and a Jack Daniels T asked for more food. He watched music TV and a movie then settled down for a transatlantic sleep. Upon waking, he saw that everyone around him had green coloured landing forms and Custom Declaration cards. All non-US citizens were required to fill them in. Tony was puzzled by documents like these they made him feel awkward and base. He could have been a stock broking whizz on the trading floor if he had been given the opportunity but his life was funding another existence now. He pressed the call button for a flight attendant. A cool brunette appeared she had a *look- but don't touch* thing going on. She was heavily made up with a jet- set flush and super - sized eyelashes.

"Can I get you anything Sir?"

"Yeah – like – what's everyone doin' baby?"

She ignored the *baby* remark and carried on in machine mode.

"You're required to fill in your Landing Card and US Customs Declaration Form."

"Are you an American or British citizen Sir?"

"I is British baby." T answered proudly.

“Well then you need to fill in one of these and one of these," she retorted with a tight lipped sneer.

“What are they?”

“Two forms you have to fill in before entry to the US Sir.” She clipped back.

“Ere what, can you do it for mi?” T enquired bluntly.

“No Sir I can’t. I’m not permitted to fill in traveller's landing cards or Custom’s declarations, and I can only explain them to you if you require help.” She said the last bit of this sentence as if he was a child of five mouthing the words slowly like a nursery school teacher. Tony was hurt and bored by the flight attendant‘s bitchy attitude. He figured she was having trouble in her private life and venting her frustration on the passengers. He may have been unable to decipher the forms but Tony knew when he was being insulted. He immediately turned away from her and seized the documents without saying another word.

He stared at the papers for several minutes and was unable to process the information. Tony had left school at the age of twelve and at seventeen; had become a professional boxer. By the age of twenty, after his accident in the ring, he had a thriving drug business. He was thankful he had stopped his brother Eunice from the same fate but was tied to the enterprise until the Herbal Pill venture took off.

A college student on her way to Camp America in earshot of the conversation thought the flight attendant was being a “crab.”

“Do you need help filling those in?” She asked sympathetically.

“Can you help mi?” Responded T.

"Of course I can I'll fill them in for you no problem."

"Sweet."

The girl took the forms from him quickly ticking boxes and filling in data but unknowingly made a blunder that went unnoticed until later.

"There all done," she chirped.

"You finished already?"

"Yup."

"Don't need no trouble with those Americans man."

"There shouldn't be any- all done," she replied with a reassuring smile.

"Let me buy you a drink."

"Great!"

They chatted politely for the next few minutes then T lost interest in her girlish life and tuned into ALI G.

Chapter 69

On arrival at JFK after retrieving his baggage, Tony stood in line for Customs and Immigration. Faced with an uptight looking Border Patrol Guard, he handed over his forms and fake passport. (this was before compulsory finger printing for all non-US citizens). A quick scan seemed to suggest everything was okay until he read T's Green immigration card.

"Would you please move to the left Sir?"

T moved cautiously to the left convinced all this negative attention was due to the old man who had bumped into him back in England.

"Ere what- what's going on?" He asked, all of the other passengers on the plane were moving forward and heading for the exit doors.

"Someone will be with shortly Sir. Please be patient and wait to be called."

"Okay," replied T

As he stood there, he saw a rubbish janitor picking up drink cartons and cleaning the floor. He felt better now.

A uniformed officer joined the desk clerk.

"This is William Bohogal – his landing card and Customs Declaration form."

T looked on with doe- eyed sweetness.

“Please follow me Sir.”

There was an x ray machine and metal detector on site.

T was frisked, and scanned for the second time. They found nothing.

“Ere what is there anyfing wrong officer?” T asked with mild apprehension.

“Would you please go into the office to your right Sir?”

T entered the room with a defiant but sullen petulance his round frame filling it with a sunshine vibe.

“Okay Mr. Bohogal your passport and travel papers are good and your hotel is one of the best in the city.”

“What’s the problem then?”

“This,” retorted the immigration officer tartly. He threw the green waiver card onto the desk.

“Is this some kind of sick joke?”

“I don’t get you,” Answered T genuinely confused.

The immigration officer leant over the table and read the question slowly with pronounced emphasis:

"Question *do any of the following apply to you (answer yes or no) have you ever been or are you now involved in espionage or sabotage or involved in terrorist activities or genocide between 1933 and 1945. Were you involved in any way in persecution associated with Nazi Germany or its allies?* Mr. Bohogal you were required to answer yes or no." T stared at the officer in disbelief as he continued.

"Sir this box is marked yes.”

“What- what – I never ticked yes I never did that I wasn’t even born in ***1933*** chah, no way I never ticked that box.”

“If you’d like to explain Mr. Bohogal ?"

"Yeah and ere what mi say – I asked the air hostess if she could help mi fill in the forms and she said no I 'ave to do it miself. Right, then this student Nicole, I think her name is she was on the flight wif me you can get 'er name, she's like on her way to Camp America- she says she'll fill them in for mi. I got her to do it she was the one what filled in *"yes"* stupid chah" I never filled that in."

The officer remained steely cool.

"Mr. Bohogal, you have over three thousand US dollars in cash with you for a 5 day trip and your UK records show you are a well known businessman. Do you really expect me to believe you were the victim of a foolish prank and never checked the form yourself?"

"Look I'll be straight with you oaky – I – I'm not that good at reading." He eye-balled him close with a velvet stare warming the humanity out of him.

"Is there anyone else in the US that can vouch for you Mr. Bohogal- any professional established associates or colleagues friends, family members anyone?"

"Yeah- I don't mean no disrespect- I never ticked that box I can't read so good I left school before I was thirteen years old ere what mi say I'm what you call 'self made.' Yeah. Let mi see here's the card for mi good friend here he's a lawyer Fred Boden here see." T gave the card to the official.

Within minutes the customs officer had returned, he shuffled some papers around and produced some new forms.

"There's obviously been a misunderstanding on the form and the young lady in question has admitted to filling the forms on your behalf. We'll just process them again and if you answer the questions now you'll be free to clear customs and immigration and enter the US. I just need to make a note of this interview okay Sir."

"Yeah – I'm not any Nazi how can I be I'm black."

"I understand Mr. Bohogal."

They went through the forms again, this time the officer verbally eliciting the correct responses to each question. After a few more minutes, the new forms were processed, and he was given the all clear.

At the arrivals gate there were two Filipino women holding a sign which simply said :

T UK

Tony was relieved.

"Hey, you T?" A bronzed beauty with loose black curls and a tight toned body approached him. She was around 5ft 5 with a killer smile and expensive heels that clicked the airport floor.

"My name's Carey- Mr. Boden sent me."

"And I'm Ria; we're here to take you to your hotel. Mr. Boden has arranged everything."

Ria was "frat girl" hot with a Minnie mouse squeak in her voice that T found cute. He gelled with both immediately.

"Ah I'm so glad to get off that plane."

"Oooh I hate flying," agreed Ria.

"Yeah they're like so poky you can't move- how was it the flight?" Cary continued.

"Okay you know it's good to be out of there I had a bit of hassle with customs some girl put me in it," T went on.

"Oh they're pretty strict in the US- wait here while I go get the car and pull over."

"Yeah cool."

"It's a great hotel you're booked into, all the big stars have stayed there, we met your guy Scoot like last week, we gave him a ride," Ria chatted on.

Carey drove towards them and they all climbed into a Black Cadillac Escalade with taupe leather interior and a private registration number.

"This is cris- man this is lush – wicked I love this car."

"Yep she's a beauty."

"Ere what she is."

From JFK they crossed the Brooklyn Bridge it was about twenty miles to the Bryant in Midtown Manhattan.

They listened to Kiss radio Sean Paul and Blu Cantrell's *Breathe.* Tony jigging along to the remixed beat in his gold coloured Adidas tracksuit and size 10 sneakers. He was rap cool.

His smile instantly putting the women at ease until the whole car was shaking with music and electric giggles.

Chapter 70

The polished skies of NYC woke Scoot and T with a dreamy nudge as they left for the Meat District for breakfast and a swim at one of the sharpest joints in the city. Lazing in the hot tub, on the third floor T was chuckling loudly as they discussed the latest converts to "Natural Highs." T's laughter, marking the air with a coral glow.

Pudge the General Manager was doing his daily rounds checking each floor and making sure everything was spotless when T's thunderous roar brought him to a stabbing halt.

The last time he had heard that laugh was back in London weeks ago:

How could it be possible? Was it him ? It couldn't be. How did he get security clearance into the US? It wasn't possible it just couldn't be him it made no sense.

Thoughts were rushing through his head like an army of red ants zipping through a dirt track.

Yes there it was, that fucking boom. No one could mistake that sound there was no other laugh like it. Oh, my God, he's here, he gasped with fear, amazement. He had nearly lost everything the last time he heard that laugh he had lost his job, reputation, his whole fucking life, and now it was back hanging over him like a death mask.

In a fevered panic, he slowly walked through all the events he had tried to forget:

He was in the purple room when little Hermonine the six year old child of a famous movie star had slipped an ecstasy tab into her mouth. She had found it on the floor and he had failed to notice it there. Thankfully, Hermonine had made a full recovery but the investigation had identified him as the culprit of that tragic mishap. The only dealer allowed entry to the club was T who denied any knowledge of the incident and blamed everything on Christian who had been skating on Ee's the whole night with Pudge. That two timing shrew if only Christian hadn't been such a hot lay. God what will I do he'll ruin everything, blow my cover he'll ruin it all oh God….

Pudge had acquired his nickname due to his doughnut shape and dyed strawberry blonde hair. It was an intentional reference to his physical appearance, and a common Private School jibe that elevated his social status; freeing him from his roots as an Australian born, silver service trained waiter to the dandy social secretary he was now, catering for the hoi polloi at one of the swankiest clubs on the New York party scene. Now T's sudden arrival was threatening his whole fantasy world he had created. He peered cautiously into the steam room.

"Oh my God it's true you're here," He wailed.

"Heh Heh Pudge bet you never expected to see me here!"

"No T er no I can't quite believe it."

"Hey Pudge this is it buwoy – this is the dream ticket life rich pickings here man hey Pudgie ripe and fresh."

"I don't want any trouble Tony not like last time it can't happen here this is America the rules are different."

He stopped talking he was finding it hard to breathe gasping for air like an oxygen-starved parrot.

"Ere what mi say don't fucking disrespect me Pudge you owe me like £2000 what I gave you to come here and now I come all this way and this is how you treat me not nice change your attitude or you'll get a boof to your head fool. Is you fried like a grasshopper?"

"I'm off drugs now T- all I meant was I don't want any stress."

"What chah don't be hassling me if I want to stay here I fucking will in fact go get me a room now bitch."

Pudge was on the point of hyperventilating his cheeks blowing up like a puffer fish.

"I don't need any trouble T," he wheezed.

Scoot stepped in:

"Just go and do your stuff Pudge he's only messing with you we're booked at the Bryant we just came her for some down time so relax okay."

"Nah I ain't messin' now go get me a room bitch boy saying all about how you is better than me you're just a servant boy. You serve people food and drink all day. You serve them all night your life is in "service" to others but nothing honourable just a fetch me this and fetch me that piggy head while they live their life and you just serve them. That's what you are everyone's bitch, everyone's water boy, serving people who get high from what I supply, so know your place man you're less than nothing man because you choose to be everyone's bitch."

T climbed out of the Jacuzzi and dried down putting on a House robe and pool slippers. He leant back on a sun lounger and read the notice:

Come and join Pudge's Roof top Barbecue 4.00pm Members Only

"Oh yes I'll be there – joining in the fun put me on the special list now bitchie."

Pudge was holding onto a pool rail for support and ignored T Scoot offered him a glass of water.

"The roof top party is already full. There are health and safety issues we can't exceed the numbers," he whined through gritted teeth.

"Chah as if I'd go anyway but watch out Pudgie you may see me there."

"It starts in a few hours I was just making sure everything was ready."

"Chah get out of mi face now I'll have some good food and ting stop blocking the sun with your gloomy – put – down face fool."

Pudge was quivering like a weeble toy likely to topple over any second. Scoot thought he should clear the air:

"Guys, come on now let's just chill there's no need for all these bad vibes we don't need to get het up over this stuff come on guys."

"Scoot, Please, I'm begging you don't bring him here. Don't let him come here ever again please or I'll have to withdraw your membership."

"Just chill Pudge. God you're so wound up it's just fucked up. Take some deep breaths and try to calm down man T's just teasing you okay."

"Fuck off bombaclott water boy that's all you is all you'll ever be. You think you is better than me at least I have no shame in who I is, I'm proud of my colour, my roots and every ting. You, you're running scared of who you are. Pudge what kind of fool fuck name is that? As if you're part of *high society* jack fuck! You is a working man's son so be proud of it and accept it. Fuck I am not even here for you man I'm doing a major deal – legitimate business of my own. I'm not here dealing I'm out of that soon. Shame man! Shame on you, you're so uppity up your own shit you've forgotten who you are. Now move on before I box you across your bombclott face."

"I think it might be best if you hung back go to another floor or something Pudge you've really upset T's feelings."

At the barbecue, T sat with various newly acquired acquaintances on the roof top slopping on fast food which he had specially brought in while Pudge tried to reclaim the la-di- da elegance of the club by playing Mozart's Eine Kleine Nacht music, which was being muffled by the politically charged rant of Public Enemy's "Fight the Power." T and his crew, mouthing the lyrics and chicken stepping to the beat until they got so close to Pudge they could see the two grey hairs sprouting from the centre of his overly coiffed head. This droll tableau of New York's social milieu continued for a full forty minutes until T got tired of goading Pudge and left with a princely smile. Pudge dialled his physician's mobile demanding Xanax and Vikadin. T had king size fish to fry and Pudge was just a minor hindrance.

Chapter 71

T was called back to London urgently leaving Scoot alone to settle the deal on the capsule maker. Richie, Bernie and Johnny Ashton had all been trying to contact him. While T was in the US Godwin had a visit from the Old Bill. There had been reports of "vagrants" sleeping in the communal areas of the property and an actual complaint lodged with the Police about disturbances and anti -social behaviour at night causing some of the residents concern. Godwin had let the police into the flat earlier in the week and Bernie had tried stalling them but now they wanted a follow up visit and a more detailed nose around. T gave the order to strip the flat from top to bottom and move all the gear to Johnny's place.

"Everything has to be scrubbed clean and cleared out you get mi?" T explained anxiously.

"Yeah they say they're coming back around 5pm when I said you'd be back." Replied Godwin, fretting and pacing around.

"That leaves you three hours Godwin to fix up this place like new, cris paint job, disinfect the floors, air out the furniture and get rid of stuff we don't need everything has to be brand new man and all the gear gone out."

Yeah Boss I understand, I tink I can do it Boss, I need a little help. The Church group will help me" He resolved brightly and picked up the phone.

"Hello Innocent it's Godwin, we need you and some of the other brothers over at the flat."

"What for?" Probed Innocent who had an open deference for his elder but didn't like to become too involved in his various dealings.

"My Boss is in trouble man we have to help him clean up his house that's it just painting and decorating that kind of stuff nothing heavy man."

"Yes Brother we need a big donation for the church for the work can you sort it?"

"Yes it's God's work it will be done brother get here before noon."

"On our way brother."

Godwin then skedaddled over to the local hardware shop for some cleaning materials.

"I need some of those white suits, masks and long washing gloves" He asked.

"Excuse me Sir?" queried the sales assistant with noticeable misgivings.

"Chah don't be stupid I need the white clean up suits and mask like on that show man" Clarified Godwin with a harassed look in his eyes.

"Got to clean out mi place or we get thrown out Landlord issues" He went on.

Relieved, the Sales Clerk guided him to the right spot where he proceeded to stock up with cleaning overalls, washing materials, paint and scrubbers.

Back at the flat, he removed all of his clothes and put on a CSI style jumpsuit with long latex gloves. Around 15 volunteers from the local church group were waiting for him, mostly black men in their early twenties. He insisted they all kit themselves out in their CSI style outfits. T left them singing Christian hymns and skinning the walls. It was a latter day miracle.

Over at Johnny's he was getting ready for an early night with "Kandice." A few weeks ago, when T heard that Johnny's girlfriend Heather had ditched him he had bought him "Kandice" a blow up life size doll for company. It was meant to be a joke but Johnny, in his junked up state had become very attached to Kandice, beginning his psycho trip to "never land," when T wheeled by. T could see him sitting over her. Stark naked except for his converse sneakers with his feet turned out at an angle. His "horse" like face a potent symbol of the Heroin he had ingested looking at her with blue glazed eyes. He was brushing her hair, petting her, kissing her but worse talking to her as if she were actually real. Tony observing this grody display with a mixture of alarm and aberrant fascination.

"Johnny come to the door and fix up yourself what the fuck are you doing with that doll bro that's like creepy shit man"

"Nothing man Kandice and I are just having some like quality time man."

"Yeah Kandice ain't real bro she's made out of specialist rubber, fuck that shit we need to load some gear in here now look sharp bro get yourself fixed up you need to do this quick like." He told him hastily.

"Yeah man I just get so lonely sometimes man you know cos Heather she' no longer here."

"SSsh ut up man I don't need no details what I saw was enough to make me puke for days man it was just fucking scary man- should never have brought you that doll, she was for fun like a joke not a substitute fuck don't go all psycho creep on me man."

"Just feeling lonely" Floated Johnny with violet bleakness.

"Get busy loading Johnny there's no time for your weird chatt" Replied T with scalding crispness.

Bernie was fielding calls from all over the place and trying to juggle drop bys and collections without sending out bad vibes or rumours about police buzz.

T agreed to speak to Rich after all he was a child hood friend and someone he looked out for :

"Tony, it's Rich. Listen, can you meet me later in Grosvenor Square? There's this charity ball thing. Should be a wicked night. I'm thinking we get a few drinks and find a quiet space to talk. It's a Venetian-themed ball but you can come in Black Tie."

"Yeah, listen, that sounds good. I know about it already it's been booked in advance for gear. The crème de la crème will be there for some society event."

"Yeah that's right" Richard replied with open- mouthed concern.

"So you're already invited?" He probed.

"Yeah yeah, before I get out of this bizzo for good I'm doing this big ball, invitation only all that stuff."

"You got your invite already?" Questioned Richard with open incredulity.

"Yeah man I got to collect from one of those aristo start ups."

"Who?"

"Some fuckwit Paulie Casino owes me over two grand."

"You going to collect there?" Enquired Richie with dismay.

"No choice he has to be told to pay up."

"Fair enough."

"Rich man I 'ave to tell you bro, I'm leaving this bizzo for good soon ere what mi say when I'm out of it I'm gone and there won't be anyone to cover your tracks anymore. You have to understand that these opportunities they only come around once and then you have to take it and run and that's what I intend to do."

"T can you stop with all the lecture bull man I don't want this pressure on my back now I'm in some serious trouble and I need to deal with it that's the sum of it man."

"Listen bro, you know you can always count on me you know I'll always help but soon I'm heading out of the bizzo and you need to get with that. Now, I was waiting on someone but 'e still 'asn't showed 'e was batting on about this and that. I don't know where the hell 'e's got to, maybe he's blown me out. I've got somethin' he dropped by, maybe you can take a look at it 'cause I don't know what the fuck it is, and you bein' a lawyer?"

"Yeah, no problem. Listen, T, we can sort this shit out, it can all be sorted. I know it can."

"Yeah, we need to.."

Tony rang Bessie a few more times; it went straight to voice mail.

Chapter 72

Pavlov was in the loop but Manny hadn't told him everything. Jimmy's was "buzzing" that night. Grim-faced locals were supping on beer, and with at least fifteen different types of Vodka on offer, Scoot was feeling loose. The only music played at Jimmy's was jazz, classic rhythm and blues and rock and roll, a concession which proved ever popular amongst those in the know and the odd tourist who stumbled into the bar. On the Jukebox was a choice selection of old Motown: Smokey Robinson and Sam Cooke numbers drenching the noisy chatter into the sweetest ball of sound. It was sublime. "This is such a banging place," enthused Scoot. The screen behind them was showing the classic Ali/Frazier fight and there was hardly any room for them to sit. Manny waved Scoot over.

"You look like an extra from Oasis, kind of British style clothes."

Manny was wearing his Ali T shirt with baggy blue jeans and a du rag on his head. He was undeniably large and had a protruding square jaw, his beautiful straight white teeth contrasting with his overcast face. They made him appear less manic and more congenial. Manny had spent a cool two thousand bucks on his teeth and was pleased with the overall result.

"So you want the Caps a dynamo, right?"

"Yeah that's the one."

"I can get that for you. It will take a couple of weeks but I can get it at a really good price, man."

"That's what we were hoping." "My contact is from Mumbai and he takes at least 50 percent of the cost price. I get my cut from you so I like cash, cleared funds at the point of sale."

"Yeah that's sounds reasonable."

"So you can have the funds wired to my account when the machine is ready to ship."

"Easy."

"Listen, man, I should tell you, it's not my business or nothin', but the feelers are out on your shit, you know what I'm sayin? You're taking some heat on this deal, man. You got some heavy interest from other sources so just watch your back and tell your people back in England, too."

Scoot was glad of the warning. They continued drinking at Jimmy's and then headed out of the Theatre District uptown to find some choice "ass" at the Plaza Hotel.

Chapter 73

Dimple swayed into the crowded party, oozing blue heat. She exuded a certain uniqueness about her, something so wickedly sensual that all of the men there and even some of the women wanted her. Dressed in vintage Dior, carrying the Kelly Longue bag a Hermes classic, she wore an Alex Gore Browne bolero, to keep the chill at bay, and floated around the Westminster Ballroom, hounded by "fans" and flashing photographers all keen to get a picture. She was submerged in a giddy mass of attention. Constantly hounded by party people, sipping on champagne, nibbling extravagant yet delicious canapés like mini anchovy tarts with roasted almonds baby hamburgers or mini chocolate puddings she was getting tired and anxious. She sashayed to the bar and ordered a Gin Daiquiris. It was super nice, fizzed around her mouth and most importantly settled her nerves.

Later that night, Richard and Tony were having a private conversation in the men's room with one Paulie Casino.

"Thought I'd find you here man" drummed T with relish.

"Er T hey man whassup?"

"Yeah like you don't know" Answered T with dry revulsion.

"The thing I hate about you isn't your jokey name or your wind up airs and graces it's your lack of respect man" He continued.

"I – I don't know what you mean" he shrinked waffling his words like a Cappacino Sundae.

"You owe me two grand" Persisted T with placid detachment.

"I told you I'm not paying the gear's shit" Paulie Casino had turned a feeble pallid colour his doughy face wrinkling up like blanched yeast.

"I don't care man you took the gear on tick and you kept taking and taking and now it's payback I want my money now."

Richard had hung back, a torpid numb nut with no interest in his friend's extracurricular activities.

T lurched closer.

"I heard on the Q.T that you might be carrying something you don't want people to know about "He ribbed.

Paulie's face putrefying to ash.

"What – what the fuck are you talking about" He crumbled.

"You know brov, don't demean yourself any further man unless you want Richie here to find out have some fucking dignity and pay up now, otherwise the whole friggin' banquet room is gonna find out that Paulie fuckwit Casino has..."

"No ! Here here's the money T I'm sorry please here it is all of it" He fell to his knees in a kind of bendy wave, stubbing his toe and recoiling to the ground in a snivelling mess.

"Get up man I got my money now I'm not Jesus Christ" He limped out like a tortured animal carrying the mark of the beast on his temple.

"What's wrong with him?" quizzed Richie with tangling consternation.

"Oh he got a Positive for HIV."

"That's rough."

"Yeah well he should pay his debts up."

"I got the stuff what Bessie left at the house" T went on changing the theme.

Dimple seeking refuge from the glare of publicity, and trying to escape from a particularly persistent female fan also made her way to the sanctity of the men's washroom.

She remained deathly silent hiding in a cubicle as they beefed up their chat.

"Look here bro me got this it's all this curious bizzo."

T pulled the bond carefully out of the bag it was in.

"Yes Tony, you've saved my life man!" Richard shouted punching the air.

"That's what I've been looking for. It belongs to that client I told you about, the one who owns me. We'll have to get out. We'll have to leave, lie low, and then try and contact him when the dust has settled."

"If what you say about 'im is true, 'e won't leave this alone."

"Fuckin' hell, man. We've got Poncho Khan's life in this package. He'll definitely try and take us out for it."

"I like how you say us, when it was you that got me into this situation. Fuck, maybe Bessie's been taken out already." Remarked T in a blue funk. He knew his friend overplayed his mobster role but he never wanted him blown out.

Dimple swung open the cubicle door.

"Ssssh, I know this man. He's here; he's going to be investing in one of my movies, a Bollywood gangster flick. He doesn't know that I only agreed to do it so I could get my revenge on him." She paused. "He raped my sister two years ago. Then, she committed suicide. I swore I'd have my revenge. Sometimes you have to fight fire with fire. I have a plan to stop him for good."

" Who who are you?" Exclaimed Richard with baking fervour.

"I'm Dimple," She vibrated with kittenish allure.

Look, I don't know what you're thinking, but..." began Richard.

"Shut the fuck up, man," warned Tony, raising his hand. "Let her finish."

"Yes, both of you should be quiet!" She went on. "Be quiet, please he's definitely here in this hotel I know it. I think you and your friend should leave the country for a while and warn your family and anyone close to you to go. I'll take care of Poncho Khan."

Richard and Tony lost no time they slipped through the back entrance, sprinting through the fashionable Mayfair district searching for a cab.

"Scoot, it's T. We've had a change of plan. Book a flight to Cancun Mexico, head for the Ritz Carlton Hotel." He left the voice message on his New York mobile.

"Right now I've got to sort Bernie and the boys out. Well, they can go to Jimmy's in Dublin for a bit and Bernie wants to go to Australia so he's sorted. Godwin can fly out to Jamaica. I'll let them know." Richard was touched by Tony's consideration for the others but only slightly so.

"Godwin, it's T. You 'ave to book yourself out on a flight to Jamaica tonight. No delays you hear me tonight, who's there now?"

"Everyone, T."

"Put me on speakerphone."

"Okay."

"Can you all hear me okay?"

"Yeah."

"Listen, an emergency's come up. We 'ave to go 'Buffalo Soldier." This was the code they used in case of rival gangs, the police, or major heat. "I'll call you soon. Bernie, you know where the cash stash is. Make sure everyone gets out. Peace."

The receiver slammed down. Tony left a message for Luke that he was going to be away for a short time negotiating the deal on the capsule maker and that Richard would be in touch regarding orders and so on.

Chapter 74

When T gave the code *buffalo soldier* a bullet of chaos struck the firm.

"We have to split up now!" Shrieked Bernie.

"Jimmy, you, Godwin and Tim come with me. Dipsy, La La and Vinnie, here's some cash. You go now! Go! Go! Go!"

Dipsy and the others raced out of the flat, hugging the guys as they said goodbye.

"Jimmy, book everyone's flight on Expedia. Once you've done that, we'll boogie onto Heathrow."

Outside Mack was waiting for them in a silver M3 BMW, hoping they would lead him to Richard.

Finally, Bernie, Jimmy, Godwin, and Tim all piled into their 4x4 Range Rover. Taking the wheel, Jimmy drove easy like a Sunday breeze to avoid police suspicion. It was warm outside, the evening shadows playing with the dappled gaze of the fading sun. He checked the rear view mirror and saw nothing. No sign of Mack. No sign of anyone.

From Denmark Street, they turned right onto Charing Cross Road and then straight up to Tottenham Court Road. About half a mile down they made a quick left turn; Heathrow bound on the A40 heading for the Westway. Now loosened up and more sanguine, they amped up the beat with some *Lethal Bizzle (London Grime music)* and got into the *groove*. Bernie lit up cracking-on spliff. He passed the weed around. Smoke was filling up the car and steaming all the windows.

"Open the sun roof you Kermit," laughed Bernie to Jimmy.

"Mi not like all this activity. I think you should stop smoking in here man…it's not good for mi at my age," complained Godwin.

"Look stop your bitching. We're on our way!"

"Turn it up!" yelled Tim. They were moving their heads in time to the music and drumming the seats with their hands, back seat grinding as the car gained speed.

Then, a knife break at the lights as the 4x4 came to a screaming stop. Mack was on their tail zigzagging through lanes cutting up other cars he was too close. The lights turned amber, Mack cranked up the music: *Fire Starter* by the Prodigy then downed some Patron, blitzed to the max – all the time getting nearer and nearer to the 4X4. He counted backwards from five in a twisted haze: four, three two one: It was rubber tarmac boom! He was like a brainsick rodeo doing seventy miles an hour in a fifty-mile zone. Slam Bam! Over in seconds before the lights hit green his M3 steaming into the back of the Jeep crushing a nearby lamppost and flipping a hundred and eighty degrees into the air. Everything stopped it was *road attack* squirting guts and crunching glass. Mack had crashed out; his cindered remains trailing the scene.

"What the fuck went on there?" Cried Bernie.

"Is everyone okay? –Godwin, you're bleeding…hold on here." He got up and gave him his shirtsleeve to mop up the blood.

"What about everyone else?" He went on spazzed out with worry.

"Fuck my head hurts," moaned Jimmy.

"Oh shit I've got blood on me, "affirmed Tim.

"Just a nose bleed – I can see it...here use this it will seize up soon."

The M3, now on the opposite side of the road was totalled; nothing of it but slices of junk, crap waste and human body parts rammed to a pulp.

"Fuck we don't need *them* here. Who was that poor bastard? He's gone...he was friggn' crazy..."

"Quick get rid of the weed. Godwin, stuff it in your bag and we'll climb out of the car. There's 5K under the dashboard, hide that in your bag too. Let me go first- keep the old bill busy. Jimmy, start unloading the boot and get **all** our luggage out."

"Sierra Oscar Foxtrot Bravo. this is P.C. No. 343 requesting back up and uniformed Response Units to Shepherds Bush Green. There's been an RTA: repeat an RTA with possible casualties."

The Policeman turned to Bernie.

"Good Evening Sir."

"Officer, the guy came from nowhere driving like a deranged wacko- complete lunatic. He was just like the *Hitcher...*"

"Sorry Sir? Take your time and calm down please."

"You know the horror movie the *Hitcher?* He was trying to butt us off the road, weaving in and out of lanes and then wallop. He just pounded into us and somersaulted through the air. We're lucky to be alive officer."

"Yes Sir, is anyone of your party hurt Sir?"

"Just a nose bleed, and a few cuts and bruises, officer. We're on our way to the airport going on holiday."

"I see Sir. My colleagues should be here shortly if you have everything you need, I think we should go to the far end of the next street sir in case the car explodes. Uniform Response units are en route sir to secure the scene."

"We um we've got a flight to catch officer," responded Bernie congenially.

"I understand Sir but until the area's secure for your own safety and other road users we obviously can't let you go just yet Sir."

"No officer, I realize that I was just wondering how long it might be."

"I'm sorry Sir, I can't speculate but it usually only takes minutes for uniformed response to arrive."

Bernie, the police officer and the rest of T's gang clambered out of the way then the police officer made a note of names and contact details. One by one, they provided fake ID's and bogus addresses as the officer dutifully scribbled the information down on his notepad.

After about ten minutes the ambulance crew, fire brigade, and roadblock team arrived when the car sparked again: a riot of flames and fury.

Godwin had the cash and the dope in his holdall. Once they'd given their statements to the old bill, they were provided with free transport to the airport and courtesy meal vouchers.

Chapter 75

Poncho was sitting at a large office style bureau his tree-trunk legs flung across the top in a lordly show of contempt. He wore a loose fitting Safari style trouser suit with long sleeves it was a sickly shade of green. His ringleted hair damped down and swept back from his brow.

Mungle his Mumbai sidekick called him on his private line.

"Poncho here," he answered with a *don't not fuck me* flourish.

"Doctor P…." the voice was strangely effeminate and raspy.

Poncho had acquired the moniker of "Doctor P" in Mumbai as he fixed things like a doctor.

"What is it?"

"There's a fly in the ointment," whispered Mungle.

"What – what do you mean a *fly?* Stop recycling lines from your *007 James Bond* movies and gangster flicks you moron. This isn't some joke, you worm. I'll squash *you* like a fly bastard bitch."

"Everything's up in smoke Dr. P., everything is kaput – all gone – everything is burnt out and destroyed."

"Explain."

“Dr. P there has been a most terrible accident it is on the radio and television. Everything has burnt and is wrecked and all gone to ashes nothing is left.”

“Always the bearer of bad news Mungle, always. You can be relied on to bring misfortune you are a *hijara* buffoon. Any idea who did it?”

“I don’t know Doctor only God knows, I got it from the wire, and from *chotta* (small) Salim nothing has remained it’s all blown up.”

Later that evening, the AP global news network reported an unidentified man had died after a “head on “ collision in London’s Shepherds Bush and that four people in another vehicle were being treated for minor injuries. Police appealed for help in identifying the man but were left clueless as to who he was, as the car had exploded at the scene of the accident and any forensic evidence that could have assisted them was likely to have been destroyed with it.

Poncho was relieved he had worn professional latex gloves when he had given Mack the order and set Mungle on Richard’s trail.

Chapter 76

TWO WEEKS LATER:

Hunt Continues For Bollywood Superstar: Dimple Sethi

British detectives continue to search for Bollywood superstar Dimple Sethi, the award winning screen actress and daughter of acclaimed Indian film director Roshi Sethi. Ms. Sethi has not been seen since the bizarre poisoning of multimillionaire film producer and property magnate Poncho Khan.

The Indian playboy, a favourite on the London party scene, was last spotted with Ms. Sethi at the celebrity- studded Blue Tiger Summer Charity Ball. Ms. Sethi is being sought by British Detectives, who urgently want to speak to her about her relationship with Mr Khan. Dimple Sethi is one of Bollywood's most famous exports, loved, and adored in her native India. She was captured on CCTV in the small hours of the morning at the exclusive party, and earlier caught on camera posing with Mr Khan for photographers while plying him with drinks. In one of the images, Mr Khan appears unsteady on his feet, confused and in a disorientated state.

At around 2:00 a.m. the pair were seen leaving together

and Ms. Sethi then enters a waiting taxi alone, leaving Mr Khan at the curb.

Mr Khan was later discovered only minutes away from London's fashionable Funky Buddha bar by party girl and socialite Georgie Wainbauer, in a small alleyway concealed with rubbish and debris. He was rushed to a local hospital where it was found he had been poisoned and had suffered chemical burns to his mouth. He does not remember anything about the incident and is in protective police custody until his safety can be guaranteed.

Detectives believe that he may have been the target of a drug related murder and his drinks could have been laced with a deadly toxin earlier that evening.

Ms. Sethi left London the same day, flying to Panama and then possibly Central Asia. Her whereabouts are currently unknown.

Both her parents are appealing for her to come forward in a bid to assist the police with their enquiries. They strongly deny any wrongdoing on their daughter's part and say she was a victim of circumstance.

Detective J. Ross has made nationwide appeals in Mumbai and Europe for anyone with any knowledge about the attack to contact the "incident room."

Bernie finished reading the story while Tony and Richard basked in the Yucatan sunshine. As the flamingo burnt sky crushed the afternoon shadows into a melting haze of Picasso warmth, the whisper of tomorrow was calling, dancing high on the folds of a Mexican breeze. Good things were on their way.

Lightning Source UK Ltd.
Milton Keynes UK
UKOW040614191112

202405UK00001B/28/P

9 780985 000356